DEAD MAN RUNNING

This novel is a work of fiction. All characters in
this publication are the product of the author's
imagination and any resemblance to real persons,
living or dead, is purely coincidental. Most of the
places herein are real, but the incidents that take
place are similarly from the author's imagination.

ISBN-13: 978-1478143840
ISBN-10: 1478143843

Acknowledgements

Much is owed to many, in particular:

Jock Holden, for driving me along most of the roads traveled in this book; to Phillip Davis, for allowing the use of his name for one of the characters; to Carolyn Whitaker, of London Independent Books, and Raymond Khoury, both of whom read early drafts and offered invaluable suggestions. There was also much-needed encouragement from Greg Dark and Bob Smith, and technical advice on the changing world of publishing from Joan Merrill, Steven Walker and Miles Pearson.

Thanks

To Brenda Oldenburg, for more reasons than there are pages in this book.

ONE

PHIL DAVIS parked the department's brown Crown Vic across the entrance to the drive that led up to the house's single garage.

Close by, Chuck Riggs, a young recent recruit, was sitting on the front passenger seat of a black and white, his feet on the concrete, elbows resting on his knees, his face bathed in sweat and pale beneath his sportsman's tan. Ben Dodgson, Chuck's partner, stood on the porch, hands on hips, glaring at a handful of neighbors who had begun to gather, curious at this early Sunday morning activity.

Phil walked up the few creaking steps. 'Morning, Ben,' he said.

Unusually, there was no grin, just a nod to acknowledge Phil's presence.

'Ben?'

Ben Dodgson had the seamed, leathery skin old-time western movie actors had and now Phil could see that his face, too, was filmed with perspiration, yellowish beneath its weathering. It would be a warm June day, but not for a couple of hours yet. What in hell did they have here?

Ben jerked his thumb for Phil to follow him into the house, then grabbed his arm to prevent him stepping into a smear of fresh vomit. Phil looked a question and Ben inclined his head towards Riggs. 'Can't blame him,' Ben said.

Phil raised an eyebrow. Ben Dodgson's contempt for the new generation of police officers was legendary. Apologizing for his young colleague's behavior came close to a papal blessing.

At six-three, Ben Dodgson had five inches on Phil and at fifty-five was a dozen years older. Now, he pulled back the fly-screen and opened the front door. Stepping into the passageway, the two men stood for a moment, letting eyes adjust.

The house was a slightly fancier version of the old shotgun houses Phil's father had grown up in down in Johnson County. At street level a passage ran straight through to the back door; both barrels of a shotgun fired from the front door would send buckshot clear through into the backyard without hitting a damn thing. To the left of the passage was a square living room with sliding doors opening into a dining area. To the right was a front parlor and behind it a kitchen overlooking the backyard. What Phil could see of the decor was plain, ordinary.

Stairs led up from the hall and at their foot stood a wheelchair, neatly folded. The sight of the wheelchair brought a frown to Phil's face. Was this the house of someone he knew?

Faintly, he heard a sound he couldn't quite identify.

Ben headed up the stairs, keeping to the right and Phil went up the same way, aware that the curious sound grew a little louder.

The house had two bedrooms at the front and across a narrow landing a bathroom and another bedroom, this one larger and with its own bathroom adjoining.

'In there.' Ben was indicating the main bedroom and from the way he planted his feet and folded his arms it was clear that he had no intention of going any further. Then he added, 'Brace yourself, Phil.'

As Phil opened the door to the master bedroom he caught the foul decaying odor of butchered meat, feces and urine and with it the unmistakable cloying, coppery smell of blood. Now, he could see that the noise came from the blue-green cloud of flies clustering on the horror stretched out on the bed.

'Jesus,' he murmured, feeling his stomach lurch.

Reaching into a hip pocket he took out a pair of thin vinyl gloves and slipped them on.

Fumbling for a handkerchief, he clamped it over his nose and mouth but the stench was already inside him.

Checking that there was nothing on the floor he stepped closer to the bed; the flies rose, buzzing and swirling madly before resetting.

The woman had been slashed four times. One cut had left a gaping hole in her throat, another had almost severed one breast, from the next her stomach wall bulged obscenely purple, and the last had ripped through her pudenda. A bone-handled carving knife was driven through her left thigh, only the yellowing white handle showing. The bedding - sheets, pillows, a thin woolen counterpane - were black with dried blood. Black blood also stained what was left of the thin cotton nightdress she wore. Her mouth was open wide in a soundless scream; her eyes staring blindly into a bottomless pit.

Phil closed his eyes for a moment, then opened them again to look around the room. That was when he saw the second body.

The boy lay wedged into the corner of the room at the far side of the bed, as if he'd crawled there, his pajama-clad legs spindly and crooked like a puppet's. One arm was flung outwards at an unnatural angle, severed at the shoulder by all but a thin strip of bloodless flesh. An axe was wedged into his skull, splitting it down to the bridge of the nose. Blood and brains had spilled down the boy's face, drying into a grayish-brown mess.

Swallowing hard, his mouth and throat suddenly dry and scratchy, Phil stared at the boy for a moment. He forced himself to see things objectively, clinically; mentally trying to formalize what else he was seeing - mostly the blood splatter on the white, pictureless walls - into the plain dry words he would write in his report. Trying but failing. What had happened here, for Christ's sake? It was like a scene from one of those movies his daughter and her friends liked to watch. Only this wasn't the freakish product of some special-effects wizard's uncomfortably inventive mind. This was the real thing, the result of a mind he couldn't begin to comprehend.

Turning his head Phil looked out to the landing where Ben Dodgson stood. Ben tilted his head and Phil looked at the part-open door that led into the adjoining bathroom. Jesus, was there more? He pushed gently with the back of his gloved hand until the door came up against something that lay behind it.

The little girl was face down on the bathroom floor, one hand clutching a gingham-frocked doll. The girl wore a nightdress colored pale lemon as were her fluffy slippers

Reaching down, Phil carefully turned the small featherlight body over. Soft, blonde hair veiled her face and for a heart-stopping moment Phil saw a resemblance to how Jennifer had looked ten or a dozen years ago.

Gently, he drew aside the strands of hair and that was where all similarities to his daughter ended.

Scissors had been driven into the little girl's left eye, angled upwards into the skull. A thin trickle of dried blood lay on the waxy cheek, ending in a dark smudge where her face had rested against the floor.

His skin crawling, Phil straightened up, turning to lean over the wash-basin. Somehow, he held back the knot that had formed in his gut from exploding and after a moment the wave of nausea ebbed a little. He straightened, carefully noting where his gloved fingers had touched the white porcelain, thinking that forensic wouldn't like him touching something the killer might have used, maybe smudging prints.

He looked at himself in the mirror above the sink. He didn't think that his appearance had really changed much in the past few minutes - no more gray in his dark hair, no deeper lines in his cheeks, no darker shadows beneath his blue eyes - it just seemed that way.

He went out of the bathroom, avoided looking again at the boy and the bloody mess that had been a woman as he walked through the bedroom, past Ben, down the stairs, this time keeping to his left, and out onto the front porch. For a moment he leaned against the wall of the house, sucking air into his lungs.

Ben had followed him but neither man spoke. After a moment there was the scrape of a match, unnaturally loud in the silence, as the tall policeman lit his pipe. Since stopping smoking five years ago, Phil had developed a mild aversion to the smell of tobacco smoke but now he eagerly sucked in secondary fumes, seeking to blanket the reek of death.

He'd seen it before often enough. Rising from patrolman to detective in Dallas, where the killing rate sometimes seemed even higher than in the country's wars, he had seen death in pretty nearly all its forms, over and over again. If he'd stayed in Dallas he might have been a lieutenant by now, maybe even reached captain, and been running Homicide. But he had grown tired of the endless violence, tired of seeing only the dark side of people, the side they kept hidden from friends and family and neighbors and passers-by, but which they showed, often violently, to the police.

He had never expected to see a scene like this in Forrest. Whoever had done this, family or friend or passer-by, someone, somewhere along the line would express surprise. 'I never would've believed it of him,' they'd say. 'He always looked like he would never hurt a fly.' If being a police officer all these years had taught Phil Davis anything, it was that when it came to mankind's potential for depravity and brutality, there was no such word as never.

Realization of that fact was one of the prime reasons he had for quitting Dallas. Violent acts committed by police officers against

8

members of their own families were far from unusual and while Phil didn't think he would ever fall victim to that kind of failing, or alcoholism, another job-related problem among veteran and some younger cops, but, then, he didn't suppose that any of his colleagues had entered the force expecting their behavior to develop darkly in the way it sometimes did.

Then there was Jennifer. He didn't think that his daughter would ever fall in with the wrong crowd but he had seen too many addicts and other examples of the walking dead from all levels of society to know that good upbringing and the best of intentions offered no guarantee of safety. To believe that such things could never happen to him or his family was to live, very nearly literally, in Never-Never Land.

That his move from Dallas to Forrest hadn't kept his family out of harm's way was something he'd known for five years. Sights like the one in this house only underlined reality.

He could hear a siren, coming fast. By now the crowd of neighbors was growing and some were edging onto the dusty lawn that fronted the house.

Phil gestured to Chuck Riggs and indicated the small crowd. The young officer scrambled to his feet and cleared the lawn, his movements and his voice unnecessarily aggressive.

Ben spoke to Phil, his voice low and bleak. 'Whatever it is, I never want to see another one,' he said.

'Who are they?' Phil asked.

'Their name's Garrett. Louise the mother, Billy and Jo-Anne the kids.'

'Father?'

'So far I only spoke to the old lady next door. She called it in. Says the father's name is Ed. Works away from home. Salesman, maybe.'

'What else?'

'She . . . the old lady, Mrs Carter . . . she hadn't seen anyone for two, three days. She's not sure how long exactly. Got worried when there were no lights in the house the last two nights. Couldn't sleep for thinking about it but didn't want anyone to think she was snooping.'

'She come into the house?'

'No. Came to the door, found it was unlocked, called Louise and the kids and when there was no answer went back home and called it in.'

'Whose is the wheelchair?'

'The boy's.'

Phil thought about that. Surprised he'd never seen the boy, or heard the name. Jennifer had used a wheelchair for five years and in that time Phil had encountered a few other users in town. But not this one.

Turning, he glanced inside the house at the wheelchair. It was basic; Jennifer's was quite elaborate. Maybe the boy's - Billy's - incapacity was not as severe as Jennifer's.

The siren wailed into the street as another police car arrived.

'Start house-to-house,' Phil told Dodgson. 'I'll call in for more help. And no one, not a damn soul, steps onto the Garrett property without a sound reason. That applies especially to the newspapers.'

'This one'll be on TV,' Ben said. 'You can bet your pension on that.'

Phil nodded. It was just the kind of thing that would hit news broadcasts statewide. More material to nourish the doom merchants who claimed that the whole damn country, and Texas in particular, was going fast to the devil.

He would have to call Chief Brodie sooner not later. If the media heard about this before Brodie there'd be hell to pay.

But first, he called Joe Carroll on his cell. Even in Forrest, people listened in to police radio. He told Joe, the dispatcher, an ex-cop whose civilian job kept him in touch with the only world he understood, to leave one man in one car on floating duty covering the whole town. Everyone else he wanted down at Lee and Jefferson. The shift was due to change soon so there would be several officers at the station. 'Tell those that are going off duty to get a couple hours sleep and then call in to see if we have something for them to do. And call in C shift right away. We need all the help we can get.'

'That's a helluva lot of overtime, Phil.'

'The Chief'll approve it.' Christ, yes. Steve Brodie would milk something like this. Somehow, he'd see past the blood and horror to the beckoning pillars of the Governor's mansion. 'And I want everything we can find on Edward, maybe Edwin, hmm, or Edgar Garrett, 220 Lee Street,' Phil added. 'I'll call in with age, description, maybe a photograph and employer's details, when I've had a chance to search the house and talk to neighbors. And try and find Sam. He was going fishing over Childress way. Call Sheriff Lansing and ask him to look out for him. Tell Lansing it's serious and urgent.'

Sam Madsen was the closest Phil had to a regular partner. Sam had taken advantage of some accumulated leave to take a trip he'd been promising himself for months.

'And call the coroner's office,' Phil added. 'Make sure Dan deals with this himself.' Dan Flory, the county coroner, was a smart and very able man but this was Sunday and at weekends he would send an assistant whenever he had the chance. 'And Joe, play dumb with the newspapers and television people.'

'Television? That bad?'

'That bad.'

'What about the Chief?'

He couldn't put it off. 'Do everything I asked, then call him. Play it cool, don't get him too excited and maybe I'll get a few hours start on this.'

'How can I get him excited, you haven't told me what you've got over there.'

'Triple-187, and as nasty as it comes,' Phil said, adding, 'And I still haven't told you.'

Ending the call, Phil turned to see another car approaching. He recognized Keiron Maloney, a sharp-eyed detective who ran the department's small forensic section. He had a feeling that this was something that would need more facilities than Maloney could bring to bear. Depending on the way this thing developed, they might need help from Amarillo. Maybe more than even they could offer

Phil turned over a few of the possibilities: the husband and father had to be top of the list if only because that's the way most homicides worked out. But the nature of the killings, three different weapons, made Phil think twice. It could turn out to be the work of a serial killer in which case the FBI would be involved. Might be smart to involve them now, not wait. Even if the husband was the man they wanted, the FBI could prove useful. Ben had said he might be a salesman. If he traveled out of state he could be any damn place, especially as it looked like the killings were at least two days old.

A sudden thought struck him and he went over to Riggs, checking the time. 'Get over to the bus depot. The seven-thirty bus for Amarillo is just leaving. A pair of drifters should be on board. One tall with red hair, the other a small, stocky Mexican-looking guy with a moustache and small beard. They spent the night sleeping off a drunk in the tank. Take them in for questioning.' He unclipped his handcuffs from the back of his belt and added them to the young policeman's. 'Cuff 'em both, separately, and search them very carefully before you put them in the car. But don't get trigger-happy. Odds are they hadn't a damn thing to do with this. Good odds. Okay?'

Riggs nodded, obviously relieved at the chance to have something to do that would occupy his mind. Phil reached out and gripped the patrolman's arm. 'You okay?' he asked.

Riggs nodded again, his jaw tense.

'You touch anything in there?'

'No.'

'Okay.' Phil let go Riggs' arm. 'Take it easy, Chuck,' he added softly.

Riggs climbed into his car and took off too fast, snaking down the street.

Ben Dodgson had already organized the other uniformed arrivals into asking questions along the street, both sides of the junction with Jefferson Avenue.

The houses on Lee were mostly timber-clad on timber frames. Outside, they were surrounded by small lawns some with old-fashioned picket fences, most still in good order. The lawn next door, the old lady's, was broken up with flower beds bright with yellow roses. Ten years back, Phil remembered this as one of the town's favored residential districts. He and Sarah had thought about moving this way but they'd decided to stay where they were on a hill on the outskirts of town. Now, five years after his wife's death, he was pleased he still had the relative isolation afforded by the few old houses his father had built more than half a century ago.

The crowd of curious and silent neighbors had been shepherded back indoors and apart from the official vehicles the street had resumed its quiet, dusty, Sunday-morning normality, the silence broken only by birdsong that was now wholly inappropriate to the darkness that weighed on Phil.

Normality. That was something Lee Street would not have for much longer, Phil thought. And maybe not ever again.

He went back into the house, taking a deep breath before pushing open the front door.

Keiron Maloney was on the landing. He had begun setting up the walkways, festoons of white plastic tape inside which everyone would remain until he had taken all the tests he needed. Maloney looked at Phil, then looked away without speaking, his lips compressed hard against his teeth.

'Don't miss a thing on this one, Keiron,' Phil said. 'If you want any help, just ask for it. And make damn sure that no one, and that includes the Chief, does anything that risks damaging evidence. You know what he's like, he'll showboat this if he gets the chance. If he gives you a hard time, call me. Okay?'

Maloney nodded his head, then looked hard at Phil. 'You ever see anything like this before?' he asked.

Phil had seen worse. Several multiple drug-related killings in Dallas where machete- and chainsaw-wielding maniacs had run amok, but he knew what Maloney meant. Outside of the drug wars, he had never seen anything even remotely like it. He shook his head.

'About help,' Maloney said.

Phil waited.

'Amarillo has facilities you can't imagine.' Maloney paused and Phil nodded agreement. 'I wouldn't want to lose control . . .'

'You won't,' Phil promised quickly, relieved that Maloney was making it easy for him to bring in outside help. 'Let me know what you want and I'll see that you get it.' He felt a sudden qualm that he was making promises he might not be able to keep, especially if this did grow into something far beyond his reach. Well, he'd worry about any ruffled feathers later. 'I touched the basin in the bathroom,' he said. 'Both sides. Not the taps.' He held up his still-gloved hands. 'No prints, but maybe I smudged something.'

Going out onto the landing, he mentally established a routine for a search of the house. He checked the time once again. He wasn't due home for a few hours and his next-door neighbor, Jane Walters, a retired nurse, was keeping a weather-eye open for his wheelchair-bound daughter.

He thought about phoning anyway because what he really wanted was to reassure himself that Jennifer was safe and well.

Not that he would let her know he was fussing. Jennifer thought she was tough. Phil thought she was tough. Their thoughts differed only in degree. Although she would soon be seventeen, Jennifer had picked up some of the habits of her mother. Unlike some police wives, Sarah had always taken an interest in his work, encouraging him to tell her about his cases. Mostly, he knew, she didn't really want know but it had been Sarah's idea of therapy for him. No bottling everything up the way some police officers did until it all blew up into drunkenness or violence or both. He still missed that release, but he didn't think he would have been able to tell Sarah about this one. Not the bloody details. And he certainly couldn't tell his daughter.

Phil looked at the bedroom door, then went downstairs to wait for Dan Flory to arrive. He would have to go back into the bedroom with the coroner but had no intention of doing so a moment before it was absolutely necessary. Already he knew that the bloody images of the dead woman and her children would remain with him for the rest of his life.

TWO

THE HUMIDITY of the Mexican night pressed down on him. Sweat ran down his neck and pooled under his arms.

Pushing aside a branch of purple-flowered bougainvillea that massed over the stucco arches forming the verandah of the house, Ryker peered through the window, listening. Above the racket of the cicadas he could hear music coming from deep inside the old rambling building.

Stepping lightly across the verandah's low outer wall, he reached the window and slid the blade of a knife between frame and casing. Moments later he was inside the house.

The room was furnished with heavy Spanish-style furniture, its varnished wood floor scattered with coarse brightly-patterned Indian rugs. A CD player was on loud, music he vaguely recognized, pop of a bygone decade maybe, masking any sound he might make.

Ryker stood for a moment, thinking. The room had the look and feel of being only temporarily empty. The music, a magazine folded open on a low table, two glasses with half-melted ice still floating in pinkish liquid. Two glasses? He sniffed at one. Campari. He could wait here until Lensky returned or he could go looking for him. He didn't like the idea of waiting.

When a voice came from behind him the surprise raised his pulse rate for the first time that night.

'Who are you? What do you want?'

It was a woman's voice and when he spun around he saw that she was young, late twenties maybe, dark-blonde hair, tallish, good figure, wearing a thin floral cotton wraparound.

He moved towards her fast and she saw the knife in his hand and opened her mouth to scream but he was too quick and hit her once with his clenched fist, stunning her. He lifted her onto the couch, dragged out the tie of her wrap, cut it, and tied her hands and feet and made a gag.

By the time he was done the young woman was coming round, her eyes unfocussed at first but clearing as she realized what was happening to her.

He should have been ready. The second glass had been a warning that someone was here with Lensky.

Lensky will be alone in the house. Just the four guards to take care of. Mexicans. Nothing to worry about.

The guards had been easy, slow and half-cut; that much was right, but Lensky wasn't alone. He didn't like surprises like this. Someone had been careless. He decided to leave the woman until he had Max Lensky under control.

He heard the slap of footsteps on the tiled floor of the hallway and moved fast and quietly to the doorway as Lensky came into the room carrying a stainless-steel ice bucket. The old man's white cotton slacks and short-sleeved bright-red silk shirt looked out of place on his sagging, out-of-shape body. Lensky was a few years past seventy but he didn't have to look like this, he could've taken better care of himself.

When Lensky saw the intruder expressions chased one another across his face, going from alarm to fear to resignation.

Lensky came further into the room, saw the girl on the couch and hesitated, the muscles along his jawline tightening under soft flesh. He walked across to the table and carefully stood down the ice bucket.

'Ralph sent you,' he said.

The flat sound of Lensky's voice raised his hopes that the old man wouldn't give him any trouble. He nodded an affirmative answer.

'How much is Ralph paying you?' Lensky asked. Ryker knew that Lensky wasn't expecting an answer. 'I can pay more,' the old man continued. 'There's cash here. And jewels. Uncut emeralds. A million dollars worth. You can have them, just leave me alone. What harm can I do? I'll just stay here in Mexico until the day I die.'

Ryker looked at the ageing body, the soft flabby muscles, liver spots on the backs of his hands, and wondered how a man like this had ever become a trusted associate of Ralph Hardy.

'You know I can't take your money,' he told Lensky. 'You have to come with me, back to Dallas. Mr Hardy wants to talk to you.'

'Talk? Kill me.'

Ryker shook his head, uneasily thinking that maybe this wouldn't be as easy as it should be. 'He just wants to talk,' he said.

'Talk.' Lensky's voice was suddenly hard. 'You dumbass sonofabitch. When did Ralph Hardy ever talk to anyone who can hurt him?' A shifty look flitted across his eyes. 'Or thinks can hurt him. Why would I do anything to cause him trouble?'

Ryker ignored the question. 'We need to get started,' he said. 'You want to get a coat, pack a bag or something?'

Lensky didn't move. His expression was guarded, close; he was figuring percentages.

Ryker swung his jacket open and showed Lensky the real odds. The heavy automatic pistol jutted from the deep inside pocket. Big enough to blow the old man half way to Guatemala.

Lensky saw the gun and sighed. 'I'll need some things out of the bedroom,' he said. He gestured with a suddenly weary hand towards the hallway.

As they started to leave the room the old man glanced towards the couch. 'She has no part in this. Let her go.'

Ryker was suddenly angry. 'For chrissake, get moving.'

'I said let her go, goddammit,' Lensky shouted, moving towards him, his hands raised, his face red with such anger that Ryker knew he had to teach the old man a lesson. How the hell else could he make the journey back if he let the old fool sound off every time he felt like it.

He backed into the room letting the old man come towards him, while he pulled out the gun, holding it high out of Lensky's reach. Then he slapped the old man across the face, then backhanded him, harder this time.

Lensky stopped short. 'Bastard,' he said, his tone cold, bleak the way Hardy's could be, and Ryker briefly caught a glimpse of how, long ago, Lensky might have been a hard man to deal with. But that was then and this was now.

'Move,' Ryker said quietly. 'I won't tell you again.'

The old man's shoulders drooped as he turned away. He started for the door but stumbled, reached out a hand to steady himself against an ornate cabinet, then pitched forward onto his knees.

Ryker watched warily, hearing Lensky gasping for breath. He heard another sound, this time from the girl on the couch. She was staring at Lensky, straining to sit up. Her expression, twisted by the gag that bit into her mouth, mingling anger and fear with concern for the old man.

Slowly, Lensky rolled onto his side then flopped over to lie face upwards.

Looking down at him, Ryker could see a blue tinge spreading across the old man's face and knew that this was no stunt. 'Ah, shit,' he said, glancing hopelessly around the room in case there was something, a bottle of pills maybe, that would put things right.

Lensky was struggling to speak, his voice hoarse. 'I wouldn't hurt Ralph. Tell him that. It was the woman. I didn't like it. Still don't. Or that shit of a brother-in-law. But I wouldn't hurt Ralph. Tell him.'

Then the old man began coughing and choking, tried to sit up, fell back and was suddenly still and silent, the blue tinge on his cheeks fading slowly to a yellowish-gray pallor.

Cautiously, Ryker knelt beside the body and felt for a pulse. Nothing. Lensky was dead.

Looking up at the girl, Ryker said, 'They didn't tell me he was sick.'

Something else he should have been told.

He stood up, abruptly angry at Hardy, then immediately shrugging off an unexpected feeling of doubt. Maybe Lensky had been right and Hardy did want him dead. Anyway, it was too late now.

The music suddenly ended. Now he could hear the slippery sounds of the cicadas in the gardens and over it the throaty rustle of breath coming from the woman.

Reaching down, he unfastened the gag, his gun warning her that screaming wouldn't be a smart thing to do.

'Is he dead?' she asked, her voice dull.

'Heart attack, I guess.'

'That's what Hardy wanted,' she said as if he hadn't spoken.

He shrugged his shoulders, hoping that he wouldn't have trouble with her, too.

She turned her eyes, dark blue and unforgiving, onto him. 'And you, you're just as bad as Hardy. A stinking rotten unforgivable bastard.'

He swung his hand, slapping her hard across the face. 'Shut the fuck up,' he snarled. Then, suddenly aroused, he ripped the cotton robe away. The girl's body was fresh and rounded and lightly golden from the sun.

He threw himself across her, his left knee forcing its way between her legs. She writhed and struggled, their bodies intertwining. 'You tramp,' he yelled at her. 'Calling me names. You think the only people can fuck you have to have a million bucks?'

He felt her hands on him, grasping at his legs and for an instant thought she was welcoming him but realized that she had managed to release the bonds and that her hands had found the .22 pistol he had strapped to his ankle.

He flung himself to one side, coming to his feet with his automatic in his hand.

But the little pistol was aimed straight at him and he saw the knuckles of her hand whiten. 'He was my grandfather, you degenerate scumbag,' she screamed at him as she pulled the trigger.

She didn't know about guns. The safety was on.

On the wall behind the couch was an old gilt-framed mirror and for an instant Ryker was diverted by his reflection. Pale blue eyes stared back at him out of a narrow expressionless face, thinning sandy hair combed back from a high forehead. He had a fleeting, unsettling sensation that he was looking into a stranger's face.

The girl was fumbling with the little gun and he slowly raised the automatic. 'Why?' he asked her. 'Why did you have to be here?'

THREE CARS stood in the garage. One was a foreign sports car, a Jaguar; one a Dodge Nitro; the third an old battered Chevy Caprice. The first was too obtrusive, an open invitation to some bored Mexican traffic cop to stop him just for the hell of it; the Chevy probably belonged to someone who came with the house and didn't look too reliable. So he took the SUV.

At the gate, Ryker turned right, then stopped and backed up until he came alongside the Ford Focus he'd rented and which now lay with its offside wheels jammed in a rainwater culvert.

Cover your tracks. Remember, the Mexicans can identify you.

He put a bullet into the gas tank and accelerated hard away as the Focus went up in a roaring explosion of flames and smoke.

He drove carefully, taking it easy until he was accustomed to the vehicle. When he reached the town it was as quiet as it had been when he'd passed through a few hours ago.

Less than hour and he was on the highway, heading for the border. The only other traffic he saw were trucks and not too many of them.

By the time he was approaching Matamoros a crack of light separated sky from land on the horizon towards which he was driving. A dull ache was building behind his eyes. He needed sleep.

On the outskirts of town, Ryker pulled into the parking lot of a motel and left the Nitro way over in one corner, then walked steadily into town, feeling the heat of the day building like a weight on his shoulders.

Along the way, he dumped his weapons except for the knife. He didn't like to be unarmed but he couldn't take the chance of a metal detector at the border finding his guns and raising all kinds of unanswerable questions.

He crossed the bridge into Brownsville. Dressed as he was in a slightly sweat-stained lightweight tan suit, he could have been anything from an unsuccessful salesman to a weary tourist. He didn't look like what he was and that usually helped.

Today it didn't matter. Not even the fact that he was on foot raised the interest of the border guards. They had already settled into the routine of another monotonous day watching tourists and truckers drifting back and forth.

Ryker didn't have to pass through a detector so he could've held on to his guns. But the risk was never worth it. Everyone knew that people seriously intent on illegally entering the USA didn't do it at busy, high profile border crossings. They preferred the odds climbing over or digging under the fence that was supposed to keep them out. Canada was easier but, then, Canada wasn't full of fucking Mexicans.

He drank coffee in the first diner on the American side of the border, the ache at the back of his eyes starting to pound. But he stayed alert, all the while watching southbound cars as they pulled in alongside the diner. Eventually, a family of four tumbled out of a dark-colored Ford Edge. All were overweight and from the way they eagerly grabbed at menu cards he guessed it would be some time before they were finished.

Outside, he used his knife to break open the crossover's door, hot-wired the ignition and drove off north towards Corpus Christi.

Remember. All the time you have to keep covering your tracks.

Ryker drove until midday and when he stopped it was at a crowded Brannigan's where he ate hamburger and fries, drank three cups of black coffee, cleaned up in the washroom, then stole another car and continued on his way. When he reached Victoria he dumped the car and picked up a Hertz rental using a credit card he'd found in the glove compartment of the crossover.

He drove until dark, zigzagging along minor roads long after he knew it was no longer necessary. Who would follow him?

You have to keep covering your tracks. Don't take chances. Don't let anyone make a connection.

No one was following him. And it would take a genius to tie the Nitro to the Edge, let alone the Hertz rental or make any of the other connections.

In downtown Houston he left the rental car across the street from a cheap hotel. Paint peeled from the façade of the hotel which looked as though it made its money from whores renting by the hour. He took a room and lay on the bed, fully dressed, smoking and thinking. He needed time before he reported to Ralph Hardy. Time to make sure that he was in the clear and that his story had no holes. He didn't want Hardy blaming him for something that wasn't his fault. Eventually, he dozed, waking when it was light.

From the window he checked that the rental car was where he had left it. It was, and would probably still be there until the rental company realized it was gone and sent out a tracer by which time the local Chicanos would've converted it into easily-traded spare parts.

He walked three blocks north before he asked directions, then headed for the bus depot and bought a one-way ticket to San Antonio, which was where he'd left his own car.

He tried sleeping but the motion of the bus made him nauseous and kept him wide awake, his headache mounting until he thought his skull would implode and when he left the bus he felt like death.

At the depot in San Antonio he collected his overnight bag from a locker, went into the washroom and cleaned up thoroughly. He used a lavatory stall as a changing room to put on clean underwear, socks and shirt. As he walked to the multi-storey garage where he had parked his car he dropped his soiled clothes into a dumper.

He caught a glimpse of himself in a storefront window and again had the odd feeling of seeing a stranger. Then, his mind, until now filled with thoughts of Hardy and Lensky and all that this entailed, cleared and he began thinking of himself for what seemed like the first time in an age.

Quite suddenly, as if someone had pulled a switch, his headache disappeared and he felt his step lighten, as if a new man walked in his shoes.

On the way out of town in his Dodge Viper he had a sudden idea and for a moment couldn't understand why he hadn't thought of it before. Pulling into a suburban shopping mall he went into a J.C. Penney and bought gifts. A silky-haired pink rabbit and a new catcher's glove for the kids. He also picked up a couple bottles of imported wine with a price tag that told him they had to be good. His wife would like that, something nice to go along with the dinner she would cook for him.

It was a long haul home, more than five hundred miles, and although he was eager to get back he would have to make an overnight stop. For one thing, although his headache was gone he knew that lack of sleep was catching up and driving non-stop, especially through the night, would be dangerous.

He picked a small motel adjoining a filling station with a diner just off Interstate 80 not far from Sweetwater. He could refuel, eat, get a few hours sleep before an early start. That way he'd be home before dark.

He spoke the word aloud. 'Home'.

It had a nice sound to it, a sound he didn't hear as often as he would like.

In his room he turned on the television that sat on a bracket screwed to the wall at a height that made the screen too high to watch in comfort. He dozed for a while and then awoke to find that he was watching a news program. A girl reporter, dark hair curling thickly around an oval-shaped face, was speaking from in front of a house.

The house looked familiar.

He heard the reporter's words, not yet paying full attention.

'So far police have no strong leads,' she was saying, 'but they are anxious to locate the husband. He is believed to be a salesman and might be out of state.'

Over the girl's shoulder he could see a street sign. The two horizontal plaques, at right angles to one another at the top of the pole, were clearly visible: Lee Street and Johnson Avenue.

Slowly, uncomprehendingly at first, Ryker came to his feet.

Now the reporter had walked over to a thick-set man, tough-looking, graying hair, standing awkwardly and glaring unsmilingly at the camera.

'Detective Davis,' the girl was saying, 'we understand that the murders were committed in a particularly brutal manner.'

The policeman's eyes shifted to the girl and away again, something like a glimmer of anger crossing his face. 'I'm sorry, Miss Nichols,' he said, his voice hard and authoritative, 'but until we have contacted the husband I'm sure you wouldn't want us to talk about the details of this crime.'

'But if he's watching . . .'

'This would be the last way he wants to learn what happened.'

'So you do not consider Mr Garrett to be a suspect.'

Garrett?

For god's sake! That was his name, wasn't it? Not Ryker. That was just the name he used when he was working. In his other life, his real life, his name was Garrett.

On screen, the policeman was making no attempt to hide his anger. 'Don't put words into my mouth, Miss Nichols.'

'Detective Davis . . .'

'It's Sergeant Davis and I have nothing else to say.'

'You haven't said very much so far . . .' But the policeman had turned away and walked out of shot.

The reporter continued speaking to camera. 'We hope to have an interview later with Chief of Police Brodie, so stay tuned. This is Barbara Nichols in Forrest, Texas.'

Reaching for the remote, Ryker hit the mute, leaving a flickering picture on the screen of a typhoon weaving its way across a stretch of flat fields beneath a threatening sky. His headache was back with a vengeance; the pain like a drill, twisting and cutting, blanking out thought.

He concentrated hard on what he had just seen and heard, replaying the newscast in his mind.

Murders, the woman had said, not murder. How many? Two, three, more? All in the same house?

For a moment he thought he was about to throw up. Then he took a grip on himself. The telephone. He would telephone the police in Forrest. Talk to the gray-haired guy. What name had the girl used? Davis. Talk to Davis, ask him just what had happened. Was it Louise? Who else? Jesus Christ. He reached for the telephone. Wait a minute. The police wanted to talk to him. To say what? He knew how the cops worked. To eliminate him from their inquiries. That was the line. Bullshit. When they talked to a man they could make him say almost any damn thing they wanted.

If they talked to him, maybe asked him about where he had been and what he'd done in the past few days, what could he tell them? That he'd been on a trip to Mexico. 'Prove it,' they'd say. How could he do that? Tell them to look up Max Lensky and his granddaughter? Anyway, Ralph Hardy didn't like people talking to the cops, not even to ask directions. Think. He had to think; but the pain in his head was worse.

On the screen above him the picture had changed and the woman reporter was back, this time with a tall, sharp-suited, sleek-haired man in his mid-fifties. Ryker turned up the sound.

'We already have a description of two people we want to interview,' the man was saying. 'One we believe to be the husband, Ed Garrett, the other a man for whom we do not yet have a name.'

'Can you give us those descriptions, Chief?' the woman asked.

The man smiled, showing white even teeth. 'I can do better than that, Barbara. We have a police artist working on drawings and photo-fit pictures right now. These should be ready in time for your early morning news and I shall be very grateful if you will use them. It will be a real help to our inquiries.'

'I'm sure we'll be able to do that for you, Chief Brodie,' she said. 'And you can confirm that there have been three deaths?'

'Yes.'

Three deaths. So his worst fears were coming true.

'And all three were especially ugly killings.'

The man's smile began to look a little strained. 'Death by violence is always unpleasant but in this case, with a mother and her children the victims, it is particularly unpleasant.'

Mother and children. Louise, Billy, Jo-Anne. Jesus. Jesus. Jesus.

'And are you able to tell us the cause of death, Chief?'

Now, the tall, smooth man's discomfort was clear. 'I think we shall have to withhold that information a little while longer, Barbara,' he said.

He continued watching the screen but learned nothing more and this time, when the woman signed off, he switched off the television and lay back in the darkness. He felt cold, shivering, his hands worst of all, their trembling uncontrollable.

He lurched off the bed and ran for the bathroom only just making it before he threw up.

His guts emptied, he leaned forward resting his forehead against the smooth tiles. The pain in his head was burning hot but his skin was cold as ice.

Louise, Billy and Jo-Anne.

After a moment he turned on the taps and splashed water over his face, then cupped his hands to drink and wash away the sweet aftertaste of vomit.

Unsteadily, he walked back to the bed and lay down, staring blindly at the ceiling.

Louise, Billy and Jo-Anne.

Suddenly he let loose some of the emotions he always tried to keep confined to a corner of his brain and they came raging out.

His hands clenched into tight, hard fists, his arms and legs forcing themselves downwards against the bed. He'd kill him. Them. Whoever did it. Kill him. Slowly. Painfully.

His teeth ground together and his head began to thrash from side to side against the pillow, his arms and legs, stiff, drumming on the mattress. Then, slowly and with considerable difficulty, he forced himself back under control.

He had to think carefully, act cautiously, tread softly.

He had to discover not only who had committed the murders in Forrest but also why.

The pain in his head began to ease just a little and with an effort he could think more clearly. He knew what he must do. First, he had to pick up money and a change of identity.

In a handful of banks, spread across Texas, he kept a safe-deposit box. All had similar contents, which included weapons, ammunition, a full set of documents: driver's license, credit cards, and everything else he might need to start a new life, each cache setting him up as a different person, usually a different name - and money. In some boxes there was as much as twenty thousand dollars.

You need an escape hatch. A way out when things go wrong. And they will. One day.

The nearest cache was at the First National Bank in Odessa. He would drive there tomorrow. From this moment on the contents of his careful bank deposits, the money, the changes of identity, and the weapons, had a purpose. They would help him discover exactly what had happened in Forrest.

And when he had all the answers, someone would pay.

Dearly.

THREE

BARBARA NICHOLS stubbed out a cigarette in the already overfilled ashtray on Doug Carlson's desk. 'Dammit, Doug,' she said, 'nobody's talking. At least nobody who knows anything.'

Carlson continued turning the pile of papers on his desk; sometimes just a flick of a glance, occasionally reading a passage, once or twice making a note. Once in a while he glanced up at the television monitors banked on the opposite wall.

He liked Barbara. If he'd been twenty years younger it might've been more than that. She had wide-spaced dark eyes, high cheekbones that hinted at maybe some Native American blood a few generations ago as did her dark-golden skin and straight, short-cut black hair. Her slimly curving athletic figure yelled out for something slinkier than the heavy woolen sweater and jeans she wore when she wasn't on camera.

'Use it,' he said.

'What?'

'The fact that the cops're covering up.'

She frowned, gnawed at her thumb and then lit another cigarette. 'It's just a feeling,' she said.

'They've been pretty reliable in the past. Your feelings.'

'The trouble is,' she said, breathing smoke through her nose, 'I don't trust Chief Brodie. He's a publicity hound. And the other one, Davis, well, I just have the feeling that he's a not-too-bright, small-town cop who's suddenly out of his depth.'

'What exactly happened in that house?'

'Goddamit, I don't know.' Barbara's cheeks burned angrily. 'Oh, I know the woman's dead and so are her two children. We picked that up from one of the uniforms before Davis gagged everybody. But no one's saying how they died. I'm sure it's something grisly, something that might help us run this up into a story the networks will pick up. But if we can't get it out fast it will be yesterday's news and then no one will want it.'

'There'll be other stories. Other killings. You can bet your life on that.'

'I know, Doug, but I have a feeling about this one. All those cops, Davis, Brodie, the big uniformed guy, the forensic officer, even the coroner for god's sake, all looked as though they were ready to throw up. Whatever's in that house has to be a real bloodbath.'

Carlson stirred uneasily. Working on a six-times-a-day television news program wasn't something for the fainthearted, physically, mentally or metaphorically, but he sometimes found himself questioning the eagerness with which some of the reporters plunged into stories that were, to put it mildly, distasteful. Especially the women. Maybe he was getting old. Maybe it was because he couldn't wholly blot out memories of the days when sudden death was part of his daily routine. That was another time; way back in the past, which was, as the saying had it, another country.

He looked over at Barbara. And another generation, he thought.

'You planning to go out there again this morning?' he asked.

'As soon as the eight o'clock news is over. I'm doing the first follow-up from the studio so we can use the police artist's drawings of the suspects.'

'Suspects?'

'Two men seen visiting the house.'

'What're they like? The pictures.'

'I haven't seen them yet. Chief Brodie's bringing them in.'

'Are you having him on the show?'

Barbara sighed. 'Not from choice but even if he hasn't said so it's clear that if we want to keep him sweet we have to give him camera-time.'

'When you go back to Forrest, try talking to Davis again. Ask him

26

if he can give you anything else.'

'I have.'

'Try again.'

'Doug . . .'

'Ask him nicely.' He grinned. 'And tell him it will be a favor to me.'

'You know him?'

'Long time ago, but he'll remember.'

'Okay, I'll try but he made it clear he doesn't like television reporters. Or maybe it's just women television reporters. On his personal scale of things, it's obvious they come slightly lower than pond-life.'

'You might be right about his opinion of television reporters.'

'Where did you know him?'

'Another time, another place.'

'Dallas?'

Carlson nodded, resuming his scan through the sheaf of news reports.

Barbara sighed again. 'Okay, I'll try but, like I said, I think he's in over his head.'

'Maybe, maybe not, but I'll tell you one thing. Your assessment of Phil Davis being not very bright is way off target.'

'Then why's he in a place like Forrest?'

Carlson shrugged. 'He hasn't always been one of Forrest's Finest. When he was in Dallas, the grapevine said he was headed for the top.'

'What happened?'

Carlson shrugged again. 'He decided to move out of the big-time. I expect he had his reasons. Phil always had good reasons for everything he did.' He thought about telling her of the tragedies that had followed Phil's move to Forrest, then changed his mind.

Barbara looked at him shrewdly, her head cocked to one side. 'What's so special about this guy, Doug?'

Carlson glanced up at the clock on the wall above the door. 'Time you put on a dress, unless you plan on showing your slavering audience what the rest of us have always known, that underneath all the gloss you're a lumberjack at heart.'

Barbara looked around at the clock, swore, stubbed out her cigarette, and went out of the office fast but controlled.

Carlson reached out to empty the ash-tray into a waste-bin - his office was the television station's designated smoking zone, his choice - then tapped the volume button on the remote control unit that lay on his desk. One of the monitors, tuned to this station, was showing the string of commercials that preceded the eight o'clock news. On the next screen he could see the studio set. Chief Brodie was already sitting at the desk angled alongside the program's anchorman, Dick Purnell. The image changed as the producer of the morning show flicked to the rostrum camera which focused on two drawings. One was a bony-faced middle-aged man with a high forehead, thin lips and long, light-colored hair. The other was of indeterminate age, swarthy, fleshy-faced, stubble-chinned, with unkempt, curling dark hair.

Numerals appeared, counting down and as the news program's logo came up he saw Barbara scurry into place. Carlson grinned at the incongruous sight of her bright, floral-patterned dress, all that would show once she was seated behind the desk, below which she still wore scruffy jeans and sneakers. She sat down, giving last-minute touches to the thick, curly wig she wore when she was working.

He knew why she was eager to find a big story that would get her network exposure. Like most of the women and men who drifted in and out of this kind of work, Barbara Nichols had ambitions that ranged far beyond the narrow scope of a small operation like WNTA. Unlike most of the others, she had some chance of achieving her ambitions. Her manner of dress and hair style apart, she looked as good on camera as she did off, managing to convey warmth and friendliness at the same time as exuding confidence that never extended into brashness.

And despite his comment a moment ago, it wasn't all surface gloss. She was very bright, researched her assignments tirelessly, and read extensively. She was constantly surprising him with the breadth of her knowledge. Local politicians were already treating her warily, as her reputation spread as someone who couldn't be fobbed off with inadequate or clichéd answers.

That was where she should be looking, Carlson thought. A political story would be the way to make an impact. Not some gruesome murder case. Still, she was young, two or three years short of thirty. There was time.

Barbara's chief problem, if problem is what it was, lay in the probably partially true stories that drifted around the studio about her sex life. Lively, was what Carlson had heard. Promiscuous, was how he would probably have put it. But for the second time in just a few minutes, he decided that was something else on which he was generationally-challenged.

On screen, Dick Purnell had handed over to Barbara who was questioning the chief of police about the causes of death. Brodie was displaying what struck Carlson as a well-practiced statesmanlike frown of concern while he explained that it was important for the police to inquire further into the case before revealing all they knew to the media.

Carlson began to experience the kind of feeling that Barbara must have had. Something about the Forrest killings was making the police edgy.

Barbara had moved on and now the first of the two drawings came up onto the screen. 'This we believe to be Ed Garrett,' Brodie said as the long-haired, thin-lipped man appeared. 'And this,' as the image was replaced by the swarthy man, 'is another recent visitor to the Garrett house.'

'You said you believe the first man to be Ed Garrett?' Barbara said. 'Does that mean you're not certain?'

Good girl, Carlson thought.

Brodie showed a lot of teeth but Carlson could tell that he was unhappy. 'The Garretts have only recently moved into the neighborhood,' Brodie said.

'Have you made contact with his employer?' Barbara asked.

'We think that he is a freelance,' Brodie replied, his smile straining now. 'Buying and selling in different parts of the state.'

'Buying and selling what?'

Now, the police chief was sweating. 'We're not sure.'

Christ, Carlson thought, this man's a joke. It was too late to do anything now but if this case continued to run, this would be the last time Chief Brodie would have his face in front of a WNTA camera. The producer would surely ease him out and on the remote chance he didn't then Kent Benson, the station boss, would ban him. Benson didn't suffer fools or incompetence on either side of the camera.

Barbara had received a winding-up signal and was inviting any member of her audience who recognized either of the two men to contact the police. Carlson breathed a sigh of relief that only a short slot had been allocated. With more time at her disposal, Barbara would probably have followed her instincts when Brodie prevaricated and gone for the throat. No one at the station would have blamed her but offending Brodie could lead to her being closed out of any further inquiries into this case and if her instincts were right she needed police cooperation. And now, Doug was beginning to think that her instincts were exactly right.

THE LAST person Phil Davis wanted to talk to was a television reporter. And of all the television reporters he could think of, which admittedly wasn't many, Barbara Nichols was last in line. He wasn't too sure what it was that had annoyed him. Well, obviously, her digging into things he didn't want to talk about was annoying. And so was the way she was trying to wheedle her way into persuading Chief Brodie to tell her things best kept quiet for the present. No, there was something else.

She looked too glossily glamorous, especially when she wanted to talk about something so grim and unpleasant.

He thought about telling Tony Rodriguez to send her away but he knew she wasn't the type to take no for an answer. 'Let her stew for ten minutes,' he told the desk sergeant. 'Then send her in.'

'Goddamn reporter,' he told Sam Madsen.

Madsen looked up from a computer print-out. 'Not the beautiful Barbara,' he said.

Phil glared at him, then slowly nodded. 'That's the one, although not my idea of beautiful.'

Madsen shook his head. 'You can't help having no soul, Phil, but there's nothing wrong with your eyesight. You know the girl is beautiful. Like a deer slipping through the forest, like a kingfisher flashing brightly above a stream, like a sweet-scented wildflower in the morning dew, like the . . .'

'For Christ's sake, spare me, Sam.'

Madsen laughed. Tall, with the sleek muscular build of an athlete, he was a full-blooded member of the Cherokee nation. Dark-haired and with coppery-toned skin, he had been with the Forrest Police Department since graduating from North Texas State University seven years ago. Although Phil had few close friends, most of whom were his own age or older, the two men had hit it off from their first meeting despite an eighteen-year age gap. Not only had they developed an easy-going camaraderie, they also worked well together. Madsen had a lightning-fast brain and a reliable instinct which blended well with Phil's more methodical approach in which close and careful reasoning played a major role.

Madsen had complained bitterly when he'd been recalled from his fishing trip but once he knew the reason had turned his full attention to the case. And, for that matter, Phil thought gratefully, so had everyone else on the force. The killings, their nature, the fact that small children, one of them a cripple, were involved was the boost that was making the force gel. But so far smooth efficiency wasn't helping solve the case or even make a dent in the armor-plated blank wall that appeared to surround the house on Lee Street and the victims within its walls.

'What're you planning to tell her?' Madsen asked.

'I wasn't planning on even talking to her so I won't tell her anything I don't have to.'

'She could be useful.'

'How?'

Madsen shrugged. When Phil wanted to be stubborn, there was no telling him anything so he didn't waste time, effort and breath, so instead he asked, 'Do you want to hear some guesswork?'

'Good guesswork, or bad guesswork?'

'Just guesswork, but it won't make you happy.'

'Go on.'

'The husband.'

'What about him.'

'There was nothing in the house. No pictures. No papers. Apart from two shirts and a pair of working jeans, no men's clothes. And a woman could wear any of those. No shaver.'

Phil leaned back, aware that Sam was putting into words random thoughts that had been flitting uneasily around his own head. 'Go on,' he said again.

'What if there isn't a husband? What if he's somebody else's husband, and Louise Garrett is his girlfriend? And his home is someplace else and Louise is someone he sees when he's on the road.'

'Louise told the old lady, Mrs Carter, he was her husband.'

'What else would she say? Mrs Carter's what, eighty-something. Louise would lie to her. A white lie maybe, but a lie. Just to explain away a man being in her house.'

Phil nodded his head slowly. 'And that would explain why there's no trace of him in the house. A few oddments of men's clothing apart. All his other stuff is in his bags.'

'Of course, if this is the way things are it means that it's a few million to one that his name isn't Garrett. So instead of looking for a man named Ed Garrett, we're looking for a man maybe named Ed, who is maybe living in the eastern half of the country.'

Phil shook his head slowly and sighed deeply. 'Oh boy,' he said.

There was a knock at the door and Barbara Nichols walked in. Except that, for a moment, Phil didn't recognize her. The immaculately-dressed, curly-haired glamour girl who had interviewed him outside the Garrett house had gone and in her place was a short-haired, very-much untidier young woman. It was only the face that was the same, strikingly pretty with alertly sparkling eyes the color of fresh chestnuts. Christ, he thought, I'm starting to think like Sam talks. That was when he noticed the slight hint of Indian blood in her facial bone structure.

He flicked a glance at his partner who winked slyly at him. Obviously, Phil thought, the tribes are banding together.

Phil pushed back his chair, making a gesture towards rising. 'Have a seat, Miss Nichols,' he told her. Sitting down, she stared at him thoughtfully and in slightly disconcerting silence for a few moments. 'How about some coffee,' Phil suggested.

'Thanks.'

He glanced at Sam who, unasked, went across to the coffee pot in the office corner and began clattering about looking for a cup that was a little less stained than most.

The woman fished into a pocket of the man's work shirt she was wearing and took out a pack of cigarettes and a throwaway lighter. 'Mind if I smoke?' she asked.

Phil hesitated. He did mind. But the no smoking rules were regularly bent when it suited the police, so he decided against saying so. She lit up, blew smoke through her nostrils, then glanced up as Madsen brought coffee for all three of them.

'My partner, Sam Madsen,' Davis told her.

She reached out and shook hands with Madsen.

There was another moment of silence during which Barbara looked around the room. New three years ago, the police station looked the way modern police stations ought to look. Official, characterless, dull. And just a little threatening. She wondered if Davis reflected the office or was as smart as Doug Carlson seemed to think he was.

Phil sensed her appraisal of the layout and guessed that she was taken in by it, the way everyone was taken in. Except the people that worked here. They knew that the money authorized for the department had run out with the construction costs. The equipment they had to work with, the things they needed to fight crime, all that was outdated and overwhelmed anytime anything happened that needed more than two men, a dog, and couple of cars. Then they had to improvise. Like the computer print-out Sam was studying. That was nothing more than a lucky break; the county Highways Department had been carrying out a traffic survey to decide whether or not Forrest needed new roads. They had used a video camera, setting it up at various points on the roads leading into town. The supervisor of the exercise had called him as soon as news of the killings broke. From the film they'd been able to make out some license numbers, which had allowed them to ask Washington for help. The computer print-out was the result of that request. What it would produce Phil couldn't begin to guess but although he hadn't said so to Sam, he wasn't hopeful.

Phil broke the silence by clearing his throat noisily. 'What can I do for you, Miss Nichols?' he asked.

'You can tell me why Chief Brodie is conniving his way onto television when he knows squat and why you, who I presume know something, have chosen to treat me as though I have a communicable disease. Put another way, why all the secrecy?'

Phil shrugged, masking his irritation. 'The police are under no obligation to make entertainment for television,' he told her. 'Especially when to do so might hinder inquiries.'

'Bullshit,' she said.

Phil stared at her. His daughter was always telling him he was out of touch. If having a deep-rooted dislike of seeing women smoke or hearing them swear was old-fashioned then he would have to plead guilty to having some of his father's attitude towards the world. After a moment, he opened the top drawer of his desk and took out a large envelope.

'Phil . . .' Madsen started to protest but Phil waved him into silence.

'What do you want, Miss Nichols? Entertainment. Is that what you want to serve up to your audience? Something to watch while they're eating their ham and eggs for breakfast or serving up the meat loaf for dinner, or simply to brighten the happy hour.' He slid a batch of large glossy color photographs from the envelope, selected one and tossed it on the desk in front of her. 'How about that to accompany the hors d'œuvre?'

Barbara had been staring irritably at him through the smoke from her cigarette and now she looked down. The blood drained from her face as she saw the close-up of the boy's head.

He slammed down a picture of Louise Garrett. 'Or that to add some flavor to the main course.'

The girl made an incoherent sound deep in her throat.

'And how about this to go with the apple pie á la mode,' Phil said softly, gently floating a picture of Jo-Anne on top of the others.

Barbara pushed back her chair, her breathing noisy, her hands bunched into white-knuckled fists pressing down on the desk top as she pushed herself to her feet.

'Down the hall, first door on the left,' Phil said.

But she didn't move. She stood there, her eyes burning into his. Then she sat down again and pulled heavily on her cigarette.

'All right,' she said, her voice not quite under control. 'So it's not something we would want to show on television. Is that why you're keeping it secret? Because you want to spare our wonderful American public from throwing up all over their living rooms.'

Phil picked up the photographs, replaced them in the envelope and returned them to the drawer. She was tough, or at least she had a strong stomach, he had to give her that. 'We don't want a copycat,' he told her. 'And we don't want hordes of time-wasters telling us they did it.

They've started already and we can weed 'em out fast if we keep quiet about the method.'

'And?'

'And we're worried.' He paused. 'I'm worried,' he amended. 'Whoever did all this is a maniac. I want him caught and I don't know yet how I'm gonna do that. If I thought that plastering the gory details of the murders over every television screen and newspaper in the country then that's what I'd do. Right now, I don't think that will help catch him.'

'Him. Just one man.'

Phil raised an eyebrow. 'Why do you ask?'

She gestured towards the desk drawer. 'Three victims, three methods of killing.'

Bright, he thought. 'Could be more than one man,' he acknowledged.

'Motive?'

'Not a whisper.'

'Suspects?'

'The Chief showed you his pictures.'

'What do you think?'

Phil hesitated.

'Off the record, Sergeant Davis.'

He looked at her in silence, then glanced at Sam who looked up briefly from studying the print-out to nod imperceptibly. But still he hesitated.

'You can trust me, you know,' she said. 'Ask Doug Carlson.'

'You know Doug?'

'He's a researcher at WNTA.'

Phil nodded slowly. 'I wondered why you came here after I made it clear I didn't want to talk to you. He told you to try again.'

She nodded.

'Why didn't you say so right away.'

'Would you have shown me those photographs just because I was a friend of Doug's?'

'No.'

'Then I'm pleased I didn't.'

'Pleased? You're happy you saw them?'

'Goddammit, of course I'm not,' she flared. 'I'm not a ghoul. But now I know what happened in that house I can begin to understand the way you're acting and maybe find a way to help.'

'Help?'

'In some parts of the country the police and television reporters have learned to collaborate. It can have results.'

Phil grunted disbelievingly.

'Who are the two men in the pictures?'

'They're composites made up from descriptions by the old lady who lives next door and other neighbors who have seen men at or near the Garrett house during the past few months.'

'And one is the husband.'

Again Phil hesitated, then decided to take a chance with her. 'Nobody knows for sure what he looks like.' He nodded his head at her change of expression. 'I know it sounds crazy but since the Garretts moved in, six or seven months ago, they've kept themselves to themselves. One time, Louise Garrett told Mrs Carter, that's the old lady next door, that her husband's name was Ed and that he was a traveling-salesman. The old lady never met him, but once or twice she saw a man at the house. Tall, light-colored hair worn long, middle-aged, which to someone like Mrs Carter could mean anything up to sixty-plus. One time, when she was asked, Louise told Mrs Carter that her husband had been home for a few hours but had to rush away again.'

'Chief Brodie said that one was Garrett.'

Phil nodded. 'That's the old lady putting two and two together and deciding he was the husband.'

Which was, he acknowledged to himself, the way their thoughts had been leaning until a few minutes ago and Sam's suggestions had shifted the perspective.

'You don't think so?' Barbara asked.

'Right now, I don't have an opinion.'

'But you're not sure,' Barbara pressed.

Phil shrugged irritably. 'Maybe she was right, maybe she wasn't.'

Barbara weighed the evasion but didn't pursue it. Instead, she asked, 'And the other man?'

'Came to the house maybe twice, three times when Louise was out. Mrs Carter saw him hanging around.'

'And that's it? No other visitors?'

'No.'

'What about school friends of the children.'

'The boy was handicapped. His mother said he received special tutoring. So far we haven't found out who his tutor was. The girl hadn't started school yet.'

'How about the husband's job?'

'Nothing we found in the house has given us a lead.' As Sam had just indicated, it would have been closer to the truth to say that they had found nothing at all about the husband. No letters, no documents of any kind, no photographs. There were not even photographs of the woman and her two children. That was strange. Everybody has pictures around the house. If the killer had taken pictures away with him then it moved the husband - the man named Ed, who maybe wasn't the husband after all - up a notch on the list of suspects.

'Have you no other leads?'

Phil shook his head. He wasn't about to tell her about the traffic video; for one thing, he was aware how weak it made their efforts appear.

'So an early arrest is unlikely?' At least, Barbara thought, this will keep the story alive. And there was more to the victims than just an ordinary suburban family. Reclusive, a crippled son. She began to think that there might be even more here than a good story for television news. Maybe there was a book in it. Maybe a motion picture. Barbara saw a sudden flash of the pictures Davis had showed her and felt a twinge of guilt at the way her mind was working. Then she buried the thought. The woman and her children were dead. Whatever happened now, they wouldn't suffer any more.

Phil saw that she didn't expect an answer to her last question and that suited him very well. In fact, there was a possibility of an early arrest. And that would be a problem. Chief Brodie had spotted Chuck Riggs' action report detailing the two itinerant drunks Phil had ordered picked up. One was tall and thin, the other short and heavy-set. Neither was even an approximate match to the old lady's description, she hadn't said that the thin man had red hair or the fat man wore a moustache and beard. But Brodie was insisting on a thorough investigation of the pair's backgrounds and alibis for the past few days. Although he was sure it was a waste of time, Phil couldn't dissuade Brodie. The down side was serious because if they arrested the two drifters it would tempt the chief to cut down the already limited resources at his disposal and probably angle to take him off the case and handle it himself. The only bright spot was that for the moment, Brodie's insistence on investigating the two men was keeping him from under Phil's feet.

The telephone rang on Madsen s desk and he answered it, then left the room.

Barbara turned her attention back to Davis, knowing that if she was to get everything she wanted on the case she would need his cooperation. 'What I'd like to do, Sergeant, is stay with you for a couple of days. Just me, no camera crew. I promise I won't get in the way and I'll quit when you say so.'

'Why?'

She wondered briefly if he ever smiled. If he did, he might be quite nice looking in a slightly worn way. 'I want to build a clear insight into how the case is proceeding. Then, when you're ready, we can look at the possibility of a special feature aimed at giving the public a chance to help all they can in bringing whoever is responsible for these awful murders to justice.'

Bullshit, he thought, but unlike the reporter he didn't say it. What she wants is a ride to glory on a triple killer's coattails. 'Let me think about it,' he said. 'Anyway, I'll have to speak to Chief Brodie. He usually handles publicity.'

'I don't want Brodie, I want you.'

She realized the double meaning almost as she said and bit her lip angrily. Then, as a slow smile spread over Davis's face, she felt herself blushing. Damn it, she thought, I'm acting like a kid. But the smile certainly helped his appearance.

'I'll get back to you,' he said.

From his tone, Barbara knew he wouldn't agree to her shadowing him. She would have to find another way in.

Phil walked with her to the door just as Sam Madsen came along the passage. 'Chief wants us,' he told Phil.

'I left my cigarettes,' Barbara said. 'I can find my own way out.'

As the two police officers disappeared through a doorway, she went back into the office to pick up her cigarettes.

Pausing for a moment, she thought about lifting the photographs from Davis's desk drawer but decided against it. For one thing it would create an unbridgeable rift; for another, the station would never use them. Of course, if there was to be a book the pictures would be a bonus. She pushed the thought aside. If that happened she could always sweet-talk Brodie into releasing pictures. In any event, right now, she wasn't sure that she could bear to look again at the vivid, gory shambles.

As she turned away from Davis's desk she glanced across to the other desk and the computer print-out Madsen had been studying. Moving closer, she peered down at it, realizing it was a list of motor vehicle license numbers, alongside which were names and addresses. Madsen had ringed some of them. Reaching into a pocket, Barbara pulled out a miniature tape recorder, flicked it on and read off those ringed names and addresses. Then she left the office, walked out of the building and climbed into her car, thinking that maybe the past half hour hadn't been such a waste after all.

FOUR

IN ODESSA, Ryker emptied the safe-deposit box, packing bills into every pocket, trading documents for those he carried in his wallet. The guns, a Smith & Wesson 340 PD, and a Glock 26, together with ammunition for them both, he put into the bag that had held the presents he'd bought for Jo-Anne and Billy.

The box emptied, he relocked it and replaced it in its slot before calling the bank guard. He would never return to Odessa but there was no point in acting in any way that would make anyone remember him.

On the way out of town, driving east, he shredded his old identification documents, scattering the pieces through the window over several miles. For a time at least, he was still Jack Ryker, but now a farm implement salesman from Laurel, Mississippi.

So far, his caution appeared unnecessary. He'd stopped at a diner on the edge of Odessa so that he could watch the morning TV newscast before going to the bank. Not surprisingly, the killings in Forrest were still big news but neither one of the two descriptions the cops were circulating was of him. Later, he picked up a morning paper. He had his own need for those police pictures.

The fact that a description of himself was absent puzzled him at first but he reasoned that it was evidence that the care he always took was paying off.

But he hadn't been careful enough. Otherwise, how would anyone have found the house in Forrest? Someone must have trailed him there. He had to be the target. Not Louise. And certainly not the kids. Someone who knew him and wanted him out of the picture had put out a contract. But the assassin had hit the house at the wrong time. And, missing him and with no way of knowing when he would be there, had decided to leave a calling card to show that he was marked and that the killer, or killers, didn't care how much he suffered.

Nothing else could explain it.

But they had made a mistake. They should have walked away, left the innocents alone. Now, he was forewarned and that meant that he wouldn't let them get near him. Until it suited him. And one day, soon, it would suit him because now the hunters were the hunted and he was driven by more than a contract price.

First, though, he needed to eliminate some names from the list of people who might be behind the murders.

Whoever was behind the killings had to come from one of two groups. One was made up of people he'd crossed. The trouble was, he couldn't believe that he'd ever hurt anyone bad enough to cause someone to kill three innocent helpless people. The other group was made up of the people he worked for. Even here, he had trouble believing it. One way or another, pretty nearly all his jobs were done for Ralph Hardy.

Couldn't be Hardy.

Could it?

Why would Hardy want him dead?

People like Hardy don't care shit for people like you. He's a user and when he figures you're all used up he'll tear you in pieces and toss you out with the rest of the trash.

What if Hardy had decided that he didn't need him any more. But Hardy would always have work for someone like him; unless it had been decided that he knew too much and Hardy wanted him silenced. If that was the reason, Hardy had chosen a hell of a way to do it.

It didn't seem like a real possibility but that was where he would start and that was why he had to go to Dallas. It was from there that Ralph Hardy ruled.

Hardy lived in a Highland Park mansion with more guards and electronic security hardware than anyone would want to go up against but most days he was driven into the city and the fortieth-floor office from where he controlled his empire. Hardy could have operated from his home, but he liked to imagine he was a businessman just like the oilmen and realtors and property tycoons and all the other wheeler-dealers who inhabited the shining black-glass tower in downtown Dallas and who either didn't know or didn't care that their office neighbor, who also happened to be their landlord, made his living out of drugs and gambling, prostitution and arms deals and people smuggling, and a whole raft of things that were similarly illegal but even more profitable than their legitimate operations.

Even at the office, getting close to Hardy wouldn't be easy but it wasn't impossible. More important, he knew the layout of the office. He'd never been allowed to visit the house.

In Dallas he left his car in the parking lot adjoining the Galleria shopping mall on the LBJ Beltway. At the mall he bought new clothes, toiletries and a plastic travel bag to carry them in. He also picked up a large padded envelope in a stationery store. Finished, he took a cab to a middle-range hotel where he paid rent on a room for the night.

Showered, shaved and changed, he put his knife and the Smith & Wesson into his coat, together with enough walking-around money for what he had in mind. The other gun, spare ammunition, and the rest of the money, he put into the padded envelope. Before he left the hotel he put the envelope in the manager's safe.

Then he set out to call on Ralph Hardy.

Yesterday's shocks hadn't lost their biting effect but his head pains had eased and he had himself under control, forcing himself to be calm and detached when a cab dropped him off at the black tower.

Among other legitimate commercial enterprises, Ralph Hardy's office building housed a couple of insurance companies and as he walked through the doors into the lobby, a huge air-conditioned plant-filled atrium, he checked the floors on which they were located. The highest was just two floors below Hardy's fortieth-floor eyrie.

He went up in a glass-fronted elevator that hung dizzily over the twelve-storey atrium.

On the insurance company's floor, Ryker found the washroom and went inside. Alone in the white-tiled room, he smoked a cigarette, staring at the walls and thinking about the house in Forrest and wondering if he would ever see it again. Except in his dreams. And nightmares.

A man like you can't have a life like those of other men. It isn't possible. Don't even think about trying it. You'll fail. You'll lose everything you've worked for.

He shook his head uneasily, aware that the pain behind his eyes was building. This was no time to be thinking about Forrest and what had happened there, what he needed was to stay sharp while he figured a way to get upstairs and into Hardy's office without too many witnesses around in case there was trouble.

He dropped his cigarette butt into the urinal and as he did so a thought struck him. Looking up, he saw sprinklers at intervals across the ceiling.

Pulling out handfuls of paper towels, he locked himself in the stall farthest from the door. He spent several minutes rolling sheets of paper into pencil-like logs and building a little pile onto which he added a few sheets of toilet paper which he first dampened in the toilet pan. That done, he put a match to the pyre.

When it was burning but before the wet sheets had begun giving off much smoke, Ryker walked out into the corridor, past the elevators and found the stairs. Halfway between floors he waited, prepared to go either up or down if anyone else used the stairs before the alarm was sounded but no one did.

It was about five minutes before alarm bells began ringing.

He walked on up the stairs, which were suddenly in use as staff from the offices above obeyed fire regulations and headed for safety. He passed the next floor and came out into the reception area of the offices of the East Texas Merchandisers Corporation, the legal front Hardy had established and which fooled no one, least of all the cops and the government who turned expensively blind eyes to big-time racketeers.

Office staff, mostly men but with a few women, all white - Hardy's ETMC was not an equal-opportunities organization - were coming towards him and he held open the door, telling them there was no need to panic, that it was a minor problem and they should just go down to the thirty-seventh floor and wait until the all-clear. Then he stepped into the room.

Large, light, airy, the room had the look of a big bucks corporation's premises. Expensively decorated and furnished, filled with computers, it looked like something out of a movie. Which he guessed was what Hardy wanted.

Three dark-suited hard-faced men were gathered outside an office door on the northwest corner of the building.

He knew the tallest of the three. A bull-necked ex-marine, Dewey Morrow probably wouldn't have reached three figures on an IQ test, but he had more street smarts than most and when the need arose he could move faster than a snake strikes. Most important of all, he was devoted to Ralph Hardy and would kill anyone who threatened his boss. Curiously enough, Ryker felt no fear of Morrow. More than that, looking at the big man who was already coming towards him, he felt relaxed and confident. And, he realized, his head was not hurting.

'What do you want?' Morrow asked.

'Tell the boss I'm here.'

'We're leaving, there's a fire.'

'Tell him.'

Morrow started to shake his head, then shifted uneasily. He glanced at the others. Like Morrow, they seemed uncomfortable and edgy, waiting for a lead. He couldn't understand why they would act this way with him. People like these ate men like him for breakfast. Ryker began to wonder if they knew something.

'Tell him,' he said again.

Slowly, Morrow turned, stepped to the office door they were guarding, knocked softly and went inside.

Moments later, Morrow came back out, followed almost immediately by a tall, broad-shouldered, gray-haired man. Expensively dressed, Ralph Hardy was in his late sixties and could have passed for a lawyer or an accountant or any one of the legitimate executives who thronged the lower floors.

Ryker remembered how things were between himself and Hardy. From the start, a dozen years ago, Hardy had made it clear that he didn't mix with people like him. He was just a hired hand, even if Hardy sought and usually followed his advice. Whatever he did, however important or dangerous, he was beneath Hardy. He hated Hardy for treating him that way, but what could he do? Ralph Hardy was the boss, what he said was stronger than the law. There was nothing he could do about it but knowing didn't make it any easier.

'What're you doing here?' Hardy snapped, then glared at the guards. 'What the hell's going on?'

'Christ, boss,' Morrow said. 'You know I don't ask questions.'

'You dumb ox,' Hardy said. He turned back to Ryker. 'What do you want?'

'To talk.'

'There's a fire, goddammit.'

'No there isn't.'

'What?'

'I fixed the alarm.'

'You did what? Why, for god's sake?'

'So we could talk.'

'To do that, you need to scare everybody out the fucking building?'

'I wanted it quiet. Just you and me. No interruptions.'

Hardy stared at him, his dark eyes impenetrable.

'Why'

'I don't know. Or do I?'

'Will you, for god's sake, stop talking in fucking riddles.'

'I figured you might not want to see me.'

Hardy gestured in exasperation, then turned back towards his office door. 'This had better be good,' he said.

He followed Hardy into the office, half-closing the door behind him. 'I went to Mexico,' he said.

'And?'

'There was a problem. Lensky had a heart attack. He died.'

Hardy's eyes didn't flicker. 'So we got lucky. So what?'

Ryker felt uncomfortable. 'You don't mind?'

'What the hell is this?' Hardy demanded.

'You tell me.'

'For god's sake.'

'Between jobs for you, Mr Hardy, you ever wonder where I go? What I do? Where I live?'

Hardy's face darkened. 'Get to the point.'

'Ever hear of a place called Forrest?' he asked.

Hardy's eyes were bleak unfathomable pools. 'What about it?'

'There was a hit there. Three, maybe four days ago. A woman and two children. One a cripple, the other four years old.'

One day you'll want to settle down. A wife, kids. Maybe a boy and a girl. You'll see, you'll change. All you'll want is to play baseball with the boy, look after the girl. Make love to your wife. Act the way other people act. Not people like you, ordinary people. You'll see. One day.

'It was my wife,' he said. 'My kids.'

Hardy watched him, an expression in his eyes he never remembered seeing before.

'Whoever did it,' he told Hardy, 'they have to be crazy because they're going to die for what they did in Forrest. To my wife. My kids.'

Hardy was studying him, the strange expression still shadowing his dark eyes. 'You think I had something to do with killing these people . . . your family?' he asked.

What was it Lensky had said, the last words he'd spoken? Something about a woman. Could that have been Louise? He shook his head, aware that the pain was coming back.

'If not you, then who?' he asked Hardy.

'I never harmed them . . . your family,' Hardy said. 'That's all I know.'

He studied Hardy's face, thinking about the kind of things that resulted from this man's orders and which never caused him to look worried or guilty or even mildly inconvenienced. But neither in his reactions nor in his voice, nor even in his almost expressionless face, did it appear as though Hardy had anything to do with hurting his family.

There was just that faint expression he couldn't quite identify.

'Okay,' he said. 'So it wasn't you. I'm sorry, Mr Hardy, but I had to know.'

He walked to the door. Glancing through into the outer office he saw that Morrow was now just a few feet away, hands lightly crossed in front of him, his jacket open. The others had spread out. Nobody could take out all three men before he was gunned down.

'Tell them not to follow me,' he said over his shoulder to Hardy. 'I don't want any trouble.'

'Trouble? You already got trouble,' Hardy said, anger now apparent in his voice as it slid towards the gutter adding, 'You know it doesn't end here.'

He knew what that meant. Nobody came up here and confronted Ralph Hardy and lived to boast about it. He looked at the older man carefully. 'I'll kill anyone, everyone, you send after me, Mr Hardy.'

'You can't kill everybody. One day, you'll run out of time. One day soon.'

He shook his head sadly. 'You know, I could've been more than what I am,' he said, aware that he would never again have a chance to talk to Ralph Hardy.

'Now what're you talking about?'

'You treat me like I was nothing. I could've done much more. Anything. I learn fast.'

That strange look was back in Hardy's eyes.

'I'm sorry, Mr Hardy,' he said again. 'But I had to do it this way. I had to know. And I have to go on until I find who killed them. Don't try to stop me.'

Hardy looked at him, his expression now the usual bleak look of the commander of a multi-billion dollar criminal empire. 'You're a dead man now. Run all you like but you're dead.'

Ryker shook his head again, then turned, went across the office, through the doors and down the stairs four floors before taking the elevator to street level.

He knew he'd made his life difficult, put it in danger. No one went up against a man like Hardy. But he'd had to do it. He had to be sure.

And now he had no time to waste. Right at this moment, Ralph Hardy would be calling in the best men in the country.

By tomorrow, not only would the police be on his trail for the killings in Forrest, there would also be hired gunmen. Men like him with nothing on their minds but killing.

It wasn't until later that he could put a name to the expression that had, for a while, clouded Hardy's eyes.

Fear.

Realization hung awkwardly with his conviction that Hardy spoke the truth when he said he hadn't harmed his family. If that was so, why did he fear him?

But there was an even more puzzling question.

Ralph Hardy was the most powerful man he had ever known, a man who ordered killings with less deliberation than some men showed when choosing the right tie to go with a suit. But for some reason, Ralph Hardy was afraid of him.

It was not only puzzling, it was also unsettling. But there was nothing he could do about it now. He couldn't go back up there and start over. If he needed to, he would have to find another way to talk to Hardy. And maybe ask him straight out, what it was he was afraid of.

In the meantime, he had to move on. Talk to the next man on his list. One of the men who might hold a grudge.

For the next visit he needed wheels of his own. Taxi drivers talked as many miles as they drove but he risked one to reach a point a few miles away from Hardy's tower. Then he walked a couple of blocks, took a bus, walked some more until he saw what he wanted. From a small-time local rental company he negotiated a good deal on a dark-green Ford panel truck. It was the kind of tub a plumber might use, or an electrician, or any kind of ordinary tradesman.

Then he headed for University Park and Senator Lucius Dillard.

Although he didn't have a clear plan he knew he must talk to the people whose lives had intertwined with his in the past. It made sense to look at the most recent people first; those who might hold a grudge that still burned hot. And there was also logic in visiting those who were close to hand; he couldn't afford to waste time.

Dillard scored on both counts; he had done a job for him late last year and he lived here in Dallas.

He couldn't remember Dillard's address but he recognized the road and when he saw it again he knew the house.

You can't miss it. White, pillars all across the front. Goddamn thing looks like a mansion on a Southern plantation that's been out in the rain and shrunk.

That was just how the house looked. A small-scale imitation of something it wasn't. Not like the huge houses that lay a mile or so to the south in exclusive Highland Park where the real money lived. They were the real thing. Dillard might like to think he lived where the oilmen who'd hung onto their money lived and where TV and movie stars and

45

sportsmen, to say nothing of men like Ralph Hardy, bought places to offset taxes, but he didn't. He never would. State Senator or not, Lucius Dillard was small change, a man always on the edge of something he never could be.

Ryker had no plan how to approach Dillard. He didn't even know whether the Senator would be home or in Washington. Surprisingly, the gates were open and he drove the panel truck up to front steps of the house, close to a badly parked Cadillac, turned off the ignition and heard dogs barking.

Big sonsofbitches. Watch 'em. If you have to, kill the bastards before they kill you.

He should have remembered the Senator's dogs. They were huge, noisy, vicious. He should've remembered that from before.

After a moment or two, when the dogs didn't come and their noise was no louder he decided that they were either inside the house or were chained up someplace. Cautiously, he climbed down from the truck and went up the steps to ring the bell beside the door.

When the door opened it was the same old man he remembered from last time. Tall, thin, white-haired and, he now recalled, English. An English butler was the kind of thing a man like Dillard thought improved his public image.

He told the old man that he wanted to see Dillard.

'Is the Senator expecting you, sir?'

'Yes,' he said.

The old man looked at him doubtfully. 'I am afraid the Senator is, ah, indisposed, sir. Are you sure your appointment was for today?'

He pushed the old man aside and walked into the cool lobby. Now he could tell that the dogs were not inside the house. That was one thing in his favor.

'Drunk, is he?'

For a moment the butler stood by the door, indecisive, then he sighed and gently closed the door and moved closer. 'Do you know the Senator, sir?' he asked. Then, peering short-sightedly, he slowly nodded his head. 'Ah, yes, you're the gentleman who was here just before the election.'

The old coot was right. It was in the run-up to the last election and Dillard had seen that his rival was gaining an edge over him. The other man, young and good looking, was making a lot of noise about the state's massive drugs problem, on exploitation of immigrant workers, and on poor housing for the lower-income groups. His appearance and his politics had given him support among women, blacks and the ever-growing numbers of Hispanic voters.

Dillard had asked Ralph Hardy for help.

It had been easy. Dillard's opponent disappeared for three days during which the media went into overdrive. When half the state was sitting on the edge of its seats at the start of every TV news program, the missing man was found, thanks to an anonymous tip-off to the police, which was mysteriously and simultaneously leaked to every TV station and newspaper in the state.

The politician was at a motel, unconscious from too much booze and a mild but effective overdose of drugs. With him in the room were an under-age black girl and an under-age Mexican boy, both naked and drugged to their eyeballs. In one unbelievable frame-up every one of the man's support groups had been targeted. It was so unbelievable that nobody believed it. Everyone knew it was a frame; the police knew it, the media knew it. Even the people who were no closer than watching it all on TV and reading newspaper reports knew it. But that didn't help the politician. Tell a lie that big and nobody dare take the risk that some little part of it might be true. Dillard won in a canter.

Thanks to a call the Senator had made to Ralph Hardy and thanks to him. He was the one who had set it all up.

'You helped us, ah, defeat our opponent,' the old butler said.

'Something like that,' he said.

'I'm afraid the Senator really is rather unwell.' The old man almost smiled. 'You might say, he is drunk as a skunk.'

'I thought you people said, drunk as a lord.'

This time the smile was real. 'Oh, drunker than that, sir.'

'I really need to talk to him,' Ryker said quietly.

'I'm sure that the Senator would be happy to talk to any friend of Mr Hardy's, but he really is very unwell.'

He leaned forward, thrusting his face into the old man's. 'You're not getting this,' he said, not raising his voice at all. 'I want to talk to him. Now.'

The butler sighed again and turned towards the stairs. 'If you'll come this way, sir,' he said.

The doorbell rang, the noise startling him and prompting an involuntary movement of his hand towards his gun.

'May I answer that?' the butler asked politely but nervously.

Ryker crossed the hall, glanced cautiously through a window, then relaxed a little. By now Hardy's men would be looking for him and might even have put eyes and ears into Dallas-Fort Worth airport, bus depots, and all the city's car rental outlets. That was why he'd rented a truck for the visit to Dillard. Hardy's people were unlikely to be that imaginative.

And they were even less likely to send a woman after him.

It was a young woman who had rung the bell on Dillard's door. Dressed in faded jeans, sneakers and a red and black check workshirt under a shapeless windbreaker, she looked as though she might be making a delivery.

'Go ahead,' he said to the butler.

As the old man tottered towards the door, Ryker went up the stairs, a curving balustraded expanse of white marble that wouldn't have looked out of place on a film set.

Below, he heard the butler clicking his tongue in resigned exasperation, then open the door and start to tell the woman the same tale he'd told him. From the sound of it, Dillard's drinking jags had made the butler word-perfect but he could tell that the woman was giving the old man a hard time. He guessed that she, too, might talk her way into the house, but he didn't care. If she was a problem, it was one he could handle.

On the landing he remembered that Dillard had a study at the east side of the building and he headed in that direction. Down below, the woman had already made it into the lobby.

He reached the study door and opened it. The morning sun had moved around the building and the room was shadowed but he could see enough to know that it was furnished expensively and tastelessly.

His back to the door, Dillard was sitting on a studded leather couch, fully dressed save for a jacket, shoes and socks, all of which were lying on the floor. The clothes were formal evening wear. Whatever Dillard had been doing the night before he was still dressed for it. And still drunk from it.

A TV was on and tuned to a channel showing cartoons. The sound was off.

The Senator was overweight, his belly stretching against the creased white shirtfront. His face was bloated and marked with red blotches against a pattern of heavy blue veins. His eyes, watery blue and small, glared angrily at the interruption.

'Who the fuck're you?' he snarled

Don't let Dillard bullshit you. As if you would. He talks big, acts big, he is big. But only if you, measure him in feet and inches and pounds. Every other way the man is chickenshit little. Jumps at his own shadow. Look at him hard and he'll walk away from you, raise your voice and he'll run. Lift a hand and he'll very likely keel over right in front of your eyes.

He walked around to the front of the couch and showed Dillard the Smith & Wesson.

The heavy face turned pale beneath the red and blue markings. Dillard tried to push himself up to his feet, rocked back again, hard, and began to cry.

'For Chrissake don't hurt me. Take the goddamn money. There, take what you want.' He waved a fat, hairy hand towards the safe which stood against the far wall, it's door open to reveal a stack of neatly packaged bills.

Ryker breathed shallowly, trying to avoid the reek of alcohol and the unwashed senator. 'Not money,' he said. 'Just a question I want answered.'

Dillard stared up at him, his mouth open, his breathing noisy and face blank.

'What do you know about Forrest?'

'Forests? Trees?'

'Not forests, you asshole. Forrest, Texas.'

Dillard frowned, laboriously thinking, then mumbled, 'North. Near Amarillo. What about it?'

'Who do you know there?'

'Know? In Forrest? Jesus, how the fuck should I know? I know people all over the goddamn state.'

Whatever Dillard was, he wasn't that good a liar. Not when he was this drunk. Faced with a gun that already had him pissing in his pants, he couldn't be faking it. Dillard clearly didn't know what the hell he was talking about.

Anyway, it was obvious that the Senator was too far gone with his drinking habit to know which way is up let alone hire a hit man to kill a defenseless woman.

So it wasn't Hardy and it wasn't Dillard.

He looked at the open safe and the money. Once it would have tempted him but now it didn't interest him.

He closed the door as he went out, slipping the gun out of sight as he walked to the top of the stairs. He couldn't see the woman or the butler.

Outside, he climbed into the truck, started the motor and drove out into the street.

Not Hardy. Not Dillard.

Next was the general. Maybe this time he'd be lucky. But he didn't know where the general lived, not anymore, not since he was busted out of the army. First he would have to do a little detective work and then get some sleep. If he could.

IN THE house, the young woman in work clothes watched the dark-green truck disappear, then read off the license plate number into a little tape recorder.

Barbara Nichols was beginning to think she was treading water but she'd come all this way and wasn't wasting any chances. Especially not now that the FBI was involved and had insisted that Phil Davis and Chief Brodie close her out completely.

'Okay,' she said to the white-haired butler. 'If Dillard really is too drunk to talk about hiring me to do his fetching and carrying, then I'll talk to you. And you can start by telling me who that was and how come he gets to talk to the Senator, drunk or not.'

FIVE

PHIL DAVIS looked up wearily as his partner brought coffee to their table and leaned back against the worn green-plaid of the bench seat.

'Cheer up, Phil,' Sam Madsen said. 'Things could be worse.'

'How?'

Sam grinned. 'That's my line,' he said.

In spite of his gloom, Phil managed a smile. As he sipped his coffee he looked out the window of the diner towards the highway. His reflection stared back at him. He looked the way he felt, tired and deflated.

The past few days had not gone well. He remembered something a veteran detective had told him when he first joined the Dallas PD. 'Right from the start get used to the fact that most crimes won't be solved. Ninety percent of the few that are, will be cracked in the first twenty-four hours after the crime is committed. After that, the chances are you're just pissing against the wind.'

Over the years he'd spent in Dallas the old cop's words had proved to be pretty accurate. Since his move to Forrest things had been a little better; most crimes in the small town were solved. But the second part of the statement, still held good; the first twenty-four hours were vital.

In the case of the Garrett killings they'd lost those and more. The coroner's report estimated the time of death as sometime on Thursday. Dan Flory had hedged on nailing the time too closely but said it was probably late that day and likely before midnight. Things might get a little more accurate when tests on larva from the flies were completed but that would take a while. So Flory's reluctant guess had to do for now. The bodies were not found until after six on Sunday morning. That meant they had lost not just the first twenty-four hours, but at least the first fifty-four.

Although Phil was still unwilling to let go his early intuition that the husband - or boyfriend - was not the man they wanted, they'd looked for him. Looked hard but had drawn blank. Not a damn thing to work on, apart from Mrs Carter's hazy description, which might or might not be of the man whose name might or might not be Garrett. No photographs, no bank account, no documents of any kind. They ran a check on the name, starting with Edward and Edwin and Edgar Garrett, then widening it until eventually they had listed every Garrett in the state who appeared in any state register. Nothing that fitted, not even a driver's license to a Garrett at this address. Phil was starting to think that Sam's theory was right and Louise had not been entirely truthful with her neighbor.

Then, the Forrest police hit a completely unexpected obstacle. They were still running down men named Garrett on the drivers license and other lists regardless of where they lived, along with motorists whose cars had been recorded by the Highways Department's survey, when control of the investigation suddenly changed hands.

From the start Phil had liked the idea of calling in the FBI and had suggested as much to Chief Brodie. The Chief hadn't agreed. Phil knew why. Brodie didn't want the Suits giving orders, something which would inevitably risk the loss of such a great publicity opportunity. Brodie had insisted they wait a while. Then, out of nowhere, the Suits were all over them and the Chief was smiling and handing out orders that Phil and Sam and everyone else cooperate fully with the Bureau.

The Chief had called Phil into his office, getting him out of his uncomfortable meeting with Barbara Nichols, and told him that the FBI was taking charge. 'We need the Bureau, Phil,' he had said, smiling with patent insincerity. 'You said so yourself and now I agree with you.'

'Not to take over, goddammit,' Phil argued. 'Yes, we can use their help, especially if our man is a serial killer. And even if he isn't, we can use out-of-state help. But help is help; you're talking about handing over the entire case. Everything but house-to-house and other routine local inquiries. What does that make us look like? Amateurs.'

Brodie had shrugged off his protests and the eagerness with which he was giving up his chance for personal publicity told Phil that someone, somewhere, had made the Chief an offer he wasn't about to refuse.

Within hours, the Garrett case was in the hands of a pair of smart-suited agents. Michael Flaherty and Jim Skerrow, promptly renamed Flatt and Scruggs by the jokers on the force, were polite and efficient and had about them an air of slightly distant superiority. Not surprisingly, morale among Forrest's Finest sank. Especially affected were those few who had seen the victims. Phil knew how they felt; more than any other crime he had ever investigated, he wanted the man who had done this found and tried and convicted and executed.

It was an unguarded remark he made to Jennifer about such a punishment that sparked a fierce argument. Momentarily, he had forgotten the outspoken attitudes she had on many things, especially contentious issues such as capital punishment. Since coming to Forrest capital crimes had ceased to be a part of his daily life and the fate of the people he arrested was never worse than a short stretch in the state pen.

The decision to leave Dallas had seemed right at the time. It had started with Phil's growing concern at how life in the city - violent, corrupt, dangerous - might affect his family. Sarah had agreed. Jennifer, then six years old, was not consulted. There was a cruel irony there, Phil now knew.

Forrest was not a random choice. Phil's father was born there and a twenty-year spell in Dallas apart, had made his home there, building houses and after Phil's mother's death and his retirement, hunting and fishing and yarning with his old friends. On his death, Phil had inherited the house and it was that, coinciding with a vacancy on the Forrest PD, that brought Phil and Sarah and Jennifer here.

Life in Forrest had been a revelation to Phil and his wife. Neither of them had lived in small-town America - he was born in Dallas, Sarah in Houston, and both had always been city-dwellers - but they took to life in Forrest easily, swiftly and happily.

Until the day of the accident it was a dream life. A drunk driver, overtaking on a blind turn, had hit Sarah's car head on. Sarah died instantly. The drunk died in the hospital the following day.

Jennifer's injuries were bad, but it was two weeks before the doctors told Phil just how bad.

Paralysis from the waist down. The form of paralysis was known as 'incomplete', a term Phil had first thought was a really sick joke but had soon learned was a minor blessing. Well, a major blessing, given what 'complete' paralysis could be. Jennifer's injury, close to the base of the spine, had left her unable to walk unaided and although there was some movement possible, with long leg braces and a walking frame, it was only something Jennifer could do under close supervision in a safe environment.

Fortunately, and for them both it counted as a blessing, Jennifer was spared the distress of urinary and fecal incontinence. And as years passed and more test were conducted, the doctors thought that in all probability the injury would not have made her impotent. Although Phil had not yet been able to think about, certainly not adjust to, Jennifer one day having a child of her own.

About a year after Sarah's death, Phil had made an uncomfortable decision about Jennifer. Although the department had willingly allowed him to adjust his working life to suit the patterns of a young paraplegic schoolgirl, it quickly proved impractical. Even in a quiet well-ordered town like Forrest, crime didn't keep regular hours.

That was when Sarah's mother, Laura Blake, had offered to take Jennifer off his hands for a few months. He hadn't liked the thought of her going away, least of all at a time when they were both still learning to cope with their bereavement, but he thought hard, discussed it with Jennifer, who had matured startlingly and at going on thirteen was smarter than many of the adults Phil met in his work. It was decided that spending time in Humble was probably a good idea, just so long as it was clearly understood by all involved that it was a temporary measure.

So Jennifer had gone to Humble to live with her grandparents for almost a year. In lots of ways it was a good move. The Blakes were alert, articulate, highly intelligent people. Sometimes, Phil thought, their minds seemed younger than his own. Laura, a former professor at the University of Houston, was an active sixty-year-old who now ran a small book store in Humble. Her husband, Sidney, still worked several days a week as a consultant at the Houston law practice he had founded forty-something years ago. Back then, the Blakes had been outspoken liberals and involved themselves deeply in numerous conflicts with state and federal authorities. Unlike a lot of people Phil knew from that generation, the Blakes had not allowed themselves to be seduced by money and success and still retained most of their old fiery enthusiasms and beliefs. Inevitably, Sarah had inherited much of her parents' philosophy and in turn had begun to pass this on to Jennifer. The spell in Humble meant that the fires were stoked.

Since then, Jennifer had spent several months each year with the Blakes. That, allied to close-to-home arrangements with his neighbor, Jane, the former nurse, and a newly-qualified young nurse, Lucy Hemmings, who was good and hit it off with Jennifer, meant that Phil and his daughter had adjusted to their new life and in several ways, some unexpected, they had become closer.

One reason for this, Phil knew, was thanks to Laura and Sidney Blake. Direct exposure to the source that had made Sarah the woman she was when Phil met her had its effect on Jennifer and over the years Phil discovered that she was increasingly ready to challenge him on almost everything he did or said. It was not challenging in an unpleasant way, but in a way that showed him in embryo form the reasons why he had fallen in love with Sarah. Not that it was always easy. The Blakes liked him personally and recognized the need for an effective police force, but they viewed many aspects of policing with suspicion. Jennifer, young and impressionable, had picked up the suspicion but not always with the necessary understanding.

That wasn't how Sarah had viewed his work. She had always known that he did what he did with care and thought and responsibility and tried hard not to let the dirt rub off on him. That had helped allow her to understand his change of heart that led to their decision to move out of Dallas.

Jennifer had yet to acquire the maturity of her mother and to understand that all authority wasn't corrupt and that most police officers had laudable ideals. At least, they had them when they started out. And they needed the support of the general public and, Phil believed, they needed the backing of a real deterrent that would make even the most violent criminal think before acting. That deterrent, he was sure, was the death penalty.

That was where he and Jennifer had fallen out when he insisted that this was the only realistic punishment for the man who had committed the murders at the Garrett house.

Of course, he couldn't tell her the details and failed in his attempt to convince her that his belief was valid. A curtain of cool irritation had fallen between them; one that Phil knew would pass, especially when he had time to spare for another, hopefully more temperate, discussion.

Then, coincidentally, Laura Blake had called and suggested that Jennifer might like to take a trip with her and Sidney. They were driving to Phoenix to visit an old friend and planned to spend a little time seeing sights on the way out and back and most especially while they were in Arizona. Phil guessed that Laura and Sidney missed their granddaughter's enlivening presence in their lives. Whatever their motives, Phil jumped at the idea, knowing that he was not good company right now and that the pressures on his time would increase. Jennifer had liked the idea, too, and after Phil had talked with the head teacher at school it was agreed that the Blakes would pick her up at the weekend.

Since then, the expected demands on his time had been dissipated by the FBI's involvement but still he was pleased that Jennifer would soon be away from Forrest. Although he was growingly certain that the killer came from outside the community he didn't know that for a fact. He had been wrong before and would be again. If he was wrong this time then his daughter would be better off someplace else.

'What do you suppose Larsen looks like?' Sam Madsen asked, cutting into his thoughts.

They were at the diner, a few miles south of the town, for a meeting. Arranged by Flatt and Scruggs, the meeting was with a senior FBI man coming in from Quantico. All they knew was that Special Agent Larsen wanted to talk to Phil out of the way of other officers, press and any idle onlooker.

'Like all the others, I suppose,' Phil said. 'Sharp suit, clean shirt, shined shoes, neat haircut. Some things never change.' He was irritated at the fact that they had been given no say in the time or place or that the meeting should take place at all. Driving out of town for a meeting struck him as an unnecessary complication. Surely Larsen would be visiting Forrest. It was partly out of his irritation that he had brought Sam along although the invitation had been for him alone. He didn't know why the Bureau wanted secrecy but he was damned if he would give them an easy ride.

He didn't think much of the venue either. The decor, green plaid carpet and upholstery, all of it worn, and with orange-brown faded curtaining hanging in sweeping curves at the windows, made the place look like a hangover from the 1970s. One that hadn't been cleaned as much as it should since then. He wondered if the county's Health Department officers ever came in here. If they did, maybe it was to use it as a guide to how things shouldn't be.

'Maybe that's him.' Sam was indicating a fat, sweating man wearing a stained polyester suit who was coming into the diner.

'No chance. Hoover would have to be one hundred years dead before they'd let complete slobs into the Bureau.'

'Or him.' Sam had seen a gangling black youth with greasy dreadlocks.

'Might be a woman,' Phil suggested.

'You think?'

'Maybe not. They would've said.'

'Sergeant Davis?'

Neither of them had noticed the man who was now standing beside their table enter the diner. He must have come in through the kitchen. Not quite six feet tall, he looked to be in his early sixties and was dressed the way they had expected: immaculately and expensively suited. Slim in a muscular way, with the pallor of a desk jockey on his long narrow face, he wore his graying fair hair longer than expected; certainly not like the neat haircuts Flatt and Scruggs wore.

'Mind if I sit down,' the newcomer said, sliding into a chair without waiting for a reply. 'Jake Larsen,' he added unnecessarily. He looked at Sam Madsen, then at Phil before turning again to Sam. 'And I expect you're Detective Madsen.' He hesitated and Phil guessed he was deciding whether or not to object to Sam's presence. Then Larsen shook hands with both policemen, called over a waitress, ordered lemonade for himself, a refill for Phil's coffee, while Sam shook his head, indicating his half-full bottle of water. Larsen sat in comfortable self-contained silence until the order was brought to the table and they were alone again.

'Thank you for coming,' Larsen said.

Phil opened his mouth to speak, felt Sam tap his ankle, and closed it again.

'Mike Flaherty says you had a good investigation going, Sergeant,' Larsen continued. 'Everything by the book, nothing missed, all real tight.' He paused.

Phil looked at Sam, then picked up his coffee cup and waited.

If Larsen was embarrassed at the silence he didn't show it. 'Before we came in,' he continued, 'we didn't know anything about the police in Forrest. We checked and I have to say we didn't expect to find men of your caliber.'

Phil stood his cup down with a sharp click.

'Small town, small crimes, small minds. Is that what you expected?'

Larsen stared at him in silence for a moment. 'If I sounded patronizing it wasn't meant that way. Just a simple statement of fact. Another fact is that Dallas lost a major asset when you decided to leave.' He turned to Sam. 'And wherever you go when you leave Forrest will gain an asset.'

'Leave? Why would I do that?' Sam asked. 'There are not too many places where a man can walk with the blessings of nature the way he can here.'

Oh, Christ, thought Phil, he's going into one of his spiritual moods.

Something approaching a smile touched the corner of Larsen's mouth. 'If you seek them out,' he said, 'you will find that there are many places where the earth is holy and the feet that walk upon it are blessed.'

Sam looked expressionlessly at the FBI man for a moment, then leaned back in his chair and laughed. 'Okay,' he said. 'So we've both read Chief Dan George.'

Larsen favored Sam with a fleeting curl of the lip that was almost a grin, then turned back to Phil. Although there was no appreciable change in his expression or voice, suddenly he was all business. 'I take it Chief Brodie didn't give you any choice in the decision to bring us in. Don't let that make things difficult between us. We can do much more than you on a case like this. You don't need me to tell you the extent of our resources.'

'Which is why I wanted you brought in at the start,' Phil told him. 'The delay wasn't my idea.'

Larsen frowned. 'I didn't know that. Sorry. Brodie plays things close to his chest.'

'Maybe he does,' Phil said, then decided to test his guess that it hadn't been Brodie's insistence that brought the Bureau into the case. 'One thing he didn't do,' he said, 'was invite you in. You invited yourself in. That isn't the way it usually happens.'

Larsen hesitated for a moment then obviously settled for not arguing against Phil's guess. 'No, it isn't,' he admitted.

'So what's special about this case? Special to you, I mean.'

'We're making great strides in the struggle to track down serial killers. The special inter-state police computer and the Bureau have done a lot of good work. One thing that's been pretty clear all along in these cases is that the sooner we are involved the better our chances.'

'Who says this is the work of a serial killer?' Phil asked.

Larsen sipped thoughtfully at his lemonade. 'You don't think it is?'

'I didn't say that. I asked why you're so sure.'

'The nature of the killings, the extreme level of violence, the absence of any other probable reason.'

'And you decided all this from your office at Quantico?'

For the first time Larsen looked uncomfortable, tugging irritably on his right ear. 'No, the agent in charge of our Amarillo office decided.'

'Flaherty?'

'A good man.'

'So good that he decided from his office in Amarillo that this was the work of a serial killer. What else did he decide without seeing the scene of the crime, the bodies, or any damn thing except what he read in the papers or saw on TV news? Did he decide the man was a psychopath or a sociopath or maybe a bit of both? Did he decide whether he was a relative or a family friend, a local man or from out of town? Just what did he decide from his office in Amarillo?'

'Can I ask you a question, Sergeant?'

'Why not? You're not very good at giving answers.'

'Why are you so angry? You just told me you wanted us involved; now you're angry because we are. Is it just because we came in anyway? Is it the protocol that bothers you? If it is, I'm surprised. From your record, you don't seem like the kind of man who worries too much about things like that.'

Phil stared at Larsen for a moment, thinking that the reason he was angry was because he sensed that Larsen wasn't being straight. Then he shrugged his shoulders. 'Okay,' he said. 'I wanted the FBI in to give us the back-up we obviously need but I don't like the idea of being edged out because I want the man who did this thing found and punished for what he did.'

'And you don't think we feel the same way?'

'You didn't see the bodies,' Phil said.

'I saw the pictures.'

'A picture is just a picture. You didn't see them, Larsen. You didn't smell them.' Or hear the flies, he thought.

'Agreed,' Larsen said. 'But I have seen bad stuff. It goes with my job, just the way it goes with yours. And you know as well as I do, that taking crimes personally isn't a smart idea.' Larsen held up a hand as if to ward off a blow. 'No, that isn't patronizing either. It's a fact.'

Phil didn't answer. The bodies had shaken him more than he might have expected. The woman alone was bad enough; the crippled boy took it onto another plane. Personal almost, although that was the kind of thinking that led to some of his arguments with his daughter.

All wheelchair users are not alike, Jennifer had drilled into him. There are nice ones, nasty ones, smart ones, dumbbells. Same with any other group. Lumping people all together because of color or creed or race was wrong; same thing went for wheelchair users.

But it was not the boy's death that affected him most. For reasons he could not evaluate, it was the little girl, not hacked, butchered, like her mother and brother, but neatly dispatched, almost clinically - cleanly, if that was not an utterly wrong word - that he could not shake from his mind.

And it was also the killing that most frustrated his attempts to try and understand the kind of man who could commit such an act.

He knew that some investigators, specialists in the field, did their work in part by putting themselves into the minds of the monsters they sought to capture. How could they do that without losing their own sanity or even cling on to their own humanity?

Looking at Larsen, he wondered if he was one of that strange band of investigators.

Now Larsen spoke again. 'Can I tell you why I wanted this meeting?'

'If you don't it'll be a waste of a day,' Phil said brusquely.

'Yes, please tell us,' Sam said to Larsen, over-polite and looking at Phil, silently urging calm.

'We are expanding the investigation nationwide. Some parallels have shown up between the methods used in Forrest and other killings. What are believed to be serial killings. We want to pursue these and because there is a limit to our manpower that means running down our operation in Forrest. In other words we want the local force to resume its principal role, at least so far as the investigation in this county is concerned. Despite what we think, a serial killer is only one angle. There may be others and they have to be followed up. And the best men for that are here. We will set up a two-way priority channel of communication so that everything we find comes into Forrest and vice-versa. We need to work together on this one. It's the only way.'

Phil stared at the FBI agent, thinking that whatever else he had expected to hear this morning, humble sincerity hadn't occurred to him. Now that he heard it, he didn't believe it.

Larsen was continuing. 'However, I have an idea that it will be more useful if you . . .' he paused, then said, 'Look, if we're going to work together can I call you Phillip?'

'Phil.'

Larsen nodded. 'And I'm Jake. If we are to work together, it will be more useful, more potentially successful, if you, Phil, can work on the case in a wider context.'

Phil looked at Sam who gave him his famous wooden-Indian look. Completely inscrutable. Which, in Sam's case, meant he was either very angry or bursting with the effort of not laughing. Phil guessed that this time it was laughter his colleague was repressing. Whatever skills Larsen might have, flattery was not one of them.

'What have you in mind?' Phil asked.

'Those motor vehicle plates you identified. How did you decide which to pursue?'

So that's what's interesting you, Phil thought.

He inclined his head towards Sam who answered the question. 'The video census points were all on roads into and out of town. The nearest was over a mile away from the Garrett house. That means that an appearance on any of the films has no particular significance. We decided that any vehicle registered to an owner living within a ten-mile radius had every right to be on these roads; put another way, we couldn't prove otherwise. We decided to eliminate them, at least for the time being, and that took care of most of the vehicles caught by the census cameras. The others we split into trucks and cars. If a truck was on what was obviously a regular commercial route, we set them aside for future inquiry.'

'There have been a number of serial killers who traveled around the country on lawful business,' Larsen said. 'They just used their free time in a way that made them our business.'

'I know,' Sam said. 'That's why we didn't discard them entirely.'

'What about the rest?'

'These were cars, and one unmarked panel truck, registered to people living out of the area, in some cases out of state. We set aside any women, not permanently but for the time being, and that left us with a handful of men we decided to check into.'

'With what results?'

'None. We never made the checks. We were just setting it up when Chief Brodie told us you people were coming in.'

'Ah,' Larsen said. 'Maybe that's where you and I should start, Phil.'

'You and me?'

'Suppose we split them, you take any in areas you're familiar with, I'll take any where I know my way around.' Larsen turned back to Sam. 'You have the list?'

'Not with me, no.'

'Can you remember any locations?'

'One in Oklahoma City, another in Richmond, Virginia. Two, no, three in the Dallas-Fort Worth area. And one in Arkansas.'

'Dallas is your old backyard, Phil. Maybe you should take those and Oklahoma City. Richmond's close to me, so I can look into that and on my way home I can go via Little Rock.' Larsen smiled, tugging again at his ear. 'How does that sound?'

'Terrific,' Phil said, not hiding his sarcasm.

'You don't like the idea?'

'For one thing, Jake, I can't look into, as you put it, anything that's over the county line. Not officially, anyway, and I have no plans to start acting unofficially.'

'You'll have the authority,' Larsen said firmly. 'I'll see to that.'

Could Larsen do that? Phil looked at Sam for support but got the wooden-Indian look again. He shrugged. 'Whatever you say,' he told Larsen.

'I'll go into Forrest today,' Larsen said. 'Talk to Brodie, make a few phone calls, and get the show on the road.' He hesitated. 'Any questions?'

'One,' Phil said. 'How did you get onto the Garrett killings?'

Larsen sipped some more lemonade, staring at Phil as he did so. 'We identified patterns in the killings that matched known serial killer methods. I thought I told you that.'

'Maybe you did,' Phil said reluctantly.

Larsen leaned back in his chair, studying Phil. 'At the risk of repeating myself, we really do need to work together.' He leaned forward again. 'Shouldn't be too hard. We have much in common, inside and outside the job.'

Phil frowned a question.

'Both experienced law enforcement officers. Both experienced in the highly specialized art of raising a daughter single-handedly.'

'You really have been checking up on me.'

'You'd do the same.'

'Would I? Okay, maybe I would.'

'How old is . . . Jennifer, right? How old is she?'

'Almost seventeen.'

'Difficult age,' Larsen said with feeling. 'What are your plans for her future?'

'My plans? I don't have any. Jennifer has her own plans.'

If she stayed on course, she would become a veterinarian, although her disability kept throwing obstacles in her way. If that didn't happen, then Plan B was politics.

'You don't have plans for her?'

Phil shook his head. 'What matters is what Jennifer wants.'

'What if she wants to be involved, at some level, in your kind of work?'

'She doesn't want that.'

'But if she did?'

'Then that's what she would do,' Phil said, with more positive emphasis than he felt.

Unbidden, an image of Jo-Anne's delicate face, hideously disfigured by the scissors in her eye, came into his mind. Did he really want Jennifer to have to see things like that?

As if reading Phil's mind, Larsen gave a little shake of his head.

'What about your daughter?' Phil asked. 'What does she do?'

'She's a police officer.'

Larsen's clearly disapproving tone prompted Phil to say, 'And you don't like that.'

'It isn't what I planned.'

'What you planned?' Sam put in.

'I thought she should be a corporate lawyer.'

'But instead, she's just a dumb cop, like us.'

'Not dumb,' Larsen said sharply. 'She's a high flier.'

For a moment, Larsen didn't speak and Phil guessed that the agent's old-school FBI antipathy towards cops in general was conflicting with his thoughts about his daughter.

'But you still don't approve.'

Larsen sighed. 'Like I said, it's not what I planned.' His eyes turned inwards for a moment. 'Not what I hoped,' he corrected himself; almost a whisper. Abruptly, he pushed back his chair and started to rise, asking, 'You coming?'

'We'll follow,' Phil told him. 'See you later, Jake.'

They watched Larsen walk out of the diner, then looked at one another.

'He's gone to get the show on the road,' Sam said in tones that imitated Larsen's incisive speech patterns. 'Christ.'

'A lot of help you were,' Phil said.

'Since when did you need help in knowing a liar when you hear one?'

'You noticed.'

'I noticed. He might have read the thoughts of Chief Dan George, but that doesn't mean he's a wholly truthful man.'

'He's also an unhappy man,' Phil said.

And still sore that his daughter didn't fall in with his plans for her, he thought. He wondered how he really would feel if Jennifer decided she wanted to be a cop. Probably he'd be unhappy, too. But he would back her to the hilt. And never, ever grumble about any disappointment he might feel to anyone.

'Another thing,' Phil added. 'He wasn't especially careful. Maybe he thought we're too dumb to notice that the Bureau couldn't compare methods with known serial killer patterns because we didn't release details.'

'Brodie could've told them.'

'No, not before they invited themselves in. Later, maybe, but at the start they must have had another reason.'

'I figured it was something else,' Sam said blandly.

'Any ideas?'

Sam grinned. 'You know as well as I do.' He reached into an inside pocket and took out the folded computer print-out on which were listed the vehicle registrations they'd requested from the licensing bureau in Washington and opened it out on the table, smoothing the creases.

'Tut tut, you had it all the time.' Phil said. 'You lied to the FBI.'

'So arrest me.'

Phil leaned over, reading the list upside-down. 'You think this is what brought Larsen out of his cozy office?'

'I can't think of anything else. The only things we did that reached outside the state were inquiries about Ed Garrett and our request for this list. Someone in Washington must've told the Bureau we requested it.'

'Why would they do that?'

Sam was silent for a moment. 'They wouldn't. Unless there's a name on here that's flagged in the computer.'

Phil knew that, commonly, various national and state authorities coded names that were of interest to the FBI, the CIA, the NSA, the police. Anyone with a legitimate interest. Then, anytime something affected that name, such as their inquiry to the license bureau, the interested party would be automatically notified.

'If you're right, in this case the name that interests Larsen must be one of those he said he'd look into. Which one do you think? Little Rock or Richmond?'

'Little Rock is my guess. All I said was Arkansas, he knew it was Little Rock.'

'Maybe he just guessed, it is the state capital,' Phil said. 'Or maybe he's seen a copy of the whole damn list and knew the places all along and was just playing dumb, then made a slip of the tongue.'

'So what do we do now?'

'One, you go back and start running the local investigation the way we should've been doing it all along. Two, I pick up my cardboard FBI badge or whatever the hell it is Larsen will give me to show my authority and then I'll head for Dallas.'

'Even though you're wasting your time if Larsen knows something we don't.'

'I'll take bets that Special Agent Larsen knows more than he's telling us. But he might be wrong about the drivers from Little Rock and Richmond. Anyway, if I stick around here I think I might very well be wasting my time, which is what you'll probably be doing.'

'Thanks. That's just the kind of encouragement I need.'

'Don't worry, Sam, I have a little task for you,' Phil said, smiling. 'Between us, we should be able to come up with someone in Little Rock and in Richmond we can trust to ask a few questions that won't alert the Bureau. That way, with a little luck, between us we can find out what Larsen knows that we don't.'

Sam nodded, brooding for a moment. After a while, he asked, 'What are we into, Phil?'

Phil, serious now, shook his head. 'Damned if I know,' he said. 'But whatever it is, I'll also take bets we're not looking for a serial killer.

I'm starting to think that whoever killed those people, crazy though it all looks, he is not what we might be tempted to think he is.'

SIX

FOR WHAT was probably the tenth time in the two hours plus she had been sitting in the lobby of the Sunset Hotel, Barbara Nichols decided that she was either wasting time or taking a dangerous risk. But if she did call it a day it would not be because of any potential danger. Taking risks of a kind had always been an acceptable part of the job. And, for Barbara, the job had always been paramount in everything she did.

She couldn't remember ever wanting to do anything but be a reporter. Growing up in Galveston, where her father had been a sub-editor on a local newspaper, she had fantasized working in the same business; but not in Galveston, and not in any place else except in New York City. Only New York would do. Single-mindedly, she directed her education towards that end. After graduating from university, majoring in journalism, naturally, she had spent two years in Oklahoma City learning the hard way that nothing in life is as easy as it looks from the outside. Then she spent three years with a Houston newspaper, getting some good breaks mainly through dedication and sheer hard work, but already beginning to acknowledge that for all her childhood fantasies, this was no longer what she wanted to do with her life. Sure, she still wanted to be a reporter but the lure of the press had been overtaken by her awareness that for really big success, and recognition from her peers and the public, she had to be in television. And she wanted success, craved for it to the exclusion of everything else in her life. Personal relationships took a poor second place to her career. Fact was, and she barely admitted it to herself, she was not above using personal relationships to facilitate a career move, or even to derail a rival. Personal relationships? Okay, so what if that was a euphemism. She was a reporter and euphemisms were part of everyday language.

One facet of Barbara's early ambition remained, she still wanted to be in New York. She spent six months there but it was crowded with too many people just like herself, just as determined, just as ruthless. Okay, not 'just as'. Some of them were tougher, no, harder, and she knew it was hopeless to waste effort trying to outdo them. So she thought long and hard and then decided that her best chance for a real breakthrough into the bigtime would come if she could enter the New York television fray with an established track record. Put another way, the networks had to want her as much as she wanted them. To achieve that aim, she went back to Texas, looked around, and landed a job with WNTA in Amarillo. That was two years ago and she knew that her reputation was already spreading. She was even more eager to make her move but she still needed to tie herself to a really big story so that the doors of those people who had heard of her, and that were cracking open in New York, would suddenly be wide and welcoming.

But those two years also meant that she was beyond being merely impatient. Her move upwards couldn't come soon enough. She needed a change, craved the excitement of big stories, hints of danger. She wanted to live life on the edge.

At first, the triple murder in Forrest looked like being the story to give her a ticket to the national networks but she was beginning to have second thoughts. If it was the missing husband who had killed Louise Garrett and her children then there was probably not enough mileage. Domestic killings were commonplace and even one as horrific as this wouldn't make the kind of impact she needed. If it was a serial killer then there might be more mileage but even then there was the possibility that audience boredom would result. Hard to believe though it might be, there were signs that the public was becoming anesthetized against stories about serial murderers. Years of headline cases had taken their toll. Books by the armful, a string of motion pictures, and even television had got into the act, not only with an occasional in-depth documentary but also using serial killings as the basis for that blandest form of dramatic entertainment, Movies of the Week. There was even a television series where the leading character was a serial killer. What did that say about the viewing public's appetites and the network's desire to indulge them?

No, her best hope with the Garrett murders was that they would turn out to be neither a simple domestic nor a run-of-the-mill serial. Something different was what she hoped for, something with an extra dimension.

When she picked up a handful of names and addresses from a computer print-out on Detective Sam Madsen's desk in Forrest she hoped something interesting would emerge. It had, but it wasn't what she'd expected and she was no longer certain that the list had anything to do with the Garrett case. If anything, she was pretty sure it did not.

She had decided to follow up those names from the list that had addresses closest to home and with the first she hit not pay-dirt exactly, just plain dirt.

When she saw the house at the Dallas address given for Luis Delgado she drove around the block twice, thinking about an approach, then put on her reporter's hat, asked some questions of neighbors, and in no time flat learned that the house was the residence of Senator Lucius Dillard. At first she'd guessed wildly that the coincidence of initials meant something but quickly learned that Luis Delgado was the senator's driver, gofer and occasional bodyguard.

Although she had never met him, she knew about Dillard. A hard-drinking, womanizing, corrupt throwback to the days before politicians tried to conceal such inclinations from the voters. Dillard openly flouted public expectations, reveling in sleaze and taking an often malicious delight in dirty politicking. But for all the bad tales she'd heard about him, she couldn't imagine a link between Dillard and the Forrest murders. But she was still cautiously curious. Dillard's driver-bodyguard might be a different matter.

While she was watching the house an unmarked panel truck drove up to it and she saw the driver ring the bell and be admitted. He could be Delgado, but the odds were that Dillard's bodyguard would have his own key to the door, even if it was in back, and she hazarded a guess that this was just a deliveryman. That gave her an idea. She hatched a hasty tale that she was canvassing for work for a new collection-delivery service setting up in the neighborhood. It wasn't a very good cover but it got her into the house and a long and rambling conversation with the old man who reluctantly admitted her.

For no reason other than the fact that motor vehicle registrations were the only clues she had, she took down the number of the truck.

From the old butler, who appeared relieved to talk to someone, she picked up hints that the man she'd seen arriving at the house was someone who was not above election-rigging and was connected in some way with Ralph Hardy. Anything that linked a United States Senator with a man like Hardy had to mean something. Surely nothing to do with Forrest, but interesting for all that. Later, when Dillard had come screaming down the stairs in a drunken rage yelling about men with guns roaming around his house, Barbara slid quietly away and used her cell phone.

Before leaving Amarillo, she had compiled a list of names and telephone numbers from her contacts back when she'd worked in Houston, updating them with some of Doug Carlson's friends and acquaintances in Dallas. It didn't take long to discover that the truck was a rental and a visit to the company, some sweet-talking and a twenty dollar bribe, gave her the driver's name and address. Then she headed along Northwest Highway towards White Rock Lake, looking for the hotel a man named Jack Ryker had entered as his base.

The truck was in the parking lot of the Sunset Hotel, an unpretentious low-rise, pink stucco building, badly in need of maintenance. She parked her car as far from the truck as space allowed, went inside the hotel, and spent another ten bucks with the clerk to learn that Ryker was in his room. And, after a brief, calculatedly flirtatious exchange with the clerk, he agreed, not surprisingly, that he would identify Ryker for her when he came into the lobby.

But, two hours later, she was still sitting in the lobby, the clerk was about to go off duty, and there was no sign of Ryker.

Then she heard the elevator doors open and glanced casually over her shoulder. One man stepped out. Tall, slender, he had medium-length sandy-brown hair brushed flat, a high forehead, eyes deep in hollows, a complexion that hadn't seen too much sun, and a wide mouth that looked as if it rarely opened let alone smiled. He wore cheap clothes, a tan suit that needed pressing, scuffed shoes, and a wrinkled shirt. He was carrying a cheap plastic travel bag emblazoned with the logo of an airline that had gone down the tubes last summer. She had seen only his back when he left the Dillard house but she was sure it was the same man. He walked across to the clerk, spoke to him and waited until the clerk went into the office in back before reappearing with a large padded envelope, which the man stuffed into the bag. Then he walked out through the main door while the clerk eagerly gave her a quick confirming nod.

She watched as the man crossed to the truck and drove out into the street. Hurrying to her car, she squealed out of the parking lot and soon caught up with him. Following the truck in heavy traffic wasn't easy and afraid of losing it she clung closer than seemed safe. Hopefully, the density of the west-bound traffic along Northwest Highway and, later, the Airport Freeway was also working in her favor, preventing the driver up ahead becoming aware that a silver-gray Honda was on his tail. Later, when the truck turned south onto Arlington Grapevine Road, the traffic fell off dramatically and, no longer buried amidst surrounding dozens of vehicles, she hung further back.

By now, the streets of Arlington were lined with middle- to upper-income housing and she was uneasily aware that she was at risk if the driver had the slightest interest in the road behind him. Hurriedly, she turned off, raced around a block and returned to park where she could see along the main road without being seen. Far off, she glimpsed the truck and spotted an intermittent gleam as it flashed a left turn.

After she had made the same turn she drove slowly until she glimpsed the truck standing in a driveway. The man in the tan suit was standing at a door that was soon opened. In the instant before she was unsighted by a high clipped hedge Barbara recognized the small man in the doorway and felt a sudden thrill of excitement. She didn't have the slightest idea what was going on, but the ingredients for a story were massing.

First, the man she was trailing had visited Lucius Dillard, a corrupt but, so far, publicly unexposed member of the United States Senate. Now, he was calling on an equally corrupt but publicly disgraced, and briefly imprisoned, former three-star general in the United States Army.

GENERAL RAYMOND K. Bohannon was smaller than he'd remembered. Five feet five or six inches tall, chunky but hard-muscled, Bohannon at sixty had almost no gray in his thinning hair. His square jaw needed shaving twice a day, his complexion was that of a healthy man. He wore gold-rimmed rectangular spectacles behind which lay narrow suspicious blue eyes. The kind of man who only looked right in uniform, or maybe a plainly formal business suit, Bohannon appeared incongruous dressed as he was in russet and fawn plaid golfing slacks, tasseled cream-leather loafers and a short-sleeved beige sports shirt.

'Well?' he asked, then looked closer, his already unsmiling expression hardening still further. 'You,' he said.

'Me.'

'What do you want?'

'To talk.'

'Our business was finished long ago.'

'Maybe, maybe not.'

Bohannon studied him thoughtfully, then stepped back, letting the door swing a little wider. Ryker went inside, waited as Bohannon closed the door behind him, then followed the ex-soldier into a room that was furnished as austerely as any army camp office.

Bohannon sat behind an uncluttered desk, inclining his head towards the room's only other chair that faced his. After a cautious glance around the room - only the one door, one window overlooking the front drive - Ryker sat down.

'What do I call you this time?' Bohannon asked.

'Ryker.'

'Well, Ryker, what do you want;?'

'Someone is making trouble. I don't know who. I have to find out.'

'Tell Hardy I no longer . . .'

'This doesn't concern Hardy,' Ryker interrupted, uncomfortably aware that he was still uncertain if that were really true.

'Who then? Who are you working for this time?'

'No one. This is my business.'

Bohannon looked at him flatly, caution and suspicion on his face. But no fear. Ryker studied the general for a moment and looking into the eyes behind the gold-rimmed glasses saw that not only was there no hint of alarm, there was not even much evidence of interest. He wouldn't necessarily have expected alarm. Bohannon had come up the hard way and knew the army better from field commands than from behind the Washington desk that had offered the temptations that were eventually his downfall. But there should have been interest, mild curiosity, if the general had any involvement in what had happened in Forrest.

'You remember the job I did for you?'

'Of course I do. Not that it did me any damn good in the long run.'

'That wasn't my fault. Hardy's neither.'

The general had been tempted by his discovery of secret funds that no one appeared to know about, maybe a hangover from the days when Oliver North and Richard Second had worked at the Pentagon. Bohannon devised ways and means of siphoning these funds into his pockets without involving international arms dealers and other unnecessary complications. It had all gone well until a Washington reporter, fired by dreams of becoming a kind of latterday Woodward or Bernstein, picked up some hints of the general's activities from a disgruntled low-echelon helper who thought he was being under-rewarded. Bohannon, born and raised in Texas, knew Hardy and decided that he needed the kind of help only the Hardys of this world could offer. The brief was simple, frighten off the reporter leaving the general to deal with the helper. But Bohannon had left it too late before calling on Hardy. The reporter was given his painful fright the same night that the helper was promoted dizzyingly to heights he never imagined possible. Unfortunately, that night was the one when the presses were already rolling with the story and the papers hit the streets at exactly the moment the reporter was being carried into hospital to have his jaw wired and a bemused former sergeant was sewing on his lieutenant's badges.

'So you don't hold a grudge?' he asked Bohannon.

'A grudge? Against Hardy? Of course not.'

'Not Hardy. I told you, this isn't Hardy's business, it's mine.'

'The answer's the same.' Now the general was frowning, and for the first time was showing curiosity. 'What's this about?'

'You know what happened in Forrest?'

The frown deepened. 'Forrest? There've been some killings there.' He leaned forward, resting his hands flat on the desk. 'What are you and Hardy mixed up in now, for god's sake?'

'Not Hardy, I . . .'

'All right, you told me, this is your business. So what is it all about?'

He looked deep into the general's eyes.

Trust no one and the chances are you'll never be disappointed. Trust one man and you're already splitting the chances fifty-fifty.

He was taking a lot on trust and on his judgment of the people he dealt with, maybe too much. He'd believed Hardy and he'd believed Dillard. Now he was believing Bohannon. All on impressions, guesswork. What other way was there? Beat the truth out of them? Or kill them anyway? He couldn't kill everyone whose path he had crossed. Hardy had said something like that. No, he had to wait until someone gave a hint of knowing something about the murders. And the general wasn't giving off any signs that hinted at even the remotest connection with what had happened to Louise and the kids.

Abruptly, he stood up and crossed the room, opening the door.

'You're going? That's it?'

He turned. Bohannon was on his feet, glaring at him.

'That's it,' he said. 'I have to go.'

'You come in here, talk nonsense, then just go?'

He looked at the general, making no attempt to mask his irritation. 'You're out of it, don't push it.'

For a moment the glare stayed in place then slowly slipped away. 'Get the hell out,' the general said. 'And stay away. And tell Hardy that goes for him, too.'

'I keep telling you, this isn't Hardy's business.' He went out of the study, closing the door behind him.

Bohannon waited until the outer door closed then turned to look out the window at the truck pulling away. Then he sat down again at his desk. For a few minutes he remained motionless, thinking, then opened a drawer, took out an address book, flicked it open, then reached out and punched a number into the telephone.

'Bohannon,' he said. 'Put Hardy on. Tell him it's important.' He waited. 'Hardy? What's going on? That man of yours has been in here talking gibberish.' He listened. 'Yes, of course that's who I mean. What the hell have you and he been up to?' He listened again. 'No, he was in a truck. Looked like a rental.' A pause. 'Yes, I got it.' He told Hardy the number he'd read off the truck's license plate. 'No, he didn't say where he was going next.' Another pause. 'Okay, consider I've forgotten all about him. Let's hope that this time I really have seen the last of him.' He banged down the telephone and sat, thinking again. Opening another drawer in his desk he took out a revolver and began to load it. Just in case Hardy was wrong.

AFTER BARBARA had recognized Raymond Bohannon she did some fast thinking, then decided to take a chance that Ryker would eventually go back to the Sunset Hotel. If he did, she could pick up his trail there, or maybe at the rental company. In the meantime, she had to talk to Eric Lundqvist.

She remembered the Bohannon scandal in detail and had been acutely envious of Lundqvist and the coverage the journalist had received for his exposé. Even the fact that he'd been badly beaten during his investigation had done no permanent harm and even added luster to the case. Lundqvist had moved on, taking a job with CNN, exactly the kind of career move she planned for herself, and was now an internationally-known face. For all his new fame, when she reached him Lundqvist was more than agreeable to talk about the case that had made his name.

'Pretty nearly everything came out at the hearing,' he told her. 'The only area we didn't get into, because we had no hard evidence, was that Bohannon had links with organized crime in the southeast. We think it was those people who arranged for my jaw to be broken.'

'Any names?'

'The men Bohannon knows are probably Ralph Hardy and Jorge Aguerre.'

'How about the man who attacked you. Did you see him?'

'I gave the police a description but it was dark and after he hit me the first time I was in bad shape.'

'Can you describe him to me?'

There was silence for a moment. 'What are you onto, Barbara?'

Lundqvist asked.

'I'm not sure,' she said, honestly. 'At the moment it's just a lot of unconnected events, people. Nothing I can tie together but I have a feeling about it.'

She heard Lundqvist laugh. 'I know feelings like that.'

'About that description,' she said. 'Was he anything like this?' She described Jack Ryker.

'Could be,' Lundqvist admitted. 'Especially the mouth. Like a steel trap that was rusted shut.'

'Thanks,' she told him.

'That's okay. Listen, Barbara, if you do tie all this together and you think there's something we can use here at CNN, call me. Maybe we can do a deal.'

'I'll remember that,' she said.

'And Barbara. Be careful. Hardy and Aguerre and the people that work for them, they're the kind that can make your life very unpleasant.'

'I'll remember that, too,' she said. 'And thanks.'

Back at the Sunset Hotel she sat in the bar from where she could see the main entrance. By eleven she was tired of fending off passes from unattached male guests, who appeared to make up the majority of the Sunset's clientele, and she had, anyway, decided that Ryker was probably not returning tonight. Or if he did come back, the odds were that he would simply go to bed. She decided to find a room for herself, not at the Sunset - that would be too risky - but nearby, and try to pick up pursuit in the morning either here or at the truck rental company.

She went out through the lobby and into the parking lot. As she turned the key in the lock of her Honda CR-V she felt something cold and smooth touch her neck and a voice, whispering, told her. 'Just be quiet, no screams, no sudden movements. Just stand there.'

She froze, thinking that it might be a mugging. Or it might be Ryker. She remembered Lundqvist and his shattered jaw and hoped it was only a mugger.

The man reached around her, opened the door, kept hold of the keys, and told her to get in. She did as she was ordered, beginning to tremble. For a moment there was no sign or sound of the man. He must have walked around the back of the car because then he was opening the passenger door and climbing in beside her. She risked a sideways flick of the eyes. It was Ryker. He still had the travel bag and he jammed it under the seat before asking, 'Who are you?'

She didn't answer and felt a sudden pain as he thrust the gun, hard and painful, into her side. 'Answer,' he said.

She couldn't lie about her name. It was on the car papers lodged behind the sun visor, on her credit cards and other documents in the car and in her handbag. 'Barbara Nichols,' she told him.

He fumbled around for a moment, then the interior light came on and he gripped her face in one hand, turning her to face him. This close she could see the thin line of his mouth and the cold shadows of his eyes. Her trembling increased. Christ, what had she let herself in for?

'I've seen you before,' he said. 'Before today.'

She forced herself to think. How much did he know about her? Maybe the hotel clerk had warned him. Or he could've been back to the rental company and heard from them that she had been asking questions. He might have spotted her today on the way to Arlington. Then there was her visit to Dillard's house or even during the long tail to Bohannon's. He could have seen her in any of several places. Whichever it was, she had a problem. Or maybe he recognized her from TV. That would be the worst. Admitting to something a little bit less dangerous might be a way out.

'I'm owed money,' she told him. 'By a man named Luis Delgado. I went to the address he gave me but he wasn't there. Turned out to be Senator Dillard's house. I saw you there and the butler told me you were mad as hell about something so I figured maybe Delgado owed you money, too. I couldn't find him on my own so I thought if I followed you I might get to him that way.'

It sounded weak, desperately weak. But he appeared to be thinking about it.

'How do you know Delgado?' he asked.

How? Think, dammit. 'He rented a car from me,' she improvised. 'That's one of the things I do. Rent out cars.'

'Why would Delgado need to rent a car.'

Why? She couldn't think of an answer. Okay, go on the offensive. 'What are you? A cop?' she asked.

'Me? Shit, no.'

Was it working? She'd had time to think of a story. Keep going. 'Delgado, he does a few things he doesn't want people to know about. So sometimes he rents a car that can't be traced back to him.'

The man made a sound that was almost a laugh. 'That sounds like Luis.'

She felt some of his tension easing and the gun moved away from her side. 'How does it work?' he asked.

'What?'

'No tracing back to the guy who rents the car.'

'For a price I lose the records. It's a service Hertz and Budget don't offer.'

'Yeah, I can see how you might find takers for that kind of service.'

Tentatively, she asked, 'Is Delgado a friend of yours?'

'I know him. And the man he works for.'

'Dillard.'

'No, not Dillard. Dillard just hires him when he needs muscle. Luis works for . . . He works for somebody else.' He was silent for long dragging moments. 'This job Luis was doing that he needed a car for. What was it?'

'He didn't tell me.'

He was silent again and she risked a quick sideways glance. His face was set hard. Out of nowhere an idea came into her head and she heard herself saying, 'But I know where he went.'

'Where?'

'A little town in the north of the state. Forrest.'

He moved faster than she would have believed possible. The gun jabbing hard into her side again and his other hand seizing her face, the fingers digging painfully deep into her cheeks as he jerked her around. His face was thrust into hers, bare fractions of an inch separating them and she felt his hot breath on the skin around her mouth.

'Forrest? Delgado went to Forrest?'

'I think so.'

'What do you mean, think? You said he did.'

'That's what he told me. I remembered it when all those murders happened.'

The fingers were tightening still more. She'd thought that when Eric Lundqvist's jaw was broken it was with a blow. If this really was the man who'd done it, maybe he had crushed it. It felt as though he could crush hers.

'Is that when he was there? At the time of the murders?'

Dammit, she was concocting the story, not recounting facts. Wait, though, the list Detective Madsen had been studying had dates scrawled alongside the names he'd circled. She forced herself to think, a fierce effort of memory. 'No,' she managed to squeeze out the words. 'Before.'

'When?'

'Some time last month.'

Imperceptibly at first, she felt his fingers ease their pressure although the pain remained.

'So,' he said, so quietly she could hardly hear him. 'Delgado was in Forrest a few weeks before Loui . . . those people were killed.'

She couldn't believe it. He'd almost spoken the woman's name.

For Christ's sake, he knew the dead woman.

So there really was a link. A link between Louise Garrett and her children, Luis Delgado, and this man. And Senator Dillard and Raymond Bohannon. And Ralph Hardy and another man Lundqvist had named, Aguerre. In spite of the danger she was in Barbara felt an almost uncontrollable excitement grip her. The Forrest murders were not merely a domestic incident and almost certainly not just another score in a serial killer's reign of terror. The whole thing was beginning to build into exactly what she'd hoped for. All she had to do now was stay with it. And stay alive.

'Maybe you can help me find him,' she said. 'Delgado, I mean.'

He moved slightly in his seat and with relief she saw he was putting away the gun. Then he reached for the switch and plunged the car into darkness.

'Maybe I can,' he said.

And maybe she could help him, Ryker thought. For one thing, she could drive him around in this little car. No rentals that might be traceable and anyone looking for him would be watching out for a man alone, not a couple.

He handed her the keys. 'Okay,' he said. 'Let's go.'

'Where?'

'Austin.'

'Austin?'

'You want to talk to Delgado and so do I. So we'll go talk to the man he really works for and he's in Austin.'

For a fleeting moment she hesitated as if she were considering refusing but just as quickly she must have recognized the fact that she had few if any options. If she had any at all. She started the engine and drove out of the Sunset's lot.

Ryker watched until he was sure she was heading the right way, following the route signs that would take them out of Dallas onto Highway 35, then allowed himself the luxury of concentrating on Luis Delgado. He was nothing. Some muscle and few brains. He had worked for Ralph Hardy for a few years but had botched too many jobs and had been handed on when Hardy set up one of his lieutenants to control the organization's activities in the south of the state. He remembered the fuss there'd been over the anointing of Jorge Aguerre. A lot of people didn't like taking orders from a Hispanic but Hardy had insisted that where there were strong links with Mexico they needed someone the Latinos would trust and who spoke their language.

Since taking over, it was obvious to anyone that Aguerre had fulfilled all Hardy's hopes. Too well, maybe. He'd heard rumors, whispers, that Aguerre was becoming ambitious. Hardy wouldn't like that. Not one little bit. And if there was to be conflict between Aguerre and Hardy then anything might happen.

But he couldn't imagine where a weak link like Delgado fitted in. Unless, of course, he'd been sent to Forrest to spy out the land. That was about the limit of Delgado's capabilities and even then he was suspect.

Don't use fools on errands where the end has a serious purpose. Serious business needs serious people all the way through. Use fools and the whole damn thing can fall apart.

But if Delgado had gone to Forrest to help plan a hit that still didn't answer the question, Why? Why would Aguerre target him? If Aguerre wanted to make a move on Hardy why would he come after him first? It didn't make any kind of sense.

Barbara concentrated on her driving, her mouth dry, her muscles tense, her face still painful from the way Ryker had gripped her jaw in his powerful fingers.

Her thoughts, wild and chaotic, were gradually becoming more ordered. She was involved in something that was messy and extremely dangerous. She knew that the smartest thing to do was to plan her escape and leave this man and everything with which he was connected behind her. But if she did that she would also kiss goodbye to the best chance she might ever have of making her name. So, what she had to do was play along, make herself useful to this man, discover all that she could, and keep an eye open for ways that she could use, when the time came, to get out unscathed.

It would also be smart, as soon as the chance arose, to let someone, Doug Carlson maybe, know where she was. Not who she was with; that might risk someone else nosing into her story. No, she would take the first chance she had of calling Doug but all she would tell him was that she was on her way to Austin and maybe whet his appetite by hinting at some of the connections she was making.

SEVEN

IT WAS more than an hour later when the car slowed and Ryker heard the indicator clicking. He glanced sharply at the woman. 'What're you doing?'

Barbara stubbed out a cigarette and gestured towards the fuel gauge. 'We're running on fumes. And I need to go to the bathroom.'

After a moment, Ryker shrugged and sat back in his seat. He was uncomfortable with this woman but he knew that for now he needed the cover her presence gave him. But having someone with him, someone he had to watch all the time, made him tense and his head was hurting. Just sitting here, without even the distraction of having to concentrate on driving, allowed time to think. Too much time, none of it helping answer the mounting questions or clear some of the troubling haziness that clouded many of his memories. The shocks and the lack of real rest during the past few days were taking their toll.

There'll be days when you can't rest, nights when you can't sleep, then more days, more nights. There's not a damn thing you can do about it because that's the life you're leading. You just have to learn to live with it.

The car turned off at the slip road, looped under the highway and eased onto the brightly-lit forecourt of a filling station-cum-diner.

'Gas first,' Ryker said.

He watched as the pump jockey, a fat youth with greasy white-blond hair, his round face bright with the effort of having to carry too much weight, washed the windshield while the pump gurgled. When the pump came to a stop the youth took the girl's credit card and disappeared into the shack. They sat in silence until her credit card was returned, then Ryker jerked a thumb at the diner. 'Pull over there,' he told her.

Barbara started up, drove the short distance and parked where he had pointed, noting that here the car was well away from the filling station's lights and even by day would have been almost out of sight of anyone passing along the service road and invisible from the highway. Whatever Ryker was up to, he was certainly cautious.

They climbed out of the car and he asked if she wanted to eat. Right now, the last thing Barbara wanted was food but she did want time to try placing a call to WNTA, preferably direct to Doug Carlson. 'Coffee would be good,' she said.

She locked the car and started to walk towards the diner but he came around the vehicle, holding out his hand for the keys. She hesitated but then handed them over with an irritable shrug.

In the diner he ordered coffee for them both while she went to the bathroom.

The face in the mirror was pale, very noticeable red marks showing where Ryker had seized her. One thing about her appearance, it was unlikely that anyone would recognize her. The way she looked on camera was always at odds with the image she projected off-screen. Today even her own mother wouldn't recognize her. She stared at her reflection, thinking hard. So far, Ryker hadn't thought of checking to see if she had a cell. But if he did, she didn't want to leave evidence of a call right now, least of all to a TV station. It occurred to her that even receiving a call on her cell might prove tricky. No, if she were to call Doug, it would have to be from a place like this, using a landline. On her way back to where he waited she spotted a pay-phone alongside a cigarette dispenser.

Sitting down, she lit a cigarette and slowly sipped her coffee thinking that she needed to relax this man, make him trust her. Talking to him was the way to start.

'Why are we going to Austin?' she asked. 'Who is this man Delgado works for?' She paused, trying to remember if she was supposed to know Ryker's name. 'And what do I call you?' she added.

He stared at her coldly and for the first time she looked into his eyes. The pupils were large, making his light-blue eyes appear darker, deep-set as they were. It was impossible to read them. He took out a cigarette pack, shook out the last one and used her lighter, slowly crumpling the empty pack with his free hand. She thought about the way he'd gripped her jaw and shivered.

Then the thin line of his mouth twisted slightly at the corner. 'Is that all you do? Ask questions.'

She forced herself to keep silent. Questions were her most important tool, it was how she did her job. But right now, though, she wasn't supposed to be a reporter, she was supposed to be something else.

After a moment he said, 'You know why we're going to Austin. That's where we'll find Delgado. Then you collect the money he owes you and I get to talk to him.' He drank some coffee. 'And you can call me Ryker,' he added. 'I figured you knew that from all the detective work you've been doing, trailing me around the way you were.'

Get into character, she said to herself. You're supposed to be someone who supplies cars to people who don't want questions asked. So you associate with tough guys, people on the edge of the straight life. And you can take care of yourself.

'Listen,' she said. 'I don't give a shit about you, your name, or any other damn thing about you. Delgado owes me money, sure, but he doesn't owe me so much that I can drive all the way to Austin and back and all the rest of the expense this'll cost and come out with a profit. So, maybe, there's something else down there that I can get into. Maybe this guy that Delgado works for can use me.'

Ryker's thin lips parted showing square white teeth in what might have passed for a smile except that nothing else on his face moved. 'I doubt it,' he said. 'Delgado works for Jorge Aguerre. You've heard of him.'

The last part wasn't a question, he expected her to know of Aguerre. Since hearing the name from Erik Lundqvist, she'd half expected he was the man Ryker was going to see. Confirmation caused a sudden bloom of excitement. The hypothetical cast list for her story was firming up and was much better than she could've hoped.

Of course she'd heard of Jorge Aguerre. A young up-and-coming superior kind of hoodlum, rumor placed him second only to Ralph Hardy who for years had been the acknowledged leader of organized crime in the southeast. Christ, it wasn't a dream, it was real; first Dillard, then Bohannon, now Aguerre and, maybe though him, Ralph Hardy. And the key element was that somehow all these characters were linked with the murders in Forrest. What had she dropped into here?

'Aguerre is connected,' she said. 'One of the new breed of

goodfellas. He's number one in the southeast.'

He was watching her, his mouth clamped shut again, his eyes bleak and expressionless. Shit. She wasn't talking right and he wasn't buying it. She sounded like someone out of a bad movie. But after a moment his lips curved again. 'Talk like that to Aguerre and he might find work for you at that. He likes to think he's number one.'

Suddenly, an unsettling look was on his face as his mind appeared to drift away. 'There's people I know would argue,' he added quietly. He finished off his coffee. 'I have to go to the can,' he said. 'Then we'll move.'

He left her there and swiftly she crossed the room to the telephone, punching in Doug Carlson's direct line. At this time of night he wouldn't be there but, hopefully, his answering machine would be switched on. It was.

'Barbara,' she said as soon as the bleep had sounded. 'I'm heading for Austin, Doug. Big break. Forrest tied to Senator Dillard, General Bohannon, Ralph Hardy and Jorge Aguerre. Don't, repeat, do not call me on my cell. Talk to you soon.'

She hung up, stepped hurriedly to the cigarette dispenser, fed in money and collected two packs. When she turned Ryker was standing by the table they'd used, watching her. How long had he been there? She walked towards him and from a few paces away tossed one of the packs of cigarettes. 'Thought you might need these,' she said, gesturing towards the crumpled pack on the table.

He caught the cigarettes, stared at her for a moment, an odd expression on his face. 'Thanks,' he said. He reached out his other hand. Her car keys. She held out a hand and he dropped the keys into her palm. 'Let's go,' he said.

Like before, they drove in silence.

Ryker thought about Aguerre. Tough, ambitious, mean with a cruel streak, Aguerre was still in his thirties. Too young for the power he wielded, was the verdict of those who disagreed with Ralph Hardy's decision to hand over such a valuable slice of territory. Maturity was what was needed, so the argument went. Ryker knew why they thought that way; most people as young as Aguerre let their emotions get in the way. Ryker never had, but he knew that he was an exception to the general rule. From whispers he'd picked up here and there, he was pretty sure that Aguerre didn't have the maturity to counterbalance the power. Worse than that, Aguerre was filled with self-importance. That could make a man vulnerable. Like being swayed by flattery. That's what he'd meant when he'd talked to the girl back at the diner.

He glanced sideways at her, watching her profile as it was

intermittently illuminated dimly by lights from cars passing on the distant side of the highway. Aguerre was the type to fall for anything a good-looking woman might say. He reached for a cigarette, thinking about the way the woman had been thoughtful enough to buy him a pack. He wasn't used to that kind of thing. He liked her for the gesture.

Don't form attachments. They can't work, can't last, can't do you anything but harm. Sometimes, you'll think you can beat it but you can't. Get used to being alone. It goes with the territory.

But he hadn't been alone. Not really alone. Not with Louise there. He tried to think about other times, long past, but clouds of forgetfulness hung unsettlingly around him. He thought again about the small gesture of companionship the woman had made and almost at once felt a sudden lurch of guilt. How could he think approvingly about anything any woman might do or say when Louise was barely cold.

Cold. What about the funeral? Who would make the arrangements? No, wait a minute, it was too soon for a funeral. Until they had someone for the murder the police would probably refuse to release the body. The bodies. Soon, when he found the man who had done it, he would go back and talk to the police. Then he could make arrangements for the burials. Not cremation. Bodies burning. Smoke. The smell. No, godammit. Not that. A burial. Flowers. He tried to remember what kind of flowers Louise liked but he couldn't and after a while he gave up, turning his thoughts back to Luis Delgado and the reasons he might have had for being in Forrest. One thing was sure, it was no coincidence.

JORGE AGUERRE did not operate out of a fancy, sky-scraping office building the way Ralph Hardy did. He used the back room of a restaurant on a side street a few blocks below Austin's Capitol building.

Las Canarias looked ordinary, just one of scores of places churning out Tex-Mex food, but over the door hung a sign, 'More Mex Than Tex', that suggested a difference. The restaurant's culinary inclinations were not the only thing that was different about *Las Canarias*. On paper, the owners were Jorge's mother and father and the manager was his younger brother, Felipe. In reality, Jorge owned every brick and stick of it. That wasn't the only reason he used the place for business. He owned scores more pieces of real estate but this one had easily-guarded entrances and the cellar linked into the cellars of other buildings on the block, all of which Jorge also owned. Anytime he wanted to come and go without being seen, he could. And he could also get out fast if the need arose. Put another way, *Las Canarias* was safe.

Most days, Jorge started his day with breakfast at the restaurant, spent the morning doing business there, then left to have lunch with visitors he wanted to impress a little by taking them to some of the city's fancier and pricier restaurants although he himself rarely ate much. Most evenings, he was back at *Las Canarias* to dine and drink and laugh it up with his friends and the people he wanted to impress a lot. At *Las Canarias* everyone treated Jorge Aguerre as if he were a king. He liked that. And he acted like a king but not one of those pussy-footing kings they had over in Europe. No, he acted like a real American king, the kind that held in their hands the power of life and death. The kind that started with men like Torrio and Capone and went on through the grand succession of the Lucianos and the Calabreses. They were the kings he emulated, and he knew how they acted because when he was a kid, in between cutting and dealing, Jorge spent all the time he could spare seeing every movie about the Mafia that came to town. From them, he knew, among many other things, that people were impressed by an earthy approach, by a man who, however rich and powerful he might become, kept close to his roots. Not like Ralph Hardy and his fancy ways.

These days, Jorge didn't do any cutting or dealing. Not directly. He had people who did that for him. Delegation it was called. The way Ralph Hardy had delegated the southeastern part of Texas to him. And Jorge had eagerly grasped the opportunity. If someone needed a lesson all Jorge had to do was mention his displeasure to one of his lieutenants and within hours a fist would fall or a knife would flash in a dark alley. As for dealing, these days it was all done by the airplane load. The days of shifting one-ounce glassine packages was a fast-fading memory. Times had changed for Jorge Aguerre and all for the better.

And he had grown smarter and sleeker with the changing times. Still well short of forty, and only maybe ten or twelve pounds over the right weight for his short, stocky frame, he liked the way he looked. Every morning he looked at himself in the bathroom mirror, brushed his long, curling black hair, shaved the blue stubble to a smooth shadow, smiled at his reflection with big square, newly-capped white teeth, and allowed himself a moment of admiration. He had done pretty damn good for an uneducated kid from the barrios of Corpus Christi. And he hadn't finished. Not yet. Not by a long way.

Some mornings, he also allowed himself the luxury of saying a small prayer to the god that had sent Ralph Hardy a moment of weakness that lasted long enough for him to grant Jorge an opportunity greater than anything in his wildest dreams. It was a moment of weakness because one day, maybe sooner than Jorge dared think, he would step up the ladder and nudge Ralph into the outer darkness of premature retirement.

He was thinking about the future and the role played in it by Ralph

Hardy that morning when the man and the woman walked into the back room of *Las Canarias* where he was eating breakfast.

It was the sudden air of tension from a table closer to the door where four of his men sat that made him look up.

He recognized the man and leaned back in his chair, studying him, knowing that this wasn't a social call. It drifted across his mind to wonder why he hadn't been told to expect a visit. Maybe Ralph was testing him out. He turned his attention to the woman. Pretty face, couldn't see the figure under the crappy clothes. She looked like she knew her way around but at the same time seemed a little skittish, edgily glancing around the room. Maybe she was the man's *puta*. He shrugged and smiled, waving an expansive hand.

'Sit down,' he told them. 'Eat? Coffee? Best damn coffee this side anyplace you ever been.'

'No time,' the man said. 'Luis here?'

Jorge looked at the man, not hiding his disapproval of the way his hospitality was ignored. 'What name you using now?' he asked.

'Ryker. Jack Ryker.'

'Okay, Jack, so what the hurry.'

Ryker leaned forward, his eyes intense and despite the warmth of the room and the presence of four of his armed men, Jorge felt suddenly very cold and afraid. 'Cut the shit, amigo,' the man said. 'Where's Luis Delgado?'

He frowned. 'Luis? What the fuck you want Luis for?'

'My business. He here or not?'

'Not now, no. Later, maybe.'

'Who sent him to Forrest? You?'

Jorge had heard whispers about Forrest and the cold chill tightened its grip. 'No. Not me. What this all about, huh?' He scowled suddenly, recognizing a problem. 'This Hardy business or maybe you moonlighting?'

'About Luis?' the man prompted, ignoring the question. 'And Forrest.'

The four men from the other table had quickly spread themselves around the room. One was by the door that led to the front of the restaurant, another beside the kitchen door, the others spaced well apart. Nobody would leave this room if they didn't want him to but Jorge did not feel any easier. He knew about this man and right now he was too close for comfort.

'Yeah, Luis go up to Forrest.'

'Why?'

'To look for someone. A woman.'

Ryker stared down at Aguerre, hardly breathing, barely aware that anyone else was in the room with them. He looked at the broad Mexican face, the brown skin, turning almost black around the eyes. Aguerre was giving off a smell that mingled strongly-perfumed aftershave with fear. The smell of fear relaxed Ryker just a little. Aguerre might think he was the big chief around here but deep down he was just another fucking spic.

'What woman?' Ryker breathed.

'Louise Garrett.'

Something wasn't right. It couldn't be. Even Hardy didn't know that Louise and the kids were a part of his life so Aguerre certainly couldn't. And even if he did, he was the target, not Louise. But for Aguerree to admit to even knowing Louise existed muddied the waters. It was the kind of lie someone would tell to conceal the fact that he, not Louise, was the real object of their interest. But if that were so, why even admit to being interested in Louise? It wasn't adding up. All it did was confuse him. Maybe if he let Aguerre talk a little more, maybe he would hang himself.

He forced himself to take a few quiet breaths, then asked, 'What's so interesting about this woman?'

'Jones see her one time. Long time ago. Last year sometime.'

'Jones?'

Aguerre frowned. 'The shadow.'

'What the fuck're you talking about now?'

'Jones. Jesus Christ, everybody know Jones. He trail people. That what he do. You want somebody trail, you hire Jones. Everybody use him. We use him, lawyers use him, private cops use him. Jesus, I heard that sometime even the heat use Jones. He the best there is. They tell me he even do it for kicks.'

'Okay, okay, so if I ever want anybody trailed I know where to come. Now what the hell has he to do with this?'

'Take it easy. Relax. Okay? One time Jones is on a job for our people. Watching a couple FBI agents who're nosing around. We want to know why they sniffing around our territory. Jones follow them a coupla days, list everybody they talk to in case they mess with our business. He see the reason they here is they watch someone. A woman. She has nothing to do with us so we not interested anymore. But Jones, crazy fucker, when we call him off he trail her anyway. Like I say, he do it just for kicks.'

'And?'

'And he end up in Forrest. That where she go.'

Ryker's mind was racing, turning Aguerre's words over and over,

86

trying to make sense of them. Louise being watched by the FBI? It was crazy. Why would they do that? Unless. Unless they were interested in him and somehow had tracked him down to Forrest, learned about his secret life and put a tail on Louise.

'Where was this? Where did this guy Jones see the agents and the woman?'

'Here.'

'Austin?' What was Louise doing in Austin? 'Where in Austin?'

'Jesus. What am I, a fucking 'cyclopedia? How do I know where he see her. So fucking important, talk to Jones.'

He forced down a compulsion to smack this flat-faced Mexican bastard in the mouth. 'You still haven't told me why Delgado was up in Forrest.'

'We been having problems with the Bureau,' Aguerre said. 'We figure it time to check all angles, so we send Luis to Forrest and see what's what.'

'And.'

'Zip.'

Now he was sure that Aguerre wasn't leveling with him. Something in his expression, the eyes maybe, shifting endlessly around the room, told him that the man was lying. But which part was a lie? Or was it all lies?

Ryker knew that here, now, with too many guns in the room, he would get nothing out of Aguerre he didn't want to give.

Changing tack, he asked, 'Where do I find this Jones?'

Aguerre glanced across at one of his men, jerked his head and waited until the man came closer, the gunman's eyes never leaving Ryker. 'Find Jones,' Aguerre said. He turned to Ryker. 'You want him here?'

'No. Someplace in the open.'

Aguerre looked at his own man, his face purposefully blank. 'You hear,' he said.

The man went out and a moment later his voice could be heard speaking fast and soft in Spanish on the phone.

'Sure you won't have coffee,' Aguerre said. 'My own mother make it.'

The man shook his head curtly and after a moment the girl did the same. Jorge could see that she looked as though she needed coffee at least, maybe something a lot stronger.

Barbara was trying to make sense of what she was hearing, trying to fit these new pieces into the jig-saw puzzle that was growing larger and more complicated.

The man Aguerre had sent to telephone came back. 'Two o'clock, the new construction site alongside the Motorola plant.'

'A construction site?' Ryker said.

'It quiet,' Aguerre told him. 'Management acting up. So the crews, we tell them to take a little vacation.'

'Where is it?'

'East side Highway 183. Need directions?'

'I'll find it.'

As Ryker turned to leave the girl spoke for the first time. 'I need the bathroom,' she said.

Aguerre jerked his thumb.

'Hurry,' Ryker said, heading for the door.

When Barbara came out of the ladies room Aguerre and just one of his men were in the back room of the restaurant.

'You his woman?' Aguerre asked.

'No. Luis Delgado owes me money. That's the only reason I'm here.'

'Luis owe you? Why?'

She couldn't tell him the same lie she'd used before. If Delgado worked for Aguerre then the story about Delgado renting a car wouldn't hold up. 'It's a long story,' she said. 'And I don't have the time.'

'Wait here,' Aguerre said. 'Luis come here most days.'

Barbara shook her head hurriedly. 'It's my car we're using. If I lose that, I'm even further out than I am now.'

Aguerre shrugged, then frowned and asked, 'I know you from someplace?'

Hastily, she said, 'I was born here, in Austin. Lived most of my life here. You maybe saw me around.'

He stared at her for a moment longer, then shrugged again. 'You know where I am,' he said, enigmatically.

Barbara turned and hurried through the door. In the front room of the restaurant one of Aguerre's men was speaking on a cell. He paused, watching in silence until she reached the street door.

Around the corner, where they had left the car out of sight of the restaurant, Ryker was waiting, the motor running, his fingers tapping irritably on the wheel.

'They're setting something up,' Barbara told him.

'Of course they are.'

'So what are you planning to do?'

'Talk to Jones.'

'But they're, I don't know, setting a trap or something.'

'And I need to talk to Jones.'

'Why? What's so important about Jones?'

He drove off without replying, turning out into the main street.

After a few moments, when it was clear that he didn't plan on answering her question, she tried again. 'It isn't Jones that's important, is it. It's the woman in Forrest. Louise Garrett. That's what all this is about. Who is she? What is she to you?'

'Shut up!' he yelled, his anger causing him to lurch the car out of its lane. He righted the vehicle, ignoring the protesting horns from other motorists.

She stared at him, for the first time beginning to feel a hint of understanding.

'Ryker isn't your real name, I already guessed that. It's Garrett, isn't it. You're Ed Garrett. You're the man the police in Forrest want to talk to.'

He turned his head to stare at her in silence, then looked back to the road ahead.

When he still didn't speak she went on. 'And you think that they have you down as a suspect so you're trying to discover who really did it.'

After another silent moment, he slowly nodded his head.

She couldn't tell him that Phil Davis had told her he didn't think the husband was responsible. She couldn't even tell him that she knew how they had died. In fact, it would not be smart for her to say or do anything. Except, maybe, to help him find the man, or men, who had committed such horrific acts.

But what had all this to do with a United States Senator or a disgraced US Army general or two of the region's leading underworld figures?

She needed to talk to someone but there was no one to whom she could turn. She'd made a decision and she was stuck with it unless she dropped out and if she did that she lost the story. A story that would make her name known in every corner of the country.

'How are you going to handle Jones?' she asked.

Garrett - no, it was too confusing and maybe dangerous to think of him with that name, she would have to stick with Ryker - turned and looked at her. He appeared calm again.

'Talk to him,' he said. 'That's all. Just talk to him.'

She remembered the man speaking on the cell in the restaurant. Setting something up, she was sure of that, something that would put them in danger. Just talking might be the hardest thing of all to do.

DOUG CARLSON played his message tape again, checking Barbara's few words against the transcript he had made.

For the past hour he had thought about little else. He'd talked to Kent Benson, WNTA's president, chiefly to take the heat off Barbara whose unexplained absence was causing problems. He had played the tape and then, when Benson, who couldn't mistake the scent of a major story, wanted to set up an investigative team, Doug argued a case for leaving it to Barbara for a little while longer. Like Benson, Doug sensed that Barbara was onto what she had wanted all along - an important story that might make her a national name. He also knew from her mention of Ralph Hardy and Jorge Aguerre that the road she was traveling was dangerous.

And speaking of traveling, someone must be with her. Why else would she warn him not to call her cell. Who was she with? And why?

He wrestled with it for a while longer, then stood up to close and lock his office door. Benson would fire him if he learned what he was about to do. And Barbara would hate him for the rest of her life. It was the thought of the rest of her life, and how short that might turn out to be, that prompted him to break his loyalty to WNTA and the trust he knew Barbara placed in him.

Picking up the telephone, he dialed the number of the police station at Forrest and asked for Phil Davis.

EIGHT

THERE WERE times when Phil Davis forgot why he had quit the Dallas Police Department. Ten minutes in the police building on Metropolitan Avenue reminded him.

The building was awash with sounds and smells that brought it all flooding back. The sounds ranged from the constant warbling of telephones, interspersed with occasional squawks from radio speakers, to the screams and whines of protesting junkies and hookers and the shouts and singing of drunks; punctuating it all were slammed doors and feet hammering on uncarpeted floors and stairs. And everywhere voices were raised to beat the racket. The smells included tobacco smoke drifting in from the smoking zones that helped relieve the otherwise prevalent stench of disinfectant, ammonia, sweat and stale piss.

Phil made his way up to the third floor office that housed the division's homicide detectives. Only one cop was in the office, a massively-built dark-suited man Phil remembered as having a violent temper allied to acute bigotry. Bob Durham hated criminals, especially drug addicts who killed in pursuit of the means of supporting their habits. In this part of Dallas, the population breakdown meant that, inevitably, the majority of the criminals were black. For that matter, so too were their victims but it was the swelling tide of black criminals Durham hated most. Phil knew that Durham wasn't unique in his bigotry but what made him unusual was the fact that Durham was himself black.

For a while, Phil had steered clear of the big man but then had met up with him at an interdepartmental conference. That evening, he'd had been wedged into a corner of the bar with Durham and couldn't avoid talking to him. Surprisingly, he'd managed to find understanding and a curious kind of sympathy for the other man's angry bigotry. 'Listen,' Durham had said. 'When I was their age the only fighting I did was either on the football field or for something real damn important. Like Civil Rights. Okay? And don't give me that shit about broken fucking homes and deprived neighborhoods. I never knew my father, and my mother was killed in a drive-by shooting when I was seven. Know what they called it? Ac-cid-ent-al. Me and my brothers and sisters, six of us, were raised by my grandma in a goddamn slum but we didn't rob and steal, we didn't drink and do drugs, we didn't do any of that shit that passes for living today. We went to school and we worked our butts off at honest jobs and we didn't go through life thinking that what's yours should be mine. And we all made good. Well, all but my youngest bro, who always was an asshole. So if me and my kin can do it then why for chrissake can't all these other evil fuckers do it.'

After that initial outburst Phil had learned a little more about the big detective. A devoted family man, a regular churchgoer, Bob Durham had pulled himself out of nowhere to a position where he could proudly look any man in the eye. But when he looked around him he saw other blacks destroying their own lives and damaging the lives of everyone in their community, bringing down the race as he called it. And when he saw how the legal system was geared to allow perpetrators of often horrific crimes to thumb their noses at the police department something inside him clicked and he began a one-man clean-up campaign, meting out his own private brand of justice.

'I never killed no one,' he told Phil. 'And nobody ever was permanently maimed. But I accentuated a little of the evidence here and there, and maybe there's been a couple of broken bones through resisting arrest, but most of all I put the fear of god into the fuckers. Maybe it's not the way it should be done, but I tell you, Phil, the streets I walk are cleaner and better for it.'

Cleaner, maybe, Phil had thought. But better? He couldn't shake his disapproval of Bob Durham's actions but after the night they'd talked he found to his surprise that in a curious way he liked the man and he certainly admired his hard-edged honesty.

He knocked on the open door and went into the office, saying, 'Hi, Bob.'

Durham looked up frowning, then smiled delightedly, standing up to tower over Phil. 'Well, look who's here. How are you, Phil?'

'Okay. How're you?'

Durham laughed, a deep rumbling that seemed to shake the floor. 'Still breaking my ass, and breaking a few heads.' He waved a hand towards a chair and Phil sat down. Durham's smile faded. 'I heard about Sarah,' he said. 'Damn shame, Phil. She was a lovely lady. And Jennifer. Jesus'

Phil nodded his head. 'How's Emily?' he asked. 'And the kids? They must be in college now.'

Durham's smile returned and he nodded happily. 'Emily's just great and both Lucy and Robert are at university. Studying law. They're both aiming to be bigtime company lawyers. That's something I taught 'em. I told 'em, don't mess with crime. I said, don't you go wasting your lives defending the scum I deal with every day. Don't mess with 'em, I said, not even as a state prosecutor.'

Phil was struck by the way Bob Durham's thinking about his children's lives resembled the way Jake Larsen thought about his daughter. 'Will they?' he asked. 'Listen to you, I mean.'

'They're smarter'n their old man,' Durham said. 'They listened and they heard.' He leaned back in his chair. 'So, what brings you back, Phil?' He frowned momentarily. 'Hey, now, you just had a big killing up there in Forrest. I heard about it. Some guy took out his old lady and the kids.'

'Those are the victims right enough. Not sure it was the husband, though.'

'What've you got on the killer?'

Phil shook his head gloomily. 'Not a damn lot,' he admitted. 'The coroner's report gives us a right-handed perp, height between five-eight and six feet, very strong and therefore probably male or a very angry female. No sexual assault.' He rubbed a hand over his eyes, thinking of the slashing wounds across the woman's breasts and genitals. Okay, so she wasn't raped but if those injuries were not sexual, what was? 'So, we're probably looking for a strong right-handed male. That limits us to around forty-five percent of the population nationwide. Apart from that, the few leads we do have are pretty damn thin.'

'Is that why you're here. Following a lead?'

'Kind of.' He explained about the tenuous hope of coming up with answers through motor vehicle numbers. 'I came down here to follow up three names and addresses in the Dallas-Fort worth area. I've crossed off two already. The third's a little odd, that's why I thought it might be useful to talk to someone about it. Someone who can keep it, well, maybe a little unofficial.'

Durham grinned. 'Sounds like me,' he said.

Phil told Durham about his discovery that the address for Luis Delgado matched that of Senator Lucius Dillard and how he'd talked with the Senator's butler, learning that someone else was asking questions the day before.

'It may be nothing,' Phil said. 'But I thought maybe you could check and see if you have any paper on Delgado. I don't want to rattle Dillard's cage if there's no cause.'

'Fuck him,' Durham said. 'Dillard's a drunk and a bum and the only reason no one's busted his ass is because he pisses in the same pot as half the goddamn brass.' The big man yawned and stretched, lumbering to his feet. 'I'll go see what we've got,' he said. From the door he added, 'You're a tad outside your area here, Phil. I take it that's the reason you want this doing unofficial.'

'No, I just don't want to make too many waves,' Phil told him. He fished in a pocket for an envelope. 'I'm temporarily attached to the Bureau,' he added, hearing a note of embarrassment in his voice.

Durham came back and read the document, then whistled and offered a mock salute. 'This'll buy you shit but it certainly impresses a poor dumbass cop like me.' He handed back the letter then paused, thinking. 'You know the Suits have this psychological profiling unit. Use it for getting a handle on serial killers. Maybe they could work something up on this.'

'Maybe they already have,' Phil said, and explained how Forrest's Finest had been elbowed towards the edge of the case.

'So you're stuck with old-fashioned police work.'

'Seems like it,' Phil agreed. 'But that isn't getting me far. Dammit, I can't even develop a motive.'

'Motive? Shit, Phil, you've been away from the killing grounds too long. Motives? How many killers you reckon have a real, solid old-fashioned motive these days? Well, I'll tell you. I maybe don't have statistics to back this up, but coming through here I reckon one in ten has a real motive, if there is such a fucking thing. These evil mothers kill for things you and me wouldn't even raise sweat over. Last week a guy shot another guy four times in the head for jumping him for a parking space. And up in Richardson some good ol' boy put both barrels of his shotgun into his neighbor's chest 'cause he didn't like the color he'd painted his house. In Irving last month there was a knifing at a school when some kid stepped all over another kid's fucking Reeboks. The victim didn't die but he lost an eye and needed a hundred and fucking seventeen stitches in his face. Know how old they were, perp and victim? Nine. Nine fucking years old. Shit. Then there's the druggies, killing for small change. And all the armed robberies last month netted less than a hundred bucks average while the victims included seventeen people shot, with eleven of 'em dead. Motive don't mean shit anymore, Phil. Unless it's buried so deep in the perp's head you'd need a drilling rig to find it.'

'Thanks,' Phil said. 'You sure know how to encourage a guy.'

Durham grinned as he turned and went out the door.

'Can I call my office?' Phil yelled after him.

Durham stuck his head around the doorway. 'With a letter like that you can probably call collect to the goddamn White House,' he said.

Sam Madsen was in the office and sounded happier than Phil felt. He told Sam about Dillard and gave him the shaky descriptions he'd had from the butler of the man and woman who'd also been nosing around.

'Anything your end?' he asked when he was finished.

'Something,' Sam said. 'Not sure whether this is as big as I think it is but see what you think.'

He had called Phil's hopefully useful contacts in the police departments at Little Rock and Richmond, Virginia, and asked them to inquire into the people whose motor vehicles had appeared on the video shot in Forrest.

'Zip in Little Rock, so we were wrong thinking Larsen was interested in that one. It was just a family driving through on their way home from vacation in Arizona,' Sam told him. With a sudden pang, Phil thought about Jennifer, by now peacefully touring the southwest with her grandparents. But Sam was continuing. 'The vehicle licensed to a name and address in Richmond turns out to be a late model Ford Escape, which is interesting because the car on the video is a T-bird.' Phil began paying attention. 'It gets better,' Sam said, as if sensing his colleague's interest. 'The owner of the Escape is given as a John Lanning but when your buddy checked the address no one of that name came up. What did come up was that your buddy suddenly found himself with an unexpected emergency and could do nothing more for us poor old country cops.'

'What are you saying?'

'He backed off, fast.'

'So . . .'

'Wait, Phil.' He heard Sam laugh softly. 'I remembered an old acquaintance of mine, someone I did a favor for one time, a guy not bound by the rules. He's a lobbyist in Washington and knows where enough bodies are buried to get information even the cops are hard pressed to deliver.'

'And?'

'John Lanning's address is a house registered to WITSEC. It's one of several houses they use as offices out of which they administer the WSP program.' Sam paused, allowing Phil time to think.

And he needed it. The US Marshal's Witness Security Program handled the problems potentially lying in wait for people who gave evidence in major trials even at risk to their own lives. Part of the deal was that the US Marshal's office and the Bureau gave them whatever protection was deemed necessary from round-the-clock guards to new identities, relocation in new homes in another part of the country or overseas, and in some cases even new faces.

'There's something else,' Sam resumed. 'My friend on the Hill asked around a little more and although it's not an uncommon name he cannot find anyone working for the Bureau in Washington named John Lanning. Now, it crossed my mind that the name John Lanning is not a whole lot different from the name Jake Larsen. Remember the description we had from the old lady for one of the visitors to the Garrett house? Bony face, high forehead, long light-colored hair. That's not a bad match to our new friend Special Agent Larsen. Maybe he was the driver of the T-bird seen in Forrest. If it is him, then it certainly answers why he was so damned eager to keep us from checking out that particular name and address. Now, I don't know what you're thinking, Phil, but I'm thinking that maybe the missing husband is really one of the FBI's witnesses, that his cover was blown, and a hit team went in looking for the guy but instead found the wife and kids and decided to . . . well, leave a pretty nasty warning to keep his mouth shut or he would be next.'

'He being Louise Garrett's . . . husband, boyfriend.'

'Who else?'

It made sense, Phil thought. The Bureau would want control so that too much attention wasn't drawn to a man they had undertaken to conceal. And they wouldn't want the cops getting hold of him first and asking awkward questions. An alternative scenario came to mind: the Bureau might even want to keep the cover in place if one of their star witnesses had freaked out and killed his own family. 'Where do you think Garrett is now, then?' he asked. 'On the run, or have the Bureau hidden him away again. That would explain why there's no sign of him in the home. Or what if whoever did the woman and kids took him with them when they left.'

'I hadn't thought of a kidnap,' Sam admitted. 'But my guess is that's he's on the run. Although the Bureau has pretty much left us on our own here, they certainly haven't eased up on the case. They're putting a lot of manpower into finding this guy.'

There was silence for a moment before Sam spoke again. 'You still there, Phil?'

'Yes. I'm just trying to decide if I'm wasting my time down here.'

'Well, while you're deciding, a guy named Doug Carlson called from the TV station in Amarillo. Said it was urgent.' The last thing Phil wanted right now was to talk to anyone connected with TV news.

'What he actually said,' Sam added, 'And he was very particular that I say this exact, "Tell Phil it's Code Brown". I suppose you know what that means.'

Phil knew. As a rookie with Dallas PD he hadn't hit it off too well with many of his fellow newcomers, but had found a surprising kindred spirit in Doug Carlson who was then a civilian researcher working in the PD's fast-growing IT section. Although a few years older than Phil, Doug knew little about real policing but felt he should learn.

Once in a while, when an opportunity arose, Phil had encouraged Doug to request permission to go on a ridealong in a patrol car and had always pushed his partner to agree that they be Doug's companions.

'Yes,' Phil said to Sam Madsen. 'I know what Code Brown means.'

Mostly for laughs, Phil and Doug had evolved their own private code for trouble and danger ranging from Code White (scared but surviving) to Code Black (death imminent). Code Brown (scared shitless) stood pretty high on the list. He wondered what Doug Carlson could have on his mind that had made him resurrect the past in this way.

'Give me his number and I'll call him when I get the chance,' he told Sam. 'And I'll let you know what I decide to do next.'

As he hung up Bob Durham's bulk filled the doorway. The big man dropped into a chair, steadfastly ignoring the creaks from the over-stressed wooden frame. 'Delgado,' Durham said, waving a thin file, 'is a smalltime shit with luck on his side. No sheet since juvenile court which means no sheet at all when we do nail him the way judges act these days.' He glanced over the few sheets of paper in the file. 'He sometimes acts as Dillard's gofer, but he really works for the Texas Mafia. Aguerre and Hardy pay his wages, call the shots.'

Phil took the file, glanced at it, shaking his head. Delgado might be a lead but he couldn't quite see how or where it might take him. Taking out his notebook, he compared the description of the second man the old lady had seen near the Garrett house with the photograph of Delgado. Fleshy-faced, unkempt black hair, three days growth of stubble; he was a good match. He copied out the few facts about Delgado the file contained. That done, he handed the file back to Durham. 'Can you fax that photo up to my office?' he asked. 'We can show it to an eyewitness.'

'Done,' Durham said.

Standing up, Phil said, 'I think I'll go get something to eat.'

'No need,' Durham told him. 'I figured you looked beat so I ordered coffee and pizza all round.'

Phil sat down again. 'Thanks,' he said. 'In that case, okay if I make another call?'

Durham waved a hand and Phil pulled the telephone towards him and dialed the number Sam had given him for Doug Carlson.

NINE

THE CONSTRUCTION site alongside the Motorola plant was large and cluttered with machinery and building materials, but there was no sign of life. If there'd been any security they had chosen to make themselves scarce.

Barbara had kept silent during the short drive. Now, Ryker steered her silver Honda carefully over the rough ground deep into the site, well away from the road and parked it alongside a tarpaulin-covered pile of insulated concrete blocks. Then, he wrestled the tarp off the blocks to drape it loosely over the car. He fiddled with the cover for a while until he had it positioned so that he could see ahead and behind. Then he sat in self-contained silence in the cave-like gloom of the Honda, hardly moving except to smoke a cigarette.

Stay in the dark places. There's safety in them. Danger, too, but not if you make them your territory, your ground. Your home. That way, the dark places work for you not against you. There's safety in darkness.

The woman was speaking, asking him a question. 'Why are we here now?'

He shrugged. 'Like you said, they're setting something up.' He wound down the window and fanned smoke out. 'How big is this town?' he continued. 'How long would it take for Jones to come from one side to the other? Half an hour? One hour tops even in bad traffic. So why four hours?'

'Maybe he isn't in Austin. Maybe he lives out of town.'

'Four hours out?'

'Maybe he was on a job. Trailing somebody. That's what Aguerre says he does.'

'Maybe.' He flicked his cigarette butt through the open window.

'So why are we here now?'

'This way, we maybe get to see just what it is they have in mind.'

Her stomach churned. 'Isn't that asking for trouble?'

He turned and looked at her and for an instant she felt a flash of fear at the bleak emptiness of his eyes. 'They're the ones did the asking,' he said. 'Now suppose you shut up and let me think.'

Two hours crawled past.

Barbara became steadily less comfortable and more tense as time moved on. She was sure that Jones wouldn't show, that someone else would. Someone who was coming here not to talk but to act, but Ryker didn't show any outward sign of concern.

Time dragged on and the interior of the little car grew smokier.

It was just past two o'clock when the man beside her sat up a little straighter. On the far side of the site, by the highway from which they'd entered, a car moved towards them. A dusty and scraped light brown Chevy Cobalt, it bumped slowly across the ground as if the driver was looking for someone. After a while the car stopped and the driver stepped out. Even at fifty yards Barbara guessed that this was Jones. A small, shabby nondescript man, just standing there he appeared to melt into his surroundings like the shadow he was reputed to be.

But Ryker also moved like a ghost, slipping silently out of the Honda and ducking out from beneath the covering tarp. He walked towards Jones, his head switching from side to side as he checked the site. Barbara scrambled hastily after him.

Jones watched them approach, his expression blandly incurious.

'Aguerre said you had some questions to ask,' he said when Ryker reached him.

'About the woman you trailed to Forrest.'

Jones's face closed up. 'Nothing to say,' he said, turning to climb back into his car.

Barbara hadn't seen the movement but suddenly a gun was at Jones's head, resting gently against his right ear. 'The woman you trailed to Forrest,' the man repeated.

Jones made no attempt to move, not even to turn his head. 'Look, mister, I can read, I seen the television. I know what happened up in Forrest and that had nothing to do with me.'

'I know,' Ryker said quietly.

Jones turned slowly and leaned against his car. He nodded his head.

The gun disappeared as swiftly as it had appeared. 'Just a few questions,' Ryker said.

Jones nodded again.

'Where was she, the first time you saw her?'

'I was tailing the Fibbies. Not local agents, these were two guys from out of town. They went out to Mabry, that's the operations base for the National Guard over on the west side of town.' Jones nodded his head in that direction. 'There's a medical unit there. Like a small hospital. That's where they talked to this woman.'

'A hospital? She was sick.'

'Not her. She had a kid with her, a boy. He was crippled, had those things on his legs, what you call them? Calipers.'

Barbara was watching Ryker and saw a shadow of pain spread over his face.

'What did they do?'

'The Fibbies? Met her, talked to her. I don't know anything else.'

'Deliberate?'

'What?

'The meeting. Was it arranged or was she just someone they happened to speak to.'

Jones thought for a moment, considering. 'Deliberate,' he said.

For another moment, there was silence and Barbara could hear the hum of traffic from the highway.

'Why'd you trail her to Forrest?'

Jones shrugged. 'I like to do it.' He tried a smile. 'Sounds crazy but that's what I do. You never know when information is gonna be useful.'

Barbara was suddenly aware that the traffic noise had altered. Now, it seemed to have a rhythmic pattern to it. She looked around, saw nothing, turned back and Ryker was no longer there. Bewildered, she looked back at her car. Empty. She looked at Jones but he was staring towards the north where the Motorola plant reared up beyond the chain-link fencing that bordered the construction site.

Then, sweeping up from behind the Motorola building, a helicopter came into view, its engine sound blotting out everything else. Within seconds the chopper was dropping towards them and she could see a figure at the open door in its near side. From the opening came a flickering of light and then Jones was hurled backwards, against his car as the windows exploded into thousands of glittering fragments.

Barbara heard herself scream as she threw herself to the ground, rolling away from the car. She looked back at Jones as he slid bloodily down the side of his shattered car to lie slumped on the ground. Blood drenched his chest and face.

By now the chopper was on the ground and two men scrambled down, both carrying what she guessed were some kind of machine pistols. Crouching low beneath the aircraft's blades, they ran forward as another, bigger and bulkier man climbed down onto the ground.

Then, from behind her, she heard an engine revving hard and as she swung around she saw her Honda hurtle out from beneath the tarpaulin which swirled up like a discarded cloak. For an instant she thought that Ryker was making a run for it but instead he launched the car towards the nearest of the two men who brought up his weapon but almost at once changed his mind and tried to run. But the car reached him, slamming into his body and tossing it up and over to crash down onto the ground in a motionless heap.

Even before the body hit the ground the car had slid to a standstill and she could see Ryker's arm protruding from the window and the gun in his hand. With every sound dampened by the helicopter, all that told her he was firing was the way the gun bucked in his hand as he fired twice. The second man was hit and spun around in a macabre dance before he too was down and still.

The big man had turned and was racing back to the safety of the helicopter but the aircraft was already lifting from the ground. She watched as he reached out, grabbing at the lower part of the fuselage beneath the doorway.

The door of the Honda opened and Ryker climbed out, his movements almost leisurely. He rested both arms on the roof of the car, aiming upwards at the man whose body flapped below the rising helicopter. This time she heard the reports as he fired. Four times. One of the big man's hands lost its grip but the aircraft was still climbing. Then the man was in the air, falling, turning once in a long, slow arc, as he fell towards the earth. Maybe he was screaming, maybe he wasn't. If he was, she couldn't hear it under the helicopter's roar. She tried to close her eyes but couldn't, horribly fascinated by his silent almost graceful descent to death.

The helicopter, still climbing, was now swinging fast to the north, but Ryker had lost interest in it. He was back in the car which slowly moved towards her. Still on her hands and knees, Barbara looked up into his face as he eased to a stop beside her.

'You coming or staying,' he asked.

She swallowed hard, her mouth dry. Somehow, she managed to find the strength to clamber into the car.

Ryker glanced away from her, looking across to where Jones lay beside the bullet-scarred Cobalt.

He stared at the body for what seemed like a long time. Then he pulled away and drove across the site and out onto the highway, turning north.

'Put your seat belt on,' he said, his voice quiet and calm. 'This is no time to be stopped by a traffic cop.'

Numb, Barbara did as she was told.

After about a mile, he took a slip road that allowed him to steer across the highway and pick up a road running westwards.

When she thought she could speak, Barbara asked, 'Why did they kill Jones?'

Ryker glanced at her. 'You don't think all that was to kill him, do you? They were told the time and the place and came looking for a man, a woman and a car. That's what they saw. From that distance, they thought Jones was me.'

'But why did Aguerre go to all that trouble?'

'Not Aguerre. The big man was Dewey Morrow, from Dallas. Tough sonofabitch. That's why it took four hours. They had to organize a chopper down here.'

'Dallas?'

'Ralph Hardy's men.'

She sat in silence as he drove, carefully and coolly, through the mid-afternoon traffic.

Nothing in Barbara's life had prepared her for the kind of danger she had just faced. And now she couldn't fully understand the mixed emotions she was feeling. The sudden, unexpected and terrible deaths of four men had left her frightened and exhausted, as if she had been running for hours. But there was something else. Underneath the fear and the exhaustion was a rising sense of excitement.

She looked at Ryker. He was extraordinary. He had come roaring out of his hiding place like a lion, protecting, attacking, all in one sustained explosion of violence. She had never met a man like him in her life. She knew that he was aware of her inspection but he didn't look at her and after a moment she turned to stare ahead through the windshield.

Uneasily, she was aware that he was affecting her in much the same way as she was affected by what had just happened. She was afraid of him; but she was also excited by him.

After a while, she lit a cigarette, shaking one loose from the pack and offering it to him.

After a moment, he took it, turning his head slightly to accept a light, cupping her hand with his.

Watch out for passengers. They just get in the way. Like excess baggage. Or prisoners. All that they do is slow you down. You'll end up looking out for them when the only person you should be looking out for is you.

But he had looked out for himself back there. Now, secured by distance and time, he could wonder about what had happened. The ease with which he'd handled himself. Jesus, it was almost as if he'd done it all before. The guns, even the helicopter for Christ's sake, he'd taken it all on and dealt with it, smoothly, efficiently, no fuss.

And no headache. For the first time in days he felt completely clear-headed and there was not even the faintest residue of pain.

A tiny nagging thought caught the edges of his mind. Jones. He'd never met him, never even heard of him before today. But there was something familiar about him. He shook away the thought. Jones looked like a million other people. That was all.

'Where are we going?' Barbara asked.

'Camp Mabry,' he said, wondering as he spoke just what the hell Louise had been doing at a National Guard hospital, for Christ's sake. He checked his watch. 'Then we either leave town or hide out. When Ralph Hardy hears what happened today, he'll be pretty mad.' He glanced at her, tense in the passenger seat. He didn't believe in luck but if there was such a thing he would be tempted to think of the woman as some kind of charm. Good luck charm or not, maybe it was time to unload. 'There's nothing more for you in this,' he said, thinking about how her skin had felt when they'd touched hands a moment ago. 'You can forget Delgado. And Aguerre won't hire you, not now. As for Hardy's people, they'll kill you without even stopping to think about it. So, you can take your car and go back home.'

Barbara didn't answer right away. She didn't know what she was waiting for. Nobody but a fool would stick around this man just for a story. And whatever she was, she wasn't a fool. So she would take the offer and quit while she still had the chance. Quit, and go back home. That was the only possible answer.

'I'll stay,' she said.

TEN

'**WE CAN'T** simply drive in there,' Barbara said.

Ryker looked down the road towards the entrance to Camp Mabry a hundred yards away. He didn't see why they couldn't just drive in. He could talk his way past the guard. He was only a National Guardsman, for Christ's sake. What could he do?

'We have to be subtle,' she said. 'Doctors have ethics, you can't simply ask questions and expect answers to come popping out.'

Ryker knew that answers popped out of anybody when they looked into the barrel of a gun. Doctors were no different.

'Let me do it,' she suggested. 'I can get in and maybe talk to one of the nurses. That will be easier. Less fuss. No hassles.'

There wouldn't be any hassles his way, either.

'The guard's what, twenty, twenty-one. He's no problem,' Barbara insisted.

Damn right he wouldn't be a problem to him, but she meant something different. Come to it, twenty-one was old enough when you had a gun. Provided you were prepared to use it. And these days, with everyone, everywhere, waiting for the other shoe to drop, a soldier with a gun was likely to shoot first and let someone else ask questions later. A little unwillingly, Ryker decided that she was making sense. After all the shooting at the construction site the cops would be all over the place and he already had too many things to think about.

'You've got an hour,' he told her.

Barbara opened the door and stepped out, her purse gripped beneath her arm, thinking fast. When she reached the entrance she turned in and walked past the guard as if she had every right to be there.

'Ma'am,' the young soldier said, almost apologetically.

'What . . . oh, sorry, I wasn't thinking.' She fumbled for her WNTA ID card with her picture and flashed it at him, already moving on. 'The hospital unit's that way, right?' she said, waving a vague hand.

'Er, yes, right,' he said. 'Straight ahead, follow the signs.'

She hurried on, stepping out confidently, feeling the young man's eyes on her back. She saw a sign and went in that direction, relieved when she at last turned a corner. Leaning against a wall, she breathed a sigh of relief, then began thinking about what she was doing. Since the shootings, less than an hour ago, there had not only been a shift in her attitude towards the man she was with, but also in the way the story was shaping. What she really needed was a chance to talk. To Ryker; and to someone else.

She needed to talk to Ryker and try to burrow into his private life. Ryker - Ed Garrett - husband of a murdered woman and father of two murdered children. Well, that's what she thought and he hadn't denied it. Hadn't admitted it either, not exactly, but there was good cause for that. Whoever else the police might be looking for, they would certainly be interested in talking to him. He was bound to be cagey, unwilling to trust anyone. So she needed to gain his confidence.

She also wanted to know more about the earlier connection he had made between the murders and Dillard and Bohannon, then with Aguerre and Hardy. All of it was still too shadowy. She had no idea why the murders had been committed, what motive there might be, or who might be behind them. One thing was clear; if those really had been Ralph Hardy's men who came in on the helicopter, then Ryker's actions were hurting someone. But why? What had he done, before today's shootings, that would upset anyone? All he had done was visit some people and ask a few questions. Okay, maybe they were important people, dangerous people even; but was that enough cause to send in a helicopter filled with gunmen? What was Ryker doing that made him the target for so much violence? A target of which she was now a part. A target she could walk away from anytime she wanted. Like right now.

It was her strange inability to walk away that prompted a need to talk to someone else, someone like Doug Carlson, to try and figure out the background of what was happening to her. But right now there was no opportunity for that although while she was here she could maybe call Doug and tell him about the shoot-out and that she was still okay.

After a moment, she started walking again and by the time she had reached the hospital unit had decided on the approach she would try.

The unit was small but what she could see of it looked well equipped. She found the office used by the head nurse; it was empty but a moment or two later a woman about her own age came along the corridor. Barbara smiled and received a friendly grin in return. Reading the woman's name tag, she went straight into her pitch.

'Hello, Nurse Adams, I'm Barbara Nichols from WNTA. Can I talk to you for a couple of minutes?'

Nurse Adams raised a curious eyebrow, and waved Barbara into the office, which was cramped with a desk, file cabinets, a table piled with what Barbara took to be case notes, and two large, comfortably sagging upholstered chairs.

Nurse Adams dropped into one, slipping off her shoes and curling her legs up beneath her. 'Take a seat,' she said.

Barbara sat down.

The nurse was blonde with a thin, lightly-freckled face that was just short of being pretty but exuded cheerfulness even through a layer of weariness. 'WNTA. Where's that?' she asked.

'Amarillo.'

'Thought I didn't know it. Although you look familiar.'

'Some of my stuff is picked up statewide.'

'What brings you here?' Nurse Adams frowned suddenly. 'Hey, I hope this isn't one of those let's-stick-it-to-the-medical-profession things?'

'No, I promise you that,' Barbara said hurriedly. Succinctly, she explained about the murders in Forrest and that she was trying to build up a picture of the victims' backgrounds.

Nurse Adams raised her eyebrows in bewilderment. 'Where do I come in?' she asked.

'I've learned that the woman and her son came here for treatment. Louise and Billy Garrett.'

The other woman's expression altered. 'Garrett? That was their name?'

Barbara nodded.

'Oh, god. I remember them.' She closed her eyes for a moment. 'They're dead?'

'Yes.'

'How awful.' Nurse Adams shook her head in dismay. 'What do you want to know?' she asked.

'Anything you can tell me.'

Standing up, the nurse opened a cabinet and pulled out a file. Back in her chair, she glanced through the file, then put it aside. 'Billy had an accident when he was about four years old. Minor spinal damage. Nurse Adams shook her head. 'Okay, maybe any kind of damage to the spine doesn't sound minor, but what I mean is, Billy could walk, although only with difficulty. He needed constant check-ups and from time to time brief hospitalization.'

'Why here?' Barbara asked. 'They lived hundreds of miles away. Do you have special facilities, or was there a connection with the National Guard?'

The nurse turned a glance towards the file but made no attempt to pick it up. 'Not the facilities,' she said. 'They're good but nothing special and so far as I know there was nothing to connect the Garretts with the Guard.'

Barbara waited, then said, 'There is something, isn't there, Nurse Adams?'

After a moment's silence the nurse nodded slowly. 'Susan,' she said. 'Call me Susan. I suppose that now she's dead it doesn't matter. The arrangements were made through official channels. I don't know the details. I remember that when Louise Garrett was here, she spent a lot of time talking with two men. I don't know who they were, their names or anything, but I'm pretty sure they were not army. They argued. More than once I had to tell them to hold down the noise. I heard Louise demanding money. More money, she said. She told them that what they'd given her wasn't enough. And she told them that she wanted a new identity.'

'What?'

'A complete change, she told them. I remember her exact words. "New name, new place, new face." That's what she said.'

Momentarily, Barbara thought that pieces were starting to come together but she wasn't sure why and the feeling faded. She studied Susan Adams, noting the deep frown lines between her eyes. 'There's more, isn't there?'

Susan nodded. It had come on the last evening before Louise and Billy had left the hospital on their last visit. The two men had finally gone and Louise was deeply upset. Susan had given her a mild sedative to help her sleep but the effect had been to make Louise talk, words spilling out in relief at being able to talk to someone.

'She knew something about a man, an important man, and that

108

knowledge put her life in danger,' Susan told Barbara. 'She was afraid for herself. She thought he might try to harm her.'

'And the children.'

Susan shook her head. 'No. She was sure about that. She said the man would never hurt Billy. She was definite about that.'

'How about Jo-Anne?'

'She never mentioned her daughter, except when she filled in her family details on the admission forms. I never saw a little girl here.'

'Are they there?' Barbara asked, indicating the file. 'The admission forms, I mean.'

Susan picked up the file, but held it close.

Sensing that the nurse was reaching the limit of her cooperation, Barbara asked, 'What about her husband?' she asked.

Susan opened the file. 'Next of kin is named as Edward Garrett. I expect he's the husband.'

'Nothing else?' Barbara asked.

Susan Adams shook her head.

'Thank you.'

'Has it helped?'

'Maybe.'

'It isn't just background you want, is it.'

Barbara hesitated. 'No. I'm hoping find out who killed them.'

'Be careful,' Susan said. 'Louise was very frightened of the man in San Antonio.'

'San Antonio?'

'The man she knew something about, she said he lived there.'

'Did she tell you his name?'

'No.'

'Nothing that would help me find him?'

'Only that he was in politics.'

'A politician?'

'No. Louise said he worked in public relations but only for the biggest people. State governors, candidates for the Senate and the House. That kind of thing.'

'Did she mention any names, people he worked for?'

The nurse thought hard. 'Yes,' she said. 'Louise said that lately he was working on the Lennox campaign.'

That was as much as Barbara could learn and after thanking Susan Adams and urging her to keep their conversation secret, she went down the corridor. Just inside the door was a payphone and she used it to call Doug Carlson.

His relief at hearing her voice was palpable and Barbara felt both gratitude and guilt. She was grateful that someone was concerned about her but she felt uneasy at telling Doug only part of what was happening.

She told him she was learning a lot more about Louise Garrett and that she would soon be heading for San Antonio.

She didn't tell him that she'd been a witness at this morning's shooting. Another important omission, made because she couldn't work out where this was leading, was the fact that the lengthening list of names linked to the killings in Forrest had now extended to include Paul Lennox, the hot Democratic front-runner for President of the United States.

PHIL DAVIS watched from a balcony as the aircraft landed and began taxiing towards the Austin terminal in the late afternoon sunshine. Then he went down to the gate to wait for Sam Madsen.

After calling Doug Carlson from Bob Durham's office, he had decided that if the message from Barbara Nichols was accurate then it would be smart to have back-up before he happened to run into any soldiers of the Hardy-Aguerre armies. Sam had sounded delighted at the chance of escaping from the office but when he walked into the arrivals lounge his expression was grim.

Moments later, Phil saw the reason why.

Right behind his unsmiling partner was Special Agent Jake Larsen. Sam looked at Phil, moved his shoulders in a barely perceptible don't-blame-me shrug, and came over.

'I hired a car,' Phil said to Sam, ignoring Larsen and turning to lead the way.

Larsen hurried to catch up. 'Okay, I should've told you we knew the victim. But it's complicated, Phil.'

'So's life.'

'Christ,' Larsen said. 'We're on the same side, Phil. Let's talk.'

Phil stopped, glanced at Sam, then nodded and led the way across to a cafeteria where Phil ordered coffee, Sam bottled water, while Larsen asked for lemonade.

After they'd taken a table, Phil said, 'Okay, let's have the story.'

Larsen looked from one to another of the two policemen, then said, 'Sam and I talked some on the flight. Your guesses are pretty close. Louise Garrett was in the WITSEC program. We gave her a new ID, set her up in a new home miles away from where she lived before.' He paused, sipped at his lemonade. 'A few months back, she called me and asked for a meeting. The boy visited hospital every few months. We handled the expenses, using hospitals where we have arrangements that assure confidentiality. One of them is here in Austin, so we fixed the

110

meeting she wanted for here when she brought the boy down.' He rubbed a hand over his eyes, and continued. 'Louise said she wanted another change of ID and relocation. I didn't think her reasons were strong enough. I thought she was just spooked at shadows, the way these people often are. I refused to agree to the changes.' He stared off into space for a moment. 'I made a misjudgment. Now my ass is in a sling.'

Sam leaned across towards Phil. 'That's the way this sucker's been talking. His ass. She's dead, her kids are dead. And he's talking about his ass.'

'Jesus,' Larsen said. 'Don't you think I feel guilty? Look, I made a judgment call and on the basis of what I had to work with it was the right call.'

'Okay,' Phil said. 'Let's forget all that blame stuff, shall we. Why was Louise Garrett in the program?'

Larsen lowered his voice. 'She'd agreed to testify against a man named Aaron Stone. Lawyer, bigtime. His clients include some people we need to close down. Ralph Hardy for one.'

'And she could've put this Stone guy away?'

'Yes.'

'For what?

'That wasn't the point. We never intended bringing Stone to trial. We just needed a threat, a real threat we could hang over him to persuade him testify against Hardy.'

'Did Louise know this?'

Larsen shook his head. 'No,' he said.

'Presumably Stone knew what you had on him.'

'Yes.'

'And knew that Louise was a danger to him.'

'Yes.'

'And a bigger danger to Hardy.'

Larsen shook his head. 'I don't think so. We hadn't put real pressure on Stone at this stage so it's unlikely he would have run to Hardy. He didn't know that all we wanted was to use Louise as a lever to get at Hardy through him.'

'So Stone's the man behind the murders.'

Larsen was silent.

'Well?' Phil asked.

'I'm not sure about that,' Larsen said.

'Go on,' Phil said.

Larsen hesitated, then said, 'If she was the only one to have died I might agree. But not the kids. That makes it different.'

'How?'

'Stone and Louise had been lovers. The boy, Billy, he was Aaron Stone's son.'

Phil looked at Sam, trying to read his thoughts and failing.

It was Sam who asked, 'What about the little girl? Was she Stone's?'

Larsen shook his head. 'Possible. Just. But based on the time when Louise and Stone split up I don't think so.'

'So, who was the father?'

'No idea,' Larsen said.

'Garrett, presumably,' Sam suggested.

By now, Larsen's gloom had deepened to bleak unhappiness and he was silent for long, dragging moments.

'If we're all on the same side,' Phil said. 'Maybe it's time to put theory into practice.'

Larsen nodded slowly. 'Sam's told me you know about the name Lanning. That isn't a name used only by me. It's a kind of house name. We use it for certain things, keep a car registered in that name, that sort of thing. But it's not a specific, messages for Lanning are handled by whomever is in the WITSEC office when messages come through. Well, Edward Garrett is the same kind of thing. A name used by the Bureau's Dallas office. When we asked Louise to choose a name for herself, she happened to choose Garrett. We explained that Garrett was a name she would have to contact if she needed to talk to someone. We told her that it might be confusing if she was using the same name. She dug in her heels. Insisted on Garrett. We couldn't persuade her.' He shook his head slowly. 'She was pretty tough.'

Phil looked at Sam but he was seeing the woman's ripped and bloody body. Tough in arguing about the name she should use, but not tough enough to face up to a savage attacker.

Phil said, 'Did you ask her why she thought of the name Garrett?'

Larsen shook his head, frowning.

'So we don't know whether or not the name Garrett belongs to someone in Louise's life.'

Sam said, 'Such as, for example, the little girl's father.'

Larsen shook his head again.

'You never checked? Even though you don't know the identity of Jo-Anne's father. He could be important.'

'Could be,' Larsen admitted.

'However you add it up,' Sam said, 'there's a hell of a lot about this case that you don't know.'

Phil nodded agreement. 'Maybe, you were paying too much attention to the Stone-Hardy target that you let the groundwork slip.'

Larsen shrugged uncomfortably.

'Where's Stone now?' Phil asked.

'Officially?'

Phil frowned a question.

Larsen permitted himself a tiny smile but succeeded only in looking self-satisfied. 'Officially, he's dead. Unofficially, he's living in San Antonio under another name.'

'Jesus,' Phil said. 'Isn't anybody in this case who they seem to be?'

'You and me, Phil,' Sam said. 'We're who we are.' He grinned suddenly. 'Although some of the time I'm not too sure about you.'

'What's that supposed to mean?' Phil snapped.

Sam held his hands in mock surrender. 'Hey, calm down.'

Phil smothered the irritation he was feeling towards Larsen and managed to smile at his friend. 'Sorry,' he said.

'When you called,' Sam said to him, 'you told me you'd had a lead from Doug Carlson. How did he get into the act?'

Phil glanced at the FBI man, then decided that by now they had probably extracted all that he was prepared to tell them. He told Sam and Larsen about the message from Barbara Nichols.

'Jesus,' Larsen said. 'That's all we need, a TV reporter running around in the middle of all this.'

'She could be in danger,' Phil said. 'In fact, given the way things are heading everyone connected with this case is probably living on the edge of something I don't like to imagine.' He thought for a moment. 'Doug seems to think that she's traveling with someone.'

'Who?' Larsen asked.

'No idea.'

'Speaking of Doug, I said I'd call him from time to time to see if Barbara makes contact again. I'll do that before we leave here.'

'Leave for where?' Sam asked.

Phil lifted his shoulders. 'How about San Antonio?'

Sam returned the shrug, then looked at Larsen.

For a moment the FBI man didn't answer, then said, 'Suits me. But before we leave, I have to go to the can.'

He walked away and Phil tossed the keys to the car he'd rented to Sam. 'The rental's in the front left of the parking lot,' he said. 'It's a . . .'

'. . . Crown Vic, brown,' Sam finished.

Phil looked at him questioningly.

'I'm a detective,' Sam said. 'Either that, or you're predictable. You don't like change.'

'Spare me,' Phil said. 'And, anyway, you're wrong.' He grinned.

'It's dark blue. The number's on the key tag. I'll call Doug.'

As he dialed he glanced over at a TV that was screening a report about a multiple shooting in the town earlier that day. Welcome to Austin, he thought. He was beginning to think that if he wanted to continue bringing up his daughter in safety, then pretty soon he would have to look somewhere other than Texas.

IT WAS late and there was no point continuing into San Antonio this time of night. Barbara was driving and suggested they stop. She was tired, she said, and needed a shower and to eat. Ryker didn't argue. She glanced at him. His face, expressionless as usual, caught by the gleam of passing headlights. She turned off the highway, her attention drawn by a cluster of illuminated signs.

The motel was middle-range, its decor a step up from merely functional. She parked outside the office and started to open the door.

'Here,' he said. He was handing her a bundle of notes.

'I have my credit card,' she said.

He thrust the money into her hand. 'Use cash,' he said. 'And don't use our real names.'

No trace, she thought. Why is he worried at my name appearing on a motel's records? Who knows I'm down here? Apart from Doug, and Ryker doesn't know that. And even if Doug came looking he isn't likely to be chasing down the exact spot. 'I'm not even sure I know your real name,' she said.

His fingers tightened around her hand. 'Don't get smart,' he said, his voice brittle. 'And get adjoining rooms.'

Barbara went inside the office and took two rooms, defiantly using the names Carlson and Purnell. If anyone from WNTA came this way, the names of the station's researcher and anchorman would hopefully raise an alert. She felt suddenly cold. If someone ever did undertake the task of searching the records of every motel between Austin and San Antonio it would be for a very important reason. She didn't like to think too much about what that reason might be.

An hour later, she had showered and put on a change of clothes. Creased from the past few days in a bag in the back of the Honda, they were at least clean.

There was no sound from the room next door and when she looked out the window the car was gone. For a moment she did nothing, then pulled out her cell, planning to call Doug again, this time to talk to him properly. But the battery was down so she reached for the bedside phone but before she had finished dialing lights flashed across the window telling her that Ryker was back. She banged the phone down and switched on the TV.

A moment later he knocked at her door. When she opened it he was holding two pizza cartons and a brown bag. 'I don't think we should go out,' he told her. The now familiar upturn appeared at the corner of his mouth. 'I got pepperoni, if that's okay. And red wine.'

She took one of the cartons, then after a moment's hesitation, took the other and stepped back to let him follow her into the room with the bag.

In the bathroom she stripped the protective wrapping off two glasses and brought them out. He was looking at the wine bottle he'd taken from the bag. He held it out with an apologetic shrug. 'No corkscrew,' he said.

'Just a minute,' she told him. In her purse she carried a miniature tool kit, a give-away from a convention she'd attended last year. It didn't have a real corkscrew but there was a gadget she had once used for the same purpose.

They ate and drank in silence. She had already learned that Ryker didn't make idle conversation.

Surreptitiously, she watched him as he ate. He wasn't good looking but about him hung an air that mingled mystery and intrigue with her knowledge that he was a man driven by powerful emotions and capable of sudden ruthless acts.

Eventually, she decided to try to persuade him to open up. 'What are we doing?' she asked.

He looked at her, frowning.

'Are we looking for who killed Louise or is there something else?'

The frown deepened. 'Isn't that enough?'

'Is it?'

He didn't answer, simply resumed eating.

'Are you really her husband and were they really your kids? If they are then I understand and I'll do what I can to help. But if there's something else I think you should tell me.'

'What else could there be?'

'Dammit! I don't know but men in helicopters don't come hunting for someone who's doing nothing more than trying to discover who killed his family.'

Again he didn't reply but he put down the remains of his pizza, emptied his glass, then stood and went to the window where he flicked the blinds and looked out into the darkness.

Ryker couldn't be sure why he had brought her along but he was getting used to having her around. She'd helped back at Camp Mabry, discovering a connection between Louise and a man in San Antonio. A

115

man Louise was afraid of. He sensed that he was getting close to learning the truth about what had happened in Forrest. But he didn't know enough to answer this woman's questions even if he'd wanted to, and right at this moment he was sure that he did not.

Surprising himself, he began speaking. 'They were mine,' he heard himself saying as if from far off. 'And they took them away from me and someone must pay for that. I don't know who but I know that if I keep following the trail I'll find the man that did it.'

'The trail? You mean Dillard and Bohannon and Hardy and Aguerre?'

He nodded, turning to look at her. Still damp from the shower her black hair reflected the light from the lamps around the walls. She was prettier than he'd first thought. And there was an underlying toughness he liked. Once again, he felt a sudden stab of guilt at thinking this way about another woman.

'They're dangerous people,' he said. 'Maybe you should drop out of it.'

She shook her head slowly. No, she'd had her chance to quit but not now. The story, whatever it was and wherever it began or would end, had gripped her. To all the other names was now added that of Paul Lennox, recently retired state governor and now presidential candidate. With a cast list like this, the story had to be big enough to explode her onto every TV screen in the land. Standing, she moved closer to him. 'No, I don't want to drop out,' she told him. 'But I need to know more than I do. Otherwise I'm just excess baggage.'

The corner of his mouth lifted again. 'Don't put yourself down,' he said. 'You're smart and you don't scare easily.' And you're pretty, he thought.

Not so smart, Barbara thought, that she hadn't taken a chance to get out of something that really did scare her. Then she was thinking again of the way he had acted that morning. Like before, she knew she should be appalled at the violence and bloodshed, the way the bodies had jerked puppetlike at the impact of bullets, the way the big man had tumbled through the air as he spiraled to his death; but instead she felt once more the clutch of raw excitement.

Suddenly, and later she couldn't remember which of them took the step or if it was both of them, they had moved closer, staring into one another's eyes. His were still the deep, cold unfathomable pools that told her nothing of what was going through his mind. And then she was in his arms. She felt the bed against the backs of her legs and she let herself go, sinking backwards, controlled by the strength of his arms around her.

She could feel the hard pressure of his gun against her breasts and then they were wrestling with their clothing until, naked, they coupled with uncontrolled urgency. Even as they were joined in a sweaty entanglement of limbs, she knew that was what it was, sexual coupling not lovemaking. And she enjoyed fucking with mindless passion. She needed it.

But afterwards, calmer and cooler, she felt a tug of alarm at how she had acted. Dammit, she was far from being a virgin but she had never before let herself go in that way, allowing herself to act in a rush of plain animal lust.

Trying to reason it out, she decided that part of it was him, the way he had acted this morning, part of it was the death and destruction and fear that he seemed to trail behind him like a black cloak. But mostly, she appeared to have uncovered in herself a desire she had never suspected existed. A desire not just for a story, however big, but for the opportunity to reach out and touch that aura of violence and danger that surrounded this man.

It was a discovery she did not like and for the rest of the night she lay, hardly sleeping, wondering where this desire would lead her next. Occasionally, she glanced at the motionless figure beside her, his chest rising and falling with his even breathing, knowing that however hard she might try there would always be some unanswered questions about him.

Ryker knew that the girl was awake but he didn't want to speak to her and so let her think he was asleep. He knew that she had needed what had happened between them just as he needed it but he wasn't sure if their reasons were the same.

Maybe, in his case it was something to do with the fact that he was sure he was getting close to the end of the trail and when he reached it who could tell what might happen.

Never start a fight unless you're confident you'll win. But never leave undone anything important until afterwards. Cover the possibility of losing, just don't believe in it.

For some reason he couldn't understand, having sex came under the heading of something important. Not with this particular woman. She just happened to be here when his need arose. Even so, he felt comfortable with her around. Relaxed, kind of, and easy. Had this been the way it was when he and Louise were together? He couldn't quite remember. Then, towards dawn, he felt his head begin to ache again. Maybe, he thought, this time it's just the wine.

ELEVEN

SAM MADSEN was driving, edging the speed limit, while Phil Davis sat in the passenger seat, glowering through the windshield at the highway stretching ahead, an almost straight line through gently undulating green farmlands. The FBI agent sat in the back seat of the dark-blue Crown Vic occasionally trying to open up conversation. Neither Sam nor Phil had much to say.

Phil had slept badly the night before and had only agreed to a stop because he knew he was tired and needed rest. But his brain didn't seem to agree with his body and kept chipping away at the same ground. And he was unhappy about Barbara Nichols. Since learning from Doug Carlson that she was seemingly one jump at least ahead and was already heading for San Antonio, Phil was seriously concerned that Larsen was still playing games. If a television reporter could discover so much, then how could they be so far behind despite access to the Bureau's massive resources? Something was missing. Larsen had to know more than he had already told them.

It was partly of out of this feeling of mistrust that he hadn't passed on something else he had learned from Doug. The Austin shooting he'd glimpsed on TV involved Ralph Hardy. The fact that the incident took place on Jorge Aguerre's territory had sparked speculation that it was nothing more than an internecine gangland wrangle. Although he had no reason to question that theory, certainly no evidence, Phil was disinclined to agree. Coincidences happened, especially in books and on TV cop shows. They also happened in real life. Otherwise, as the man said, if there was no such thing, why have a word for it. But in real life true coincidence was rare.

Eventually, Phil turned his mind to what lay ahead. 'What name is Stone using?' he asked Larsen.

'Lewis Kant.'

'And who knows he's really Aaron Stone?'

'The Bureau knows, now you do.'

'That's it?'

'Of course.'

Phil twisted in his seat to look at Larsen. 'You were supposed to be the only people who knew Louise Garrett wasn't who she seemed.'

Larsen looked out the window for a moment before answering. 'Stone is different. The cover is deeper. We arranged for a very convincing death.'

'Why?'

'What?'

'Why go to all that trouble? What's so important about Stone?'

'I told you, he was Ralph Hardy's lawyer.'

'And that's enough for a more elaborate cover?'

Larsen's eyes flickered. 'He was legal advisor to a lot of very important people.'

'All of them criminals?'

Larsen looked out the window. 'Yes,' he said, unconvincingly.

'Bullshit,' Phil said. He turned to Sam. 'Pull over.'

Sam slowed the car.

'What're you doing?' Larsen asked.

'We're letting you out,' Phil told him. 'You can walk from here. Find someone who believes all your lies, Jake. Let them take you the rest of the way.'

'For Christ's sake, Phil . . .'

'No. For my sake, Jake, because if I have to listen to any more of this crap I'll throw up.' The car stopped. 'Get out,' Phil said.

'Now listen . . .'

'Out.'

'All right,' Larsen snapped. He sat in silence for a moment, then said, 'Okay, I hope you know that in telling you all this I am putting my job and my pension on the line.'

'I know,' Phil said, 'if you tell us, you'll have to kill us. Well, tough shit, because the way I'm starting to feel I might very well shoot first.'

Larsen sighed for sympathy, was given none, and started to speak. 'Stone had a small legal practice in Waco, only eight partners, but very bigtime and specializing in taxation. His list of clients read like a who's who in different fields. They were divided pretty equally between three areas. One third were very rich independent businessmen. Owners of private companies, not CEOs of corporations. Some of them were major oilmen in the state, men who'd made their pile before the fall in prices and had diversified into real estate and electronics and computers and aeronautics and any other damn thing that turned big bucks. These were men who were up to their asses in money and were very grateful to Aaron Stone for figuring out ways for them to keep a tight hold on most of it. He did this through a variety of ways including forming ironclad offshore companies and negotiating favorable tax deals in the Caymans and anyplace else he could figure an angle. But it was all legitimate. Sometimes the firm strayed pretty close to the edge, but was never actually illegal.' Larsen paused, thinking. Clearly he hadn't finished, but Phil sensed that this silence was not evasive. Larsen was marshalling his thoughts, so he motioned to Sam to start moving again.

As the car slipped into its lane, the FBI man resumed. 'We were not involved although it turned out that the IRS had been interested in Stone for about twenty-five years. They knew that somewhere along the line money laundering was taking place but they could find nothing to back up their assumption. So it remained nothing more than a hunch. Then, about eight or nine years ago, they discovered that Stone's firm's legitimate deals were being used as cover for the needs of another third of their clients. This was the laundering of cash generated on a massive scale by organized crime. Not just from here in the southeast but from all over the country. Operations in Florida, Vegas, New York, New Jersey, the mid-west, everywhere these criminals, what we used to call the Mob, had large sums of cash. Cash from casinos, prostitution, and mostly drugs, was being channeled through maybe a dozen small legal firms like Stone's in different parts of the country. You remember, there was a book about it.'

'One of John Grisham's,' Sam said.

Larsen wasn't interested in novelists. 'Whatever,' he said. 'It was a smart idea, using lots of little outfits. For one thing, if one of these law firms took a tumble the people generating all this money - and it was incalculable billions - didn't suffer too badly. For another thing, a small firm was certain to attract less attention. Especially in a place like Waco, for god's sake. I mean, who in hell would think of looking in Waco for an organized crime laundering operation? Well, when the IRS stumbled on this they decided that it was time to call us in.'

Larsen was silent again and after a moment Phil said, 'Louise Garrett?'

Leaning forward against his seat belt, Larsen said, 'We had Stone and all his partners under tight surveillance for maybe two years before we got a break. Seems that while they all probably knew what was going on, had to, only Stone and his brother-in-law, a guy named Max Lensky, directly handled the organized crime business. Then Lensky retired, ill-health, old age, whatever. So we focused on Stone. We knew he had a mistress, Louise O'Brien was her real name, and they had a kid, a little boy named Billy. The kid was already a cripple when we came on the scene; some kind of accident the story went. Stone also had a grown-up son, Harry, to his wife. There could never be a divorce. Religious reasons, would you believe. The wife was a devout Bible-thumper and brought Harry up the same way. Harry was a loser who hated his father, sentiments Stone returned. The wife, Sonia, was an alcoholic who spent most of her time in drying-out clinics. About five years ago, there was a bust up between Louise and Harry. He beat her, telling her she was to blame for his mother being a drunk, which wasn't true by the way, she was that way long before Louise O'Brien came along. We had Louise's place bugged and got it all on tape. Including the son, Harry, raving that the little boy, Billy, hadn't been crippled in an accident, Stone's wife had done it in a drunken rage. The way Harry Stone put it, it was clear that he and his mother both thought that was a pretty fair exchange. One busted marriage equals one crippled kid. Not exactly eye for an eye, but close enough for a Bible freak.'

Phil watched the roadside flowers flowing past like a silent blue tide, thinking that on a scale of one to ten, Louise Garrett's life had to measure somewhere around minus fifteen.

'The taping,' Larsen said, 'wasn't live. I mean, we didn't have anyone listening in, just an arrangement where we picked up the tape every twenty-four hours. It was just for information. The bug, I mean.' He shook his head. 'So there was no way we could have stopped it.'

'Stopped what?'

'Harry's beating of Louise. And what it escalated into. He raped her.'

Jesus. The measure of Louise's life had just sunk to minus twenty.

'That night,' Larsen said, 'Louise told Stone she was leaving, and she told him why. Stone is an unscrupulous bastard but he has a weak spot. That kid. He loved little Billy. When Louise told him how Billy had been crippled, he went crazy. He stormed out, saying he was going to kill his wife. Louise went after him . . .' Larsen's voice trailed off.

After half a mile had ticked by he resumed. 'And we fucking lost them. It was hours before we picked them up again and by then Aaron Stone's wife and son, Harry, were dead. The next day, Louise left town, taking Billy with her. We went after Stone for the two murders but we couldn't prove a thing. Not without Louise, and she'd vanished. As far as we knew then, maybe we could've made it stick with her. It might have been strong circumstantial evidence, but not good enough in court if she got herself a smart lawyer.' Larsen sighed. 'Stone was, still is, a smooth operator. Hard, resilient, but all this had shaken him badly and in an off-guard moment he let slip that he had talked to his pals in the crime families and they were hunting Louise.

'It took us a year, but we got to her first and by then she was a very frightened woman. Stone had killed his wife and when his son, Harry, tried to intervene he shot him, too, and Louise saw it all. So we did have a solid witness to the killings. By then, we'd thought a lot and knew that we wanted more than just putting Stone in prison. We did a deal with Louise. Her testimony against Stone in exchange for a new identity. Once we had that, we went to Stone and offered *him* a deal. His testimony against the Mob and in return we would not proceed with the murder counts, which here in Texas meant the death penalty, and he, too, would go into the WITSEC program. In his case, we offered to go the distance and stage his death. Outside of Stone and the Bureau nobody would know he was alive, except Louise.' Larsen sighed again. 'Or so we thought.'

Phil glanced at a road sign stretched over the highway. Another half hour and they would be in San Antonio. He wasn't looking forward with any pleasure to meeting Aaron Stone. How did you talk to a man who was being protected by the FBI from prosecution for major involvement in organized crime and the murders of his own wife and son? And how could the Bureau countenance such a deal? They must have figured that they would get a huge return to make that kind of compromise.

Beside him, Sam Madsen glanced at Larsen through the rear-view mirror. 'What about the third third?' he asked.

'What?'

'You said one third of Stone's practice was legit, and one third wasn't. What about the rest?'

'That was legit, too, but different. Stone acted for a string of politicians. Big boys, a handful of state governors, senators.' Larsen leaned back. 'And I think we should get used to calling him Lewis Kant. Aaron Stone is dead, remember.'

'Why did he pick San Antonio to hide out?' Phil asked.

'It's a big place and he wanted to stay in the state. It suited us, so we agreed. And he isn't exactly hiding out. He owns a public relations company that specializes in political campaigns.'

'Isn't that dangerous?'

'Not really. Like I said we went the distance. We gave him a new face. Not even his own mother would recognize him.'

If he had one, thought Phil. He said, 'That isn't what I meant. I would've thought it was dangerous letting a man like that near politicians.'

Larsen shrugged his shoulders. 'I guess they can take care of themselves. Most of them are tough nuts. Lennox certainly is.'

'Paul Lennox?'

'Right.'

'Jesus Christ,' Phil said, swinging around to stare at Larsen. 'Are you telling me that a former associate of organized crime, a man who murdered his wife and son, is helping elect a man who will almost certainly be the next president of the United States.'

Larsen stared back. 'What do you want me to do? Run up to Lennox and tell him who he should pick for his staff? It's a free country, Phil. And, anyway, the FBI's not political. That's the other crowd.'

'The hell it isn't political. And whatever you call it, this is just plain dangerous and, worse than that, it's fucking stupid.' He paused. 'Oh, wait a minute. I know what you're doing. You plan to just sit around until Lennox is elected and then the Director goes along to the White House and says, "Good morning, Mr President, now you're ours." Right?'

'Come on, Phil, that isn't the way things are done and you know it.'

Phil turned his back on the FBI man, thinking that either Larsen was a naïve fool or was even more duplicitous than he'd thought at the start. And he was pretty damn certain he wasn't a fool, certainly not a naïve one.

'So where do we find Stone-Kant?' Sam asked. 'Taking tea with the mayor, or chatting to the local branch of the DAR?'

'Funny,' Larsen said flatly. After a moment, he said, 'We'll head for Lennox's campaign headquarters. Take the exit for Flores, then south until we reach Dolorosa. You'll see the building. Can't miss it.'

'How come? Covered in Old Glory, is it?' Phil asked.

Larsen turned to stare out the window, ignoring the last remark.

Phil worried away at the fact that a presidential candidate, a man you could happily risk a month's pay wagering he would win in November, was being compromised through his unwitting employment of a very nasty criminal. It smacked of dirty tricks in the making. And, he didn't like it.

He didn't know much more about Paul Lennox than he did about any politician and that only ever amounted to what he read in newspapers or gleaned from TV. But Lennox had an aura, the kind that the Kennedys had exuded with effortless grace and which press and pundits and campaign managers had subsequently and always mistakenly hung on almost any other young, fairly presentable politician who didn't actually eat babies in public.

Whether or not Lennox was truly what he appeared to be on the surface he couldn't know. Nobody would until some years into his presidency, if then. Certainly Lennox, the former mayor of San Antonio and until last year state governor of Texas, carried the aura in a confident manner that made it look genuine and many people had real hope that he might be the answer to long-unanswered prayers, especially from those party faithfuls who had baulked a few years back, quietly of course, when color had crept into the reckoning. But however good the candidate looked, Phil was sure he couldn't withstand being soiled by linkage to Aaron Stone.

When Lennox's campaign headquarters loomed up, the candidate's image was plastered all across the facade up to the top storey of the building. Young, a few years short of fifty, dark-haired and athletically handsome, Paul Lennox smiled down a hundred times onto the street where Sam managed to slip into a parking space right out front as a delivery truck pulled away.

At street level, the building was awash with bright-eyed, fresh-faced young volunteer workers, most of them teenage girls, and Phil felt a momentary pang for Jennifer. This was the kind of thing she would love to do outside of classroom hour if she didn't live in a small out-of-the-way town like Forrest.

Larsen led the way through the building, being directed from one person to another until they were finally in a corner of a large third-floor room busy with the noise of printers pouring out updates on the candidate and his activities. Phil picked up a leaflet, glancing at its handful of quotable quotes. Right at this moment, he knew, up in Michigan, at the incumbent president's campaign HQ in a building much like this one, there'd be similar leaflets telling similar stories in bite-sized pieces. He could guess what President Ethan Roberts' fliers would read like if he got wind of the information about Aaron Stone. They would be a lethal mixture of poison and dynamite. Worst of all, the stories would be true. Roberts had never been known to give quarter to any opponent and now, running a very poor second in the polls to Lennox, he would go unhesitatingly for the jugular.

Larsen was talking to a tall, skinny young man with an expression of eager anxiety who was telling him that Lewis Kant was out of town.

'Until when?' Larsen asked.

'He'll be back late afternoon, early evening,' the young man said. 'It's just a quick fence-mending visit out in Medina County. That's an area where we're a little weak. We intend to take Texas with not even a hint of opposition.' He grinned, showing large, horsy teeth. 'We damn well will, too.' He looked from Larsen to Phil and Sam, his expression shifting a shade uneasily. 'Why do you want to see Mr Kant?' he asked.

'We represent a large organization that is looking to make a substantial contribution to the campaign,' Larsen said smoothly, coming close enough to the truth, Phil thought.

'That's great,' the young man said. 'We're running way out in front but we need to keep up the pace all the way through to November. That means we need all the money we can raise and all the publicity, too. That's what I tell the TV people who come along.'

Phil leaned forward. 'Any TV people been here today or yesterday?'

'They're in and out all the time.'

'How many? Yesterday and today.'

The young man frowned, his eyes flicking uneasily at Larsen who looked inquiringly at Phil. 'Why's that important?' the young man asked.

Phil tried a casual grin. 'What's your name?' he asked.

'Danny. Danny Reynolds.'

'Well, Danny, our client doesn't want the media getting wind of his contribution. He wants it kept just between us for as long as possible. You know how some of these rich people are.'

The young man nodded in uncertain agreement.

'So, who's been here?'

'Yesterday there was the local station, KWEX, and this morning someone from Amarillo.'

'Man or woman?'

'Woman.'

'What was her name?'

Danny was looking worried now. 'I forget.'

'Barbara Nichols,' Phil said. 'Was that the name?'

Danny nodded unhappily.

'Shit,' Larsen said while Sam grinned.

'Is that a problem?' Danny asked.

'Not for you,' Phil said. 'Where'd she go?'

'She went out to see Mr Kant. She said she wanted to shoot some footage out on the road, so I told her where to find him.'

'And where is that?'

'Out around Devine.' Danny glanced at his watch. 'But by now I expect Mr Kant will have moved on and, like I say, he'll be coming back in tonight. He has to go over the arrangements for a ceremony tomorrow. Mr Lennox is making a presentation in Alamo Plaza. Mr Kant will be checking that everything's the way it should be.'

'That's okay, Danny,' Phil said. 'We'll see Mr Kant this evening and we'll just have to make sure we see Miss Nichols before she sees us.' He paused. 'Was she alone?' he asked casually.

'Yes.'

'No one waiting outside?'

'Oh, I don't know about that. All I know is she came in here on her own.'

'Okay, Danny, thanks for your help.'

'That's okay, glad to be of service. If I see Mr Karat I'll tell him you want to see him. What name shall I say?'

Larsen flicked a glance at Phil, saying to the young man, 'Bennett, Jerry Bennett. He'll know me. We've done business before. He'll know it's important. I only call on him when there's good cause.'

'I'll be sure to tell him.'

'Alamo Plaza,' Phil said. 'That's where Kant will be this evening?'

'Yes, sir. I'll be there, too. I'll look out for you.'

'That'll be nice,' Phil said, turning to thread his way through piles of leaflets.

Outside, he waited by the car for Sam and Larsen. Looking at Sam, Phil shook his head slowly. 'Are you keeping track of all this?' he asked.

'Just about.'

Phil looked at the FBI man. 'Jake Larsen, John Lanning. Now Jerry Bennett. Any other names you're known by?'

Larsen shrugged. 'Security,' he said.

'How about Louise Garrett who's really Louise O'Brien? Then there's Aaron Stone now known as Lewis Kant. How many other people in this mess go by more than one name?'

'We have to be careful,' Larsen told him.

'But maybe not careful enough,' Phil said.

Larsen frowned questioningly.

'Apart from the fact that your security is so filled with leaks that Louise and her kids are dead, we're running as fast as we can and we're still behind a goddamn TV reporter. What's she got that we haven't? Who's she talking to?'

'Maybe,' Sam said, 'she's just doing what all good Indians do, and sniffing out the trail.'

'It's no joke, Sam,' Phil said. 'And I thought we're supposed to call you people Native Americans these days. '

'Like you say, that's for you guys. We can call ourselves any damn thing we want.'

'Well, whatever you call yourself, if she can sniff out a trail, why can't you?'

'Because, as you've already worked out for yourself, Miss Nichols has got herself a companion who maybe knows more about this than all of us put together.'

Phil nodded. 'I guess you're right,' he said. As he often did, Sam had targeted a central point. 'Okay, let's go find someplace to stay and decide what we plan to do tonight when Kant reaches the Alamo. The Alamo, for Christ's sake. What am I doing here? Confrontations at the Alamo. What comes next? Gunfights at the it-ain't-all-okay corral?'

'Look on the bright side,' Sam said. 'It could be worse. We could be re-fighting the Battle of the Little Big Horn. At least, unlike that encounter, the way things are down here you're not certain you're gonna lose.'

BARBARA TURNED the Honda onto a dirt road, not sure that the directions she'd been given were working out right. They'd been chasing from one farm to another, each time just missing the man they wanted. Then, up ahead, in the dusty yard in front of a dark-green-painted farmhouse, she saw a cluster of cars, one of them a lime-green Chevrolet Traverse she'd been told to look out for.

Back in San Antonio she had persuaded Ryker to let her talk to the people at the Lennox campaign headquarters alone. Presumably because she'd been successful at the hospital at Camp Mabry, he'd agreed and once again she'd used her real ID, guessing rightly that her status would bring results. It had but it was quickly apparent that none of the young helpers was likely to be the man they were looking for. When a toothy young man named Danny told her that Lewis Kant ran the campaign she decided that he was the man she should talk to first. If he wasn't cooperative, then she would try someone else but she didn't know how long she could keep Ryker in the background.

The trouble was, out here, in the quiet and calm of farming country, Ryker was unlikely to sit quietly in the car while she talked to Kant and she didn't want him to know that she'd lied to him all along.

Especially not after last night.

She had woken, sore from fierce sex, to find he was gone from her room. But she could hear the TV in the adjoining room and after she'd showered away the night's excesses, she went next door and called him.

His greeting was distant, not unfriendly, but as if he barely knew her. He had said little on the road down to San Antonio and although he was not intimidating the way he had been at first, his silence was oppressive and worrying. One thing was sure, their sexual encounter had no meaning for him above that he would have gained from a visit by a call girl.

Barbara wasn't sure how she felt about that. Yesterday, the excitement had urged her into the situation that had developed. Today, the excitement was dimmed and in its absence the sex seemed almost distasteful.

She eased the Honda to a stop beside the Chevy Traverse and climbed out, telling Ryker she would find Kant and ask him some questions. She started walking towards the farmhouse when she heard the slam of the car's other door. Damn, she thought.

Ryker caught up with her and took her arm, stopping her. 'Take it easy,' he said. 'What's the name of this guy we're seeing? Kant?'

'Lewis Kant.'

He shook his head thoughtfully. 'I never heard of this guy. You sure he can help?'

'No, of course I'm not sure. All I know is that Louise was afraid of a man who works for Paul Lennox. Kant runs the show down here, so the chances are he'll know our man. What we do is ask him some polite questions about the people on his team and try to figure out which one is the man who fathered Billy Garrett.'

His fingers dug sharply into her arm. 'Don't fucking say that,' he said.

She stared at him, some of the fear coming back.

Ryker stared back, thinking that she was different this morning. Had changed somehow since last night. It had happened before. Let a woman get close and somewhere along the line they start getting ideas that they own a piece of you or want to change the way you are. All the goddamn same. No, that wasn't true. Couldn't be. He didn't remember Louise ever acting that way. She was different, wasn't she? He tried to bring a memory out of the past but so much of it swirled mistily. Jesus, it was hard to recall any damn thing without his head hurting.

You should avoid strings. Any relationship, whoever it is, man, woman, child, even a fucking dog, ties strings to you. Some guys, they let it happen. They think they can break the strings anytime they want. But

128

that isn't the way it works. Before you know it, the strings have become chains and then you're in real trouble. Take my word for it, relationships are poison.

Poison? Not all of them. What about the kids? Okay, so maybe Billy wasn't his son but he cared for him, didn't he? And then there was the little girl. Jo-Anne wasn't poison. Jesus Christ, anyone could see that.

Take my word for it, before you know it, strings become chains and then you're in real trouble.

Barbara watched his eyes, aware that she was seeing the reflection of some strange, tortured inner struggle. Contrasting with her thoughts a few moments ago, now she wanted to help him. She had forgotten what he must be going through, trying to find and now maybe getting closer to the man who had butchered his wife and the two little children. Christ, no wonder he was mixed up and had shown her so little emotional response. With what he had gone through, was still going through, it would be a miracle if he had any emotional slack left for anyone to take up.

Impulsively, she rested a hand on his arm. 'Let me help,' she said. 'I want to. And I can, believe me.'

His eyes slowly focused on hers and for a moment something she hoped was a smile glimmered deep inside but then she heard another voice and instantly his eyes shifted and she felt the muscles in his arm tense under her fingers.

Turning, she saw someone coming from the farmhouse. Small, barely a couple of inches over five feet, he was skinny, had thick dark-gray hair and a deep tan. His eyes were gold-flecked hazel, his nose flat like a prizefighter's, his face youthfully unlined, although close up she could see that he must be in his sixties. Whatever his age, he looked fit and moved energetically.

The little man was smiling with professional affability, showing unnaturally white and even teeth. 'Are you Barbara Nichols?' he asked.

She stared at him in surprised silence.

The smile widened. 'I'm Lewis Kant,' he said. 'Danny Reynolds called from the office. Said you'd been asking for me and were on your way out. Didn't know if you'd catch up with me. Move pretty fast on these visits. Have to. A lot of territory to cover.' He held out a hand and Barbara took it, conscious that for all his professionalism the little man hadn't managed to cure damp palms. Then he made the same gesture to Ryker and after a hesitation that seemed to her to last for minutes, the two men shook hands.

'So, I guess you want to talk about Paul Lennox,' Kant said, looking from one to the other of them, still exuding affable good humor.

Almost before he spoke again, Barbara knew that he was about to say something that would make her life very difficult.

He did.

'After all,' Kant continued, 'why else would a TV reporter come all the way down here from Amarillo?'

TWELVE

STANDING ON the steps of the post office at the northern edge of the plaza, looking across an array of canvas awnings, Phil Davis spotted Sam Madsen. He waved a hand, then walked down the steps and the two men wandered among the stalls set out across the plaza.

Phil had just mailed a postcard to Jennifer, knowing it would sit in the Blakes' mailbox until they returned from their trip to Arizona. It depicted the plaza but without the picturesque market stalls; just the statue mightily paying tribute to the long-ago of defenders of what was now a revered museum on the left-hand side of the plaza from where he now walked.

He wasn't sure if Jennifer would approve of the image on the postcard. She might prefer the plaza as he was now seeing it with no historical or political message, just the stalls and the people thronging among them.

It was an exhibition-cum-market for local artists. Mostly, the stalls carried paintings, and the majority of these were watercolors that bravely tried to capture the landscapes of the surrounding country. A few stalls had home-made jewelry, trinkets would be a better description, he thought, that also tried to be something they were not. The makers had vainly hoped to recreate the vivid color and imagery of the ancient Mexican and Native American craftsmen whose land this once was.

'Ain't real,' Sam's voice murmured in his ear.

Phil knew that Sam had an on-off relationship with a Native American painter whose work threw a contemporary light on ancient traditions. From things Sam had said in the past, Phil knew that some of her contempt for touristy art had rubbed off.

'Pretty, though,' Phil said. He smiled at the lady seated on a low stool behind the stall and asked the price of a brooch, then asked her to wrap it. 'Think she'll like it?' he asked Sam.

'Who?'

'Jennifer, who'd you think?'

Sam shrugged. 'What do I know about your private life,' he said. 'Maybe you got something going.'

'I'm too old to start over,' Phil said as he paid for the brooch. They walked through the stalls, shaded by awnings and trees from the warming sun. 'Nice place,' he added.

Sam nodded agreement but didn't take the hint. 'Who told you you're too old?' he asked.

'Some things,' Phil said, 'you just know.' Glancing around, he asked, 'Where's Larsen?'

Sam thought about pursuing Phil's private life, then gave in and said, 'Told me he needed to check in with the Bureau's local office. Seems the Suits have a protocol to follow. Of course, he might just be reporting to Quantico or Washington. Or asking for instructions. Or maybe calling in reinforcements. Who knows?'

'What did you make of what he told us? You reckon this time we know the truth?'

Sam stopped and leaned against a tree, his face shadowed and ruminative. 'Well, look at it this way, he couldn't have made it up. Not all of it. So I guess what he told us was close to the truth. Whether it's the whole truth is another question entirely and I have an uneasy feeling it maybe calls for a different answer.'

'Meaning?'

'Meaning, he has to be hiding things from us, Phil. There are pieces of this that don't make any kind of sense. For one, why are we still involved? Every day we're further away from Forrest and more deeply entangled in things that are no business for a couple of hick cops like us.'

'Maybe you're right, but just so long as we are here, are we expected to sit back and let all this drift along? Aaron Stone working for

Paul Lennox. I mean, Christ, Sam, the guy's blindly heading for disaster and we're supposed to just sit here and do nothing about it.' Answering his own question, Phil shook his head. 'Larsen said that no one else knows, now that Louise is dead, it's just the Bureau. And now us.' He paused, thinking. 'Of course, if I was paranoid, I might start jumping at shadows, just in case one of the instructions Larsen might be taking right now is to make certain we don't talk about it.'

Now Sam shook his head. 'No. I know it's expected that cops like us don't hit it off with the Bureau, but they're not dumb. Not all the time and not all the way up. They know they can't close off the fact that Lewis Kant is a supposedly-dead lawyer named Aaron Stone who made his name doing dirty business for dirtier people and probably being paid dirty money. They know that somewhere along the line word will leak out. Maybe not before November, it could even be years, but sometime, somewhere, somebody will blow the whistle on Kant and if by then Lennox is president his pack of cards comes tumbling down.'

'You're right,' Phil said. 'So what game is the Bureau playing?'

'The present Director of the FBI was President Roberts' first appointment. Seems like they're real close. Maybe they're playing a game of their own.'

'Conspiracy? At that level? Christ, Sam, please don't talk conspiracy.'

'Hey, I never used the word,' Sam said. Then he shrugged and added, 'Maybe we'll get an angle when we talk with Kant.'

Across the plaza carpenters were finishing off a bank of benches for the people expected to attend tomorrow's ceremony. Paul Lennox, who had long been San Antonio's favorite son, and former mayor and state governor, was scheduled to present awards to a select group of the town's leading citizens.

'We need to do something about Barbara Nichols,' Phil said. 'Whatever she's doing, she's taking chances. Especially if bullets start flying.' Speaking of which, he told Sam about the shooting in Austin the day before.

'You think there's a connection?' Sam asked.

'Who can tell? But all the links that we're making, and Larsen's making, and Barbara's making, tie together a lot of people that have no business even knowing one another. Links like that lead to trouble.'

'Maybe we'll get to talk to her tonight, if we can find her.'

'Unless she's picked up yet another lead ahead of us and goes chasing off someplace else.'

'We could find out what car she's driving and put out an APB. Larsen could fix that for us, even if the local force won't play.'

'Maybe later,' Phil said. 'You know, Doug Carlson's certain she's not alone. If Doug's right then whoever Barbara's friend is knows most of the people involved. Also, the first time Barbara called Doug, she tied everything to Forrest. Now what does that suggest?'

'She's talked to Louise Garrett's significant other.'

'Right,' Phil agreed.

'He's still a suspect,' Sam said. 'Which puts her in a very bad position.'

Phil shook his head. 'You know I was never hot for the husband or boyfriend or whoever he is as the killer. I mean, if he did kill Louise and the children, why chase around the country the way he is? And with a TV reporter for god's sake.'

'He's looking for someone,' Sam said.

'Could be.'

'And maybe he doesn't know she's a reporter. That could be why she doesn't want anyone calling her.'

They had reached a bridge and Sam leaned on the parapet, looking down into the water. Phil stood for a moment, thinking over their conversation. 'If that's the way it is,' he said, 'he won't be too happy if he ever finds out that she's been keeping secrets from him.'

HE SHOULD have known better. The bitch. The fucking treacherous bitch. A fucking reporter. Jesus Christ. That was why she'd been cozying up to him, driving him around wherever he wanted to go, buying him cigarettes. Letting him fuck her. Shit. He should have known.

But he kept it all inside. For now. This wasn't the time or place. Not here, out in the fucking boonies talking to this old guy with his artificial smile and greasy palms.

Anyway, the old guy was maybe a lead to the man he wanted. And for now the woman was the best one to do the asking. Smart, he had to give her that. Too smart for her own good, but smart enough for this. He kept his feelings bottled up and nodded at her, then towards Kant, making it clear that she should start the questions.

They were inside the farmhouse. Sitting on cushioned rockers. Place smelled like a fucking barn. He could imagine all the farmers coming in and out with pigshit on their boots or whatever the hell they raised here.

Cattle's better'n pigs, and pigs're better'n hens, and hens're better'n wheat, and wheat's better'n alfalfa.

Jesus, he hadn't thought about that for years. What Zack had called the old man's al-fucking-falfa speech. It must be the fact that he was on a farm again, for the first time since god knows when, that had stirred up

134

old memories. Brought his brother back into his mind.

He tuned in to what the woman was saying now to Kant. She was telling him they needed urgently to meet a man, talk to him, about the fact that there was a problem that could blow up in the candidate's face at anytime. She made it sound convincing, he had to admit to that.

But Kant wasn't buying. Shrewd, and cagey, he was looking from her to him and back again.

Barbara started again. 'Look, Mr Kant,' she said. 'I'm not doing this just for a story. There's more to it than that. This is something that concerns my friend here, deeply concerns him.' Her friend, get that. Betrayal one minute and the next she's calling him her friend. 'And it also concerns Paul Lennox because it could damage his chances in November. Look, I can't prove this, but I want Lennox to win. We need to make changes in this country and one of the changes we need most is to be rid of Ethan Roberts. Lennox can do that but he has to be clean, squeaky clean, and it's possible that someone on your staff down here is connected with something very unpleasant. Now, we don't know who that someone is. It could be a nobody, someone who stuffs campaign leaflets into envelopes, in which case all you do is quietly fire him and there's an end to the problem. But if this man is high up, close to Lennox, then you need to take steps to make sure your candidate is completely isolated and the connection is scrubbed clean.'

Kant was watching her closely now, a slight vertical crease forming between his eyes and making the only lines on his oddly smooth face. 'This problem that could blow up into something very unpleasant. What is it exactly?'

Barbara glanced at Ryker, thinking that he appeared to have taken the revelation that she wasn't what she'd claimed to be very calmly. And he was letting her direct the meeting with Lewis Kant. All of which should have made her feel easier than she did. Maybe it was knowing that any moment now she would have to start talking about the murders in Forrest that was making her edgy.

'Have you heard of a town called Forrest?' she asked.

Kant shook his head slowly, the line etched between his eyes remaining.

'In the north end of the state,' she told him. 'A few days ago the police discovered three bodies there, a woman and two children. They'd been murdered.'

Kant looked bewildered. 'Go on.'

'We've learned that the woman once told someone else, a nurse at a hospital, that she was afraid of a man who was working on Paul Lennox's campaign.'

'Who?' Kant asked. 'What's his name?'

'We don't know. That's why we've come to you.'

'This woman, the one who was murdered, what was her name?'

'Louise Garrett,' Barbara said.

His eyes widened. 'Louise?' The word was little more than a grating whisper.

She stared at him, thinking, No, it can't be.

'Garrett? You're sure that's her second name?'

Barbara flicked a sideways glance at Ryker but got nothing.

Then Kant was speaking again, straining to make the words come. 'You said there were children.'

She glanced again at Ryker but he was sitting immobile, hands on knees, staring hard at Kant. 'The other victims were a boy,' she told Kant. 'Billy, and a girl, Jo-Anne,' she said to the old man.

'Billy. Was he crippled?' There was a desperate urgency in his voice.

She knew the answer he wanted to hear but she couldn't give it to him. She nodded slowly.

'Oh, my god.' Kant closed his eyes. 'Billy, my little Billy.' The blood drained from his face, his tan turning to a sickly yellow.

Oh, Christ, Barbara thought. It's him. For no reason at all she had assumed that Louise's lover would be a younger man.

Kant was motionless, then his hand moved as he crossed himself and his lips moved in what was obviously a prayer.

From another room Barbara could hear voices, faint and peppered with bursts of laughter. After several moments, she leaned forward to rest her hand on Kant's arm. 'Can I get you anything?' she asked. 'A glass of water?'

He shook his head sharply, eyes still closed.

She needed a cigarette but decided to wait. Looking at Ryker, she saw he was still staring intently at Kant and for once she could read his expression. There was a curious mix of disbelief and acceptance. He must have known, as she did, that Kant's reaction meant that he was the man they were looking for and that equally clearly he had played no part in the murders. She wasn't at all sure what part of it he disbelieved.

Ryker couldn't believe it. This old man, false teeth and face lift, a fucking midget for Christ's sake, had been Louise's . . . he couldn't even think the word. But he had to believe it. For a minute there he'd thought the old goat was about to keel over, the way Lensky had. Nobody could pull a stunt like this, not the best actor in the world. This was the man. And however much he didn't want to believe the other part of it, the old man was Billy's father.

Eventually Kant's eyes opened and he looked from one to the other of them, some of his color returning. 'No point in pretending, is there,' he said. 'I'm the one you're looking for. I knew Louise. She was Louise O'Brien not, what did you call her, Garrett? She left. Ran away.' He shook his head, his light brown eyes filling with tears. 'She didn't need to run. I would never let her be harmed. I would've found a way to protect her. I know Max hated me for what happened to Sonia but I would've found a way.'

Max? Sonia? Who the fuck're they? Max Lensky? Is that who he's talking about? Ryker leaned forward to ask a question but the old man was babbling on again.

'Who did it? Do they know who did it? The police, I mean.'

Barbara shook her head.

Kant's mouth tightened and he wiped a hand across his eyes. 'She shouldn't've run away. Not from me. I wouldn't harm her for the world and certainly not Billy.'

Kant's mind was racing. Was it a coincidence, or was it a hit? He couldn't know the answer, but he knew that the Feds had got to her, convinced her that after what happened to Sonia and Harry she wasn't safe around him. He knew how they worked. They would've told Louise they'd protect her against him if she would testify. Against him, for god's sake. But they're convincing, those bastards. He knew that. They'd worked hard on him, trying to convince him to testify against Ralph Hardy. As if he would. That bastard from the FBI, Jerry Bennett he'd called himself, worked on him for months, but he'd suckered him along. The face job, the new ID, everything he needed to put him where he wanted to be and all the time Bennett breathing down his neck telling him Louise was going to say this, going to say that. Bastard. And they'd screwed up. The Bureau with all its bullshit had screwed up and now Louise was dead.

He pulled back a thought that had floated through his mind, unbidden. Was it really a hit? Why would he think that? Who would put out paper on Louise? Not him, and he was the only one she could hurt. Except Ralph. No. They were partners. Ralph would never have ordered it. Would he?

He looked at the man sitting there boring holes in him with his eyes, remembering what the woman had said. She'd said this concerned him. Deeply concerned, she'd said. 'Where do you come in?' he asked the man.

The man didn't answer and Kant felt his palms sweat. He knew the type, thought he did. Hard case. No time for talk. Then he took a guess. 'You knew Louise. Right?' He looked at the woman. 'You said there was another child. Louise had another child.' Back to the man. 'Yours?' That drew a flicker. 'And the cops think you did it.' This time there was a reaction. The eyes changed, blanking out everything. 'And you're trying to find out who really did it.'

Barbara nodded. 'That's part of it,' she said.

'And the other part?'

'Paul Lennox.'

Kant frowned, then slowly nodded his head in agreement. 'Right,' he said. 'When all this shit hits the fan, it isn't only me that's covered. Everyone I work with gets their share and in Paul's case, he's buried.'

He'd always known there was a risk but he'd hoped there'd be a way through it. That bastard Bennett had assured him that so long as he stayed clean they wouldn't blow his cover. Their cover, the FBI were the ones who'd built the new ID. Conmen. He knew they wanted a handle on Lennox. But he'd conned them. They didn't know what he was really doing. That he was really doing all this for Ralph Hardy so that when Lennox was elected Ralph could call him up one day and tell him, We own you.

Then another thought slowly coalesced in his mind Something else this TV woman said. Louise had told someone that she was afraid of a man who worked on the Lennox campaign. Justified fear or not, that had to be himself. But how could Louise know he was with Lennox? Nobody knew that. Except the Bureau. It had to be them. They'd told her. But for god's sake, why?

Barbara was looking at Ryker, trying to get a sense of where he wanted to go with this but there were no indications. Nothing. Just the blank stare pinned on Lewis Kant.

'We're looking for the man who did this,' she said to Kant. 'The man who killed Louise and the children. That's all. We're not interested in the rest of it.' That wasn't true. She had to use all this new information and Kant must know it. He'd spent his life, both his lives, dealing with the media. But right now, she was uneasy at Ryker being here with Kant. Two men, both tied to Louise, and Ryker completely unpredictable.

That's all? Kant was thinking. That wasn't all. If this pair had found him then so could others. He would have to talk to Ralph, make plans. And much as he hated the idea, he needed to talk to that FBI bastard, Bennett. The Bureau had a stake in this. They'd protect him.

Glancing at his watch, Kant pulled himself to his feet. 'I have to talk to these people,' he said, jerking a thumb in the direction of the hum of voices. 'Then I'm heading back to San Antonio. There's something I have to do ready for a ceremony tomorrow. After that.' He paused, took a breath, swallowed. 'After that, I have to do some thinking.'

Then Ryker spoke. 'Sit down.'

Kant looked at the man who slapped a hand hard down on the arm of the rocker.

The sound hit Kant like a bullet and he dropped back into his rocking chair as if he'd been shot. The man was looking at him as if he wanted him dead and Kant felt his spine go cold and the moisture on the palms of his hands turn to ice

'You're not listening,' the man said. He jerked a thumb at the TV woman. 'She told you we're looking for who did it. We're following a trail. This is where the trail leads. So far, this is where it ends. Convince me it goes on from here.'

He didn't say 'or else' and he didn't have to. Kant pushed himself back in the chair, trying not to think what the unspoken 'or else' might mean.

'I don't know where it leads,' he said. 'I haven't seen Louise or Billy since she ran out. That's going on for five years ago. Since then, nothing. No word, no letter, no sign, nothing. Not a damn thing.'

'Who're Sonia and Max?'

'Sonia was my wife.'

'Was?'

'She's dead.'

No reaction which meant that they didn't know how she'd died. And he guessed that meant they didn't know his real name. Maybe they could find out, maybe not. Either way, it wouldn't do for them to start sniffing around. All this was bad enough but it could get worse. He would have to talk to Ralph about these two.

'Max?'

'Sonia's brother.'

'Lensky?'

Kant swallowed hard, his mouth uncomfortably dry. How in god's name did this guy know about Max? Sitting there, dead-eyed, letting the woman do all the talking until now. Waiting. What did he know? What did he want? He wanted a lead, that's what he'd said. A lead that would take him away from here. So give him one.

An idea hit him. 'You want my opinion?' he asked. 'Louise went to the FBI. They hid her. Gave her a new ID.' He looked at the man, trying to fathom what was going on behind those eyes. 'She never told you, right. It happens. Don't feel bad about it. It's the only way the program can work. The Witness Security Program. So they screwed up. The Bureau did. A leak. Someone found out where she was and thought she could be trouble.'

'Trouble? Who could she hurt?'

Shit. He'd dug a trap and walked right into it. 'She knew things about my former business,' he tried. 'Knew some things that could be dangerous if they got out. Could be one of half a dozen.'

Who could he give them that wouldn't backfire? Not Ralph and this guy already knew about Max. Jorge Aguerre. The spic was trouble in the making, he'd told Ralph often enough and recently Ralph was starting to agree.

'There's a guy in Austin,' he said. 'Name's Jorge Aguerre. Bigtime operator but smalltime mind. A lot of times people talked about him to me. Louise heard it all. She knows where some of Aguerre's bodies are buried. You should talk to him.'

'We did.'

Kant struggled to think of someone else but the intensity of the man's stare had lessened. Maybe he was taking the idea on board.

Ryker was thinking, Louise and the FBI? That's crazy. He would've known. Wouldn't he? Surely he couldn't have missed that. Nobody's perfect but that was too much to miss. But what was it the nurse in Austin had told Barbara? That Louise had talked to two men, asked for a change of ID. That fitted in with what Kant was saying. Crazy or not, it tied together.

Now this business about Aguerre. Had he slipped up? Had he let that fucking spic blindside him? He already knew that Aguerre had set up the meet with Jones so that Ralph Hardy could send in a team but what if Aguerre had done all that to make smoke. If that's what he'd done it had worked. Set up a lead from Jones, just in case he got clear of the hit team, a lead that sent him to Camp Mabry and then down here. All the time moving further away and giving Aguerre and Hardy more time to set up another attempt to blow him away.

He didn't like this little bastard sitting opposite him, but it was sounding as if there might be something in what he was saying.

He was doing it again. Believing people. He'd believed Ralph Hardy when he said he'd had no part in the killings. He'd believed Dillard and Bohannon. He'd let Aguerre sucker him. He believed Jones. Now he was believing Kant. He believed everybody. He'd believed the woman. And that had been a mistake. Maybe it was all a mistake, believing any of them.

Barbara glanced at Ryker and he was looking her way, his eyes cold and thoughtful. She was in trouble, she knew. Somehow, she had to explain away her role in all this.

Then Kant was speaking to her. 'How did they die? Louise and Billy.'

Again, Barbara flicked a swift glance at Ryker. Now that he knew she was a reporter was there any point in further pretence? As far as she knew, the police hadn't released the cause of death, at least they hadn't up to the time she'd walked out of Phil Davis's office a thousand years ago. But Ryker wouldn't know that. What troubled her was how he would react, hearing it. And Kant, for that, matter, because whatever lay behind the façade it was clear that he had real feelings.

'Answer the man,' Ryker said.

Momentarily, she closed her eyes, thinking of the photographs Davis had shown her. 'Louise was killed with . . .' She didn't know but it had to be a knife of some kind. She described what she had seen on the photograph of Louise, her eyes moving from one man to the other. Kant was pale again, Ryker's expression unreadable.

'Billy?' Kant asked, obviously not wanting to hear but needing to know.

She told him, the words cold, like hammer blows. Axe blows.

For a moment she thought Kant would pass out but somehow he held on. Ryker was studying her face, still nothing telling her what he was thinking. Or feeling.

'Someone has to pay,' Kant said, his voice uncertain but bleak.

Barbara looked again at Ryker and this time there was a response. A slow, deliberate movement of his head. A nod. Affirming Kant's statement.

Barbara shivered, hoping, praying, that she wouldn't be around when the price was paid. And relieved she hadn't had to describe what happened to the little girl.

Suddenly, startling her, Ryker was on his feet and heading for the door. Hastily, Barbara stammered a farewell to Kant, thanking him, aware that they needed to talk some more if her story was to be complete. But that could wait. Had to wait. She followed Ryker outside, hurrying to catch up as he walked fast towards where they had left the car. Abruptly, he stopped, staring at a high-roofed barn, his head cocked as if he was listening.

In the opening above the door on the gable end of the barn, Ryker thought he saw a movement. From a distance, rising and falling, came a sound, a faint high-pitched wailing. And there was a smell. Burning. And another sound, a crackling. What is it, he wondered, what is it?

'What is it?' the woman was asking him.

The sounds and smell vanished and he realized that he was mistaken about movement in the barn. He shook his head and walked on, climbing into the driving seat of the Honda, starting up the motor. The woman scrambled into the car and he drove off immediately, spinning dust clouds as he turned and headed back along the dirt road.

'Are we going back to Austin?' she asked.

He shook his head. 'Tomorrow. We wait and see what Kant does. See what he says to Lennox, see if he quits, see if it's all talk.'

Try to understand, he was thinking. Try to get a handle on all of it. Any of it. Things were happening that didn't make sense, others that did but which only added to the confusion.

Most of all, there was the problem he was having trying not to think about what he had just heard Barbara describe. Drawing pictures in his mind, pictures of what had happened in Forrest. Pictures he did not want to imagine but which he could see with awful, startling, sickening clarity.

THIRTEEN

RYKER KNEW that it was his visit to the farm, the smells and the sights, that had prompted an unexpected rush of images from the past. The farm here in Texas, huge and reeking of money, was nothing like the broken-down dump where he was born and raised in Iowa but that hadn't stopped his mind opening up a store of long-buried memories.

Most of them were about Zack. Of course they were. His brother was the best thing about his youth. The only member of the family worth a damn. His mother had thought the same. It was always Zack this, Zack that, never him. He didn't blame her. Zack was her first-born and, anyway, he was smarter, taller, tougher, better looking, overflowing with effortless charm. Maybe Zack reminded his mother of how her husband had been when she married him although how the old man could ever have been charming was hard to imagine.

The old man hadn't given a shit for either of his sons, lecturing them and working their asses off when he was sober, and using his fists to make his points when he'd been drinking, which was often. They'd all suffered, the old man usually taking it out on his wife before turning to the boys.

Family life. What a fucking joke.

He'd told Ma he was the end of the line. He would never marry, never raise kids of his own. Let the blood die out with him. He knew Zack felt the same but he didn't tell her so.

Ma had listened, then told him, 'That's the way you're thinking now. You'll change, you see if you don't. One day you'll want to settle down. Take a wife and have kids. A boy and a girl if you're lucky. You'll see, you'll change your ideas. All you'll want is to play basketball with the boy, look after the girl. Make love . . .' She'd broken off there, coloring up in embarrassment for a moment, then gone on. 'Make love to your wife. Act the way other people act. Not people like us, ordinary people.'

That's what she'd said: Not people like us. But what she'd meant was: Not people like his father.

Apart from that one time, his mother had said little to him all the years he was growing up. Not talked to him the way he thought mothers were supposed to. Most of the time she simply handed out chores and kept quiet, especially when the old man was around. That was only wise, keeping out of the old man's way, especially when things went wrong - or at least went against the way the old man thought they should go - which was when he took it into his head to hit out at someone.

Even so, there were some days on the farm when life wasn't too bad, a handful of times it was even enjoyable if the old man wasn't there or when he was going through a dry spell. He'd talk to them, to him and to Zack, most of it lecturing, like the al-fucking-falfa speech, passing on his half-assed ideas about how to make a way in the world.

'Everybody has to pay their own way,' the old man had told them, time after time, as if justifying the fact that he used his sons like slave labor. 'Passengers just get in the way. Like excess baggage. Or prisoners.' That was to remind them that he'd fought in a war. 'All that they do is slow you down. You end up looking out for them when the only person you should look out for is yourself.'

He knew, even when he was only five or six years old, that the old man resented them all. The woman he'd married and Zack and him. Then, he didn't know why. Only later did he realize that the old man blamed them for the life of hardship and failure he endured. The old man probably thought that if he'd stayed alone things would've been different. 'Avoid strings,' he'd lectured his sons one time, ignoring the fact that one was twelve, the other only seven. 'Any relationship, whoever it is, man, woman, child, even a fucking dog, ties strings to you. Some guys, they let it happen, think they can break the strings anytime they want. But that's not the way it works. Before you know it, the

144

strings are chains and then you're stuck. Take my word for it, relationships are poison.'

He remembered talking to Zack about that particular lecture. 'Does he think we're poison, Zack?' he'd asked.

Zack had looked at him for a long time, then grinned that secretive little smile he had and told him, 'So what if he does. Maybe one day we'll get the chance to prove to him how wrong he is.' The grin had faded. 'Or how right.'

He didn't know what Zack meant by that and his brother wouldn't explain. He could be like that, silent, sometimes for uncomfortably long periods, holding himself in real tight. He did his best to copy from his brother, somehow sensing that Zack's way was the way to survive. Once in a while, Zack would tell him things. In some ways these were oddball versions of the old man's lectures but there were enough differences to know that they were worth hearing, and remembering. And acting upon. Like the time Zack had stopped him from trying to prevent the old man from hitting their mother.

'You're too little,' Zack warned. 'Not strong enough. Me too. Now. Remember, never start a fight unless you know you can win.' Then Zack had stared towards the house from where they could hear the faint wailing of their mother. 'But never leave undone anything important until it's too late. Then, you do what you have to. But if you're not completely confident, cover the possibility of losing. Just don't believe in it.'

They were older that time, he was eleven, Zack sixteen and already the same height as the old man but still rail-thin. Something in Zack's voice had worried him. He wasn't sure why but he was afraid that one day Zack might take it into his head to leave. That was unthinkable. The old man would go crazy if the strongest pair of hands left the farm. Life for those who remained would be intolerable.

'Don't leave us, Zack,' he'd blurted out.

His brother had looked again towards the house, silent now, their mother probably unconscious. Then he'd looked down at him and smiled the secret smile. 'I'll never do that,' he'd told him. 'One thing you can be sure of, I'll always be with you.'

For years that had been true, even when they were hundreds of miles apart his brother was with him. But these days he often went for long periods of time never so much as thinking about Zack. Until something happened to stir up a memory. Like today and the visit to the farm and the sight of the barn and the sounds and smells. Except there hadn't been any sounds or smells. Not really. They were just in his mind. He shook his head uneasily.

From the adjoining room he heard the woman moving restlessly on the bed. Soon, Ryker knew, he would have to make a decision about her.

They'd seen Lewis Kant waving his arms and bossing a crew of teenage helpers around the plaza where in the morning Paul Lennox planned on making a speech. He didn't trust politicians. Didn't trust Kant. He believed him, the way he seemed to believe just about everyone who talked to him. But he didn't trust him. Come to think of it, he didn't trust anyone.

That was one of the old man's lectures that he had believed and he knew that Zack had believed it too. The old man had told them, his eyes fixed malevolently on his wife, 'Trust no one and the chances are you'll never be disappointed. Trust one person, man or woman, and you're already splitting your chances fifty-fifty.'

The old man had been right about that. Look at the way he'd trusted Barbara Nichols. A goddamn TV reporter. From here on, until he decided what to do with her, he wouldn't let her out of his sight. That was why he had taken a two-bedroom suite at the Lexington a couple of miles off San Antonio's Loop. He lay stretched out on the couch in the living room, aimlessly watching TV and trying to make some sense out of his thoughts and what had happened to him during the past few days.

His eyes drifted around the room, and for no reason another hotel floated into his mind. The Menger. He'd passed it earlier, when they were down in Alamo Plaza. Now, in his mind, he caught a sudden, fleeting image of the hotel's interior. Old-style heavy furniture, a galleried hall, a big painting on the wall showing a cattle drive. And then there was the bar, like something out of an old western movie.

He swung his legs to the floor, standing to pace suddenly and anxiously across the room and back again.

This really was crazy. How could he know all that? He'd never been inside the Menger in his life. Had he? Christ, until he made the visit to Mexico he'd never even been in San Antonio and then all he'd done was pass through. So how could he know what the inside of the hotel looked like?

Shaking his head, he sat down again. He was letting things get to him. Maybe the pictures he'd just seen in his mind were nothing more than imagination. He'd just invented the hotel's interior; even if it was right, then sometime he must have seen pictures of it. It couldn't be any other way.

After a while, Ryker drifted off into a half-doze, his mind refusing to let him sleep as it conjured up disconnected memories of long ago, the Iowa farm, his parents, and Zack. Most of all, they were of Zack and beneath them lurked an unsettling feeling that something bad surrounded

146

his brother. Something that, however hard he tried, he couldn't quite bring to the front of his mind.

In the next room, Barbara lay on the bed, staring at the doorway and the sliver of blued light that flickered with the pictures of a TV screen.

Ryker still hadn't said anything about the lies she'd told him. She didn't want the confrontation but the longer he went without bringing it up, the worse she felt. When he did, she didn't know how she would deal with it. The balance in the mixture of excitement and danger she felt in his presence was slowly tilting towards danger.

Maybe the time had come to get out. Before danger became fear of his capacity for sudden, extreme violence. But their relationship was no longer the way it had been. Anytime up to yesterday, she could have simply walked away. But it was no longer that simple. He wasn't making a big deal about it, but it was clear that he was watching her carefully, ensuring that he was always between her and an escape route. Escape. Until now, she hadn't been prepared to let the word form a part of her thinking but that was the only way she could leave. She would have to escape.

Well, he had told her that tomorrow he planned to go along to see and hear Lennox, then talk to Kant once again. There would be a lot of people around. That might be her opportunity. An opportunity, she repeated to herself, trying not to think that it might be more accurate to call it her last chance.

PHIL DAVIS leaned against the wall at the northwest corner of the Menger hotel, looking at the crowd starting to gather in the plaza. Sam Madsen stood to one side of him, upright, arms folded, lost in thought but his eyes watchful. Phil glanced around, interested that the uniformed police presence was low key. Uniforms apart, he would have bet that numerous plain clothes detectives drifted casually around the area but there was nothing to make the occasion anything more than what it was, an appearance by a presidential candidate at a semi-formal presentation. He knew there would be tight security, much more - these days it went with the territory - but the local law enforcement people were keeping it admirably low key.

A uniformed sergeant had spoken to them earlier and had been interested in their identities, asking if they were here on business. Kind of, Phil had said, telling the sergeant that he and Sam were working with Special Agent Larsen of the FBI. Earlier, Larsen had been with them but had drifted maybe thirty or forty yards away along East Crockett to talk to an agent from the Bureau's local office who was liaising with the San

Antonio Police Department. Phil pointed out Larsen, but the sergeant clearly knew the local agent and wasn't disposed to waste time pursuing the matter and left them alone.

'What are you thinking about?' Phil asked Sam.

For a moment Sam was silent then turned and came closer, leaning against the wall alongside Phil. 'I've been thinking about all the things we might've done if the FBI hadn't come into the case. And then there are things they should've done. Like working up a psychological profile of a man who would commit a crime like that. Killing the woman and the children in that way.'

'And?'

'And I'm surprised Larsen hasn't mentioned it.'

'Maybe he hasn't had one done.'

'You think so? One of the things he said to us, that first time we met, was that the Bureau had all kinds of computer facilities for helping track down serial killers.'

'I thought we'd convinced ourselves that we're not looking for a serial killer. '

'Beside the point,' Sam said. 'It's something that needs checking out. And, anyway, whatever the killer is, a psych profile would help. So why hasn't he had one done?'

'Maybe he has.'

'In which case, why hasn't he mentioned it to us?'

Phil glanced along the street towards Larsen. 'Well, we've already guessed he's still keeping secrets.'

'But why that particular one?'

'If it is one,' Phil gently reminded his partner.

Sam grinned. 'Okay, maybe I'm becoming paranoid. Anyway, I've been thinking. Remember when Chief Brodie brought that professor over from NTU, Lassiter, his name was, to talk to us about the principles of psychological profiling.'

'I remember.'

'But do you remember what Lassiter told us?'

Phil thought for a moment. 'Some of it. People who kill the way serial killers do, are often outwardly completely normal, apparently stable, well adjusted individuals. Friendly, like to charm the birds off the trees. Absolutely no frothing at the mouth. But underneath, a thoroughgoing psychopath or sociopath, vicious, ruthless, completely intent on control of his chosen victim up to and including controlling whether the victim lives or dies. Usually the latter. And then dictating how he or she dies.'

'That's some of it,' Sam agreed. 'There were other details. Like all that crap the movie-makers like to include, about deep down really wanting to be caught, doesn't apply. These guys have no intention of being caught and usually have the brains to make sure they're not. At least not for a long while. That's something they achieve by very careful planning, taking no risks.'

'So?'

'So, taking a TV reporter along seems pretty risky.'

'We already considered that, Sam. Maybe he doesn't know that's what Barbara is.'

'Whatever he thinks she is, it's still a risk,' Sam said. 'Unless she's his next victim.'

Phil looked at him. 'Oh, shit,' he said, thinking about Sam's earlier suggestion that they should try to find Barbara's car. Then he shook his head. 'No, I'm not convinced this is what our man is. I remember Lassiter saying that serial killers live in a world they alone make, seeking out victims either by chance or because they can fit them into their private fantasy world. He also said that their acts follow patterns, become ritualized. They start out imagining what they're going to do, then one day they finally do it, then they have a real event to fuel their imaginations, and they go out and do it again. Living off the thrill and excitement of the killing and using that excitement to make them kill again. And again.' And even if they were caught, Lassiter had told his audience, imprisonment is no real hardship because any time they want, whatever their surroundings, they can bring into their minds the acts they have committed and re-live them, over and over again in the seclusion of a prison cell.

'So why are you convinced that our man isn't in this category?' Sam asked.

'Because he didn't just kill Louise. He killed the children as well. If there was a pattern like that, other deaths like these, we'd know about it. It would be in the system.'

'Would we know?' Sam asked.

Phil looked momentarily doubtful. 'Surely,' he said.

'What if no one has spotted a pattern because it isn't obviously a pattern? Or what if Louise and the kids were the first time he put his fantasy into action? Either way, the information would not be in the system.'

Phil stared unhappily at his partner. 'If that is the case, if he is a beginner, then Barbara doesn't fit into the ritual he's starting to establish for himself.' He could hear the lack of conviction in his voice and tried to shake away a suddenly persistent image of the pretty, strong-willed young woman who'd sat in his office, superimposed over little Jo-Anne's image and those of Louise's mutilated corpse and Billy's butchered body.

'Here we go,' Sam said, breaking into his grim thoughts.

Phil followed Sam's gesture towards a small motorcade coming around the corner from Commerce Street and across the front of the hotel. The cars passed them, stopping just short of the newly-built platform and seats where a crowd was already eagerly applauding the presidential candidate. From where he stood, Phil couldn't make out Lennox as the cars emptied, the crush of men, bodyguards he guessed, gathering close. Looking around, he spotted Danny Reynolds, the horsey-faced youth from the candidate's headquarters beaming toothily. Then Lennox appeared, bounding up the few steps onto the platform to a welcoming cheer. Close behind Lennox, dwarfed by the candidate's lanky build, came the diminutive figure of Lewis Kant.

Last night's expected meeting with Kant hadn't taken place. Or, at least, that was what Larsen had told them when he had pointed the man out earlier. Whether Larsen had used his connection with Kant to talk to the man privately Phil didn't know. What Larsen had said was that Kant would meet them after the ceremony.

Lennox had begun speaking but the sound system was aimed out across the plaza and Phil could make out only an occasional word borne back by the light breeze. He decided to move to where he could hear the candidate's words.

He had taken no more than about six paces when he heard a sudden shout from across the street behind him, a woman's voice, panicky, and almost simultaneously a soft yet sharp crack from somewhere above his head. He recognized the sound and spun around, looking up, aware at the same time that Sam was already in motion, sprinting to Phil's right, heading towards the hotel entrance. There was nothing to see at any of the windows but out of one, overlooking East Crockett, hung a curtain, lazily flapping in the breeze. A woman, probably the one who'd shouted, was pointing at the window, her mouth open wide in a face white with shock.

Kaleidoscoping on top of the visual images were sounds. Screams and shouts echoing around the plaza. By now, Phil was already following Sam who had disappeared into the hotel but he risked a backwards glance over his shoulder. Tumult. Men and women running in all directions. Then he was inside the Menger Hotel.

Bursting through the doors he ran the short distance to another set of doors that took him into the lobby. Across to his left he saw an open-mouthed group of people clustered near the reception desk and then heard Sam call his name.

Sam was already on the first landing, gun in hand now, racing past a huge painting of a cattle round-up and heading towards the northwest corner of the building.

Phil saw a string of uniformed police officers rushing towards him along the long, wide corridor that led to the reception area from the entrance along East Crockett. The leading cop saw the gun in Phil's hand and skidded to a halt. Frantically, Phil waved his badge, gesturing upwards and trying to make the man understand that Sam was not the target.

By now a handful of armed men had followed Phil in from the front door and were spreading around the Menger's lobby, one of them, tall and dark-haired, taking charge with calm authority.

Suddenly, from over their heads, came a muffled fusillade of shots. By the time Phil reached the next floor Sam was talking to a group of men, some uniformed. He glanced towards Phil as he approached and gave a small shrug. A few yards away, Phil saw a body stretched out, face up, a handgun a few inches from outstretched fingers.

Sam came over to him.

'That him?' Phil asked.

Sam nodded. 'Came right at me, shooting. Gave me no choice.' He didn't look too well and Phil realized that learning his trade in Forrest hadn't prepared his partner for this. It was the first time he'd killed a man, was very probably the first time he'd drawn his gun for any reason other than to shoot at targets.

'Take it easy,' Phil said. 'If you hadn't got him, he would pretty certainly have got you.'

The take-charge man Phil had seen below walked up, still looking calm and relaxed, as if what had just happened was an everyday event. 'You're Madsen,' he said and Sam nodded. 'Lucky you guys were here. We owe you.' He held out a hand to Sam, then turned to Phil. 'And you're Davis. Larsen told me your names. I'm Mike Caceres. Lieutenant, SAPD.' He glanced back to the group of men behind him and gestured.

One man walked over, thick-shouldered and red-haired, he looked like a bruiser but had a surprisingly soft voice when he spoke. 'Rifle, telescopic sight, the whole assassination kit. In the room on the corner. Perfect position.'

'So how come the room wasn't cleared and sealed?' Caceres asked mildly, his eyes angry.

'It was searched. The man sent to seal it is still in there. On the bathroom floor. Alive, but he'll have a headache he'll be able to hand on to his grandchildren.'

'What about the candidate?' Phil asked.

151

'He's okay,' Caceres said. 'Shocked and covered in blood, but not a scratch on hint.'

'Blood,' Phil said. 'Whose?' He was looking at Sam and knew that they had both already guessed the answer.

'Lennox's campaign manager,' Caceres said. 'Guy named Lewis Kant.'

'Dead?'

'Blew the top of his head off.'

Sam shook his head slowly. Caceres was looking from one to the other of them, then asked, 'Something we should all know?' he asked.

'This is Larsen's show,' Phil said. 'Best if you talk to him.'

Caceres shrugged. 'Okay,' he said. For a moment he was silent, then he added, 'I guess you noticed there's something odd about this set-up.'

Phil looked inquiringly at him.

'Even if you hadn't nailed the guy,' Caceres said to Sam, 'someone would've got him. There was no way he could get out of here. We had the building secured within a minute, two minutes max. No way the shooter could've made any of the exits. We would've got him even if we'd had to nitrate test everyone in the hotel. Goddamn suicide mission.'

Maybe, Phil thought, unhappy at an alternative scenario that had lodged in the back of his mind. 'Where's Larsen?' he asked.

Caceres shrugged. 'Probably with the candidate,' he said. 'I'll need a statement before you head for home,' he told Sam. He grinned suddenly. 'You'll be a goddamn hero, back in wherever the hell it is you guys come from.'

As Caceres walked away Sam turned to Phil but as he made the movement his eyes picked up an image and hardened. 'There,' he snapped, gesturing down into the lobby. 'Barbara.'

Phil looked, saw only a cluster of people, most of them looking upwards towards them. Except for two, a man and a woman heading out through high glazed doors into an inner courtyard.

Sam was moving again, fast but not running. Phil caught up to his shoulder. 'Sure?' he asked.

'Positive,' Sam said.

'What about the man?'

'Medium height, sandy-colored hair, high forehead. Never seen him before.'

When they reached the courtyard the only people in sight were a handful of hotel guests excitedly discussing the events of the past few minutes and a couple of employees propping a ladder against a wrought-iron pole from which were festooned strings of colored lights. Phil spoke to the guests, Sam to the maintenance men.

'Phil,' Sam called, already moving towards a door in the far corner.

Phil followed and moments later they were in the noise and bustle of the hotel kitchen. Within moments they heard an uproar from the service entrance and found an irate supplier whose delivery truck had disappeared.

Lieutenant Caceres arrived, asked a few brisk questions, but he had already given orders to lift the cordon around the hotel. Getting it put back would cause confusion and it was probably already too late. 'Who are they?' he asked Phil.

'People we need to talk to.'

'You want help? We can set up roadblocks,' Caceres offered but without much conviction.

Phil shook his head, thinking that until he knew more about the man with Barbara, he didn't want to take the chance of putting him in a position where he might feel threatened.

'How are they connected?' Caceres asked.

'Not sure. But the woman's a reporter so maybe it's not top priority.'

He wasn't convinced of that but Caceres seemed to be okay with it.

About ten minutes later, the delivery truck was found but by then the truck's apparent owner had vanished. Half an hour after that, Caceres told them that the truck had been stolen earlier that morning from a repair shop.

'You know what I think?' Caceres said. 'I think that was the getaway vehicle for the shooter.' He looked at Phil and Sam, waiting for a comment. When neither said anything he continued. 'Okay, okay, so I already said this looked like a suicide mission. But you have to ask, did the shooter know that's what it was.' He shook his head, then asked, 'So, did those people you're interested in, this reporter lady, get lucky or did they know something?'

Phil looked at Sam, then at the lieutenant. 'I don't know,' he said. 'I hope they got lucky, because if they knew, then this thing's getting a whole lot more complicated than it already was before today.'

BARBARA'S SILVER Honda was where they had left it when they walked the last few hundred yards to Alamo Plaza. Since abandoning the truck Ryker had been edgy but seemed to relax when they reached the car.

'You drive,' he told her.

She started up the motor, asking where they were going, actions and words coming automatically.

The shooting in the plaza had shaken her worse than that in Austin. They had been close enough to the platform to see the bullet hit Lewis Kant. The shock of the sight, blood everywhere, the screams and shouts, the sudden panic, had built instantly into a state of mind that made her want to run. But Ryker had never left her side, most of the time his fingers wrapped tight around her arm.

'Just drive,' he told her now. 'I'll tell you where later.'

She moved off, turning onto Broadway. 'You knew about the truck, didn't you,' she said.

'Yes,' he said, speaking without thinking.

'What else did you know?'

'The hotel. I knew the hotel. I'd seen it. Not really, just pictures.' He had known it exactly. Just like the images in his mind last night, the interior of the hotel was exactly the way he knew it would be. The wrought-iron rails around the balconies overhanging the lobby, the painting on the wall, even the grand piano. Every part of it was etched in his mind before he stepped through the door.

'And the set-up,' he said. He shouldn't tell her this. But he had to talk to someone, either that or his head would explode. 'The platform, the angle the shooter would work from. I knew it. Knew it was bad. From that position the shooter would have to lean right out the window, someone would see him. I told them that, told them it wouldn't work. Even the getaway was wrong. Not the truck, that was okay, but there was no way the shooter could reach the truck before the heat would be all over him. I told them that.'

'Who? Who did you tell?'

Who had he told?

Then he knew.

'Ralph Hardy,' he said.

That was it. He'd told Ralph Hardy. He'd been supplied with the details; layout of the hotel, pictures, everything he needed. He'd worked out a way in and a way out but he didn't like the shooter's position. He'd wanted it changed but Hardy had said it would have to do. 'So pick somebody to do it who doesn't mind committing suicide,' he'd told Hardy. 'Or who's too dumb to see what will happen.' Had he really talked to Ralph Hardy that way? He couldn't believe it, not him, but now it was coming clearer. He and Hardy often talked about methods, worked out arrangements. Hardy would get the background. Like Dillard's house, where it was, the layout, the goddamn Dobermans. Then it was up to him to make the plans and decide who would do the job. Some of the jobs, those that were interesting or difficult, he did himself. He'd told Hardy the importance of picking the right man for a job. 'Don't use fools on errands,' he'd told him. 'Not where the end is serious. Serious business needs serious people all the way through. Use fools and the whole damn thing can fall apart.'

Jesus Christ, had he really laid it on the line to Ralph Hardy of all people? Yes, he had, because he was important, a top man in Hardy's empire. What had he been thinking about these past few days, acting as though he was just the hired help. No wonder Hardy had looked at him as if he was crazy that last time they had talked. What was he doing, letting his mind play tricks that way.

He saw a street sign up ahead, Jones Avenue. Jones. Same name as the man who'd been shot in Austin. He remembered the dead man's face. Featureless, easily forgotten, but at the same time vaguely familiar. Like he'd known him. Yes, he'd used Jones in the past. Then somehow forgotten him completely, just the way people always forgot seeing Jones. Christ, his mind was a mess. 'Pull over,' he told Barbara.

He needed to think. And he also needed to know if the cops were looking for them. Switching on the radio, he flicked from station to station until he found local news.

A man's voice, strident with barely suppressed excitement. Going over the shooting in the plaza, the death of the gunman. Then, suddenly, the newsman's voice went up a notch. 'I've just been handed an update. The San Antonio Police Department has announced that they are holding Paul Lennox for questioning about this morning's shooting of his campaign manager, Lewis Kant.'

He stared at the radio, as if trying to see the speaker's face.

'That's insane,' Barbara said.

It might sound crazy to her but it made sense to him because in that same instant he realized that Lennox's implication in the shooting wasn't unexpected. It was the way it had been planned. He and Hardy had planned it that way. In the room used by the shooter there would be phony evidence implicating Lennox. How could he have forgotten? What was happening to him?

He turned down the sound on the radio.

'Not insane,' he heard himself saying to Barbara. 'It's a set-up. '

It was all dropping into place. 'Lennox has to be stopped. This was the way to do it. Framed for arranging this hit.'

Doors were opening in his mind, light flooding into darkened corners. It was planned like something out of a movie. It would play out as though Lennox had set it up to make everyone think that he was the intended target but the shooter missed and hit the guy standing next to him, whoever he happened to be. Just like in *The Manchurian Candidate*. And Lennox's supposed motive was that it would give him an unstoppable boost at the polls.

She was staring at him. 'Who wants Lennox stopped so badly they'd do a thing like this?'

He knew the answer to that. 'Who? The President of the United States, that's who. Ethan Roberts. He's the one who wants Lennox stopped. Not killed, stopped. Killing him is only half the answer. Stop him this way and it doesn't just stop Lennox, it stops all of Lennox's people for the next decade. Maybe for a generation.'

Barbara shook her head. She couldn't believe any of this. Most difficult of all to accept was that the man sitting beside her was a part of a massive conspiracy. It was - she'd used the word already - insane. But the trail she'd followed since leaving Forrest had no breaks in it, at least none that she could see.

'The shooter's dead,' Ryker was saying now. 'By now, the guy who stole the delivery truck will be dead. That's the way it was planned Everyone who knows anything is taken out of the picture. It's the only way.' He turned to look directly at her. 'And now I'm on the list. That's the reason Hardy put out paper on me. Not because I braced him in his office. Jesus. We argued all the time. No, he has to take me out because I know what's happening and who's behind it.'

He thought for a moment. Then the voice on the radio caught his attention and he turned up the sound.

'We hope to have a statement on today's event's from President Roberts very soon. The President is on an official visit to Mexico and is due in Chihuahua in about an hour .'

Reaching down, he snapped off the radio. An idea was starting to form in his mind. The woman would call it crazy but if he was to prevent them from killing him, then he would have to take drastic action. He would have to cut off the head of the snake.

'Let's go,' he said. 'Take a left up ahead, then pick up the signs for Laredo.'

'Why?' she asked. 'Where are we going?'

'Mexico,' he said. 'That's where we end it.'

FOURTEEN

THEY HAD picked up the interstate, heading south, and Barbara was finding it steadily more difficult to concentrate on driving. She couldn't believe that Ryker was making sense. But, then, only a few days ago, she wouldn't have believed any of the events of the past few days. This, though, was beyond even that. How could she accept that what he had told her about Ethan Roberts was the truth. Since taking office, the president's words and deeds had confirmed her suspicions that he was a ruthless, self-centered demagogue. But to believe him capable of plotting to destroy Paul Lennox's chances to unseat him in November's election by having him framed for murder was too much. Wasn't it?

Despite her doubts, most of her earlier excitement in hunting down a big story had returned. Whatever the truth about Ethan Roberts, a dynamite political element had emerged back in San Antonio. An image of Lewis Kant formed in her mind, the blood flying as his head exploded, and earlier she had to bite down hard on her lip to keep from throwing up but she was handling it. And that was worrying. She knew that people could become inured to even the most dreadful sights. Cops. Soldiers. OR and ER doctors and nurses. Some journalists were on the list, too, but

157

only rarely at the sharp end. She forced herself to think of other things but, as if her mind was feeding on blood, she helplessly conjured up more dreadful images; the men dying in the gun battle in Austin, the savage killings in Forrest. With a start, she realized just how far they had come since then. More than that, how far had she come? How could she have allowed the pursuit of a story to take charge of her life in such a way? Like the way she had surrendered to sudden, and now inexplicable, lust. The physical attraction she had felt towards Ryker had faded. Faded so badly that she found it hard, cruelly distasteful, to imagine that she had allowed herself to have sex with the man.

She tried to convince herself that what had happened in her motel room outside Austin was a variation on the Scandinavian Syndrome. Although the actions of a hostage in forming an attachment to a bank robber seemed very different from what she had done. Maybe this was closer to Patti Hearst and the Symbionese Liberation Army. But even that didn't measure up. She was not an initially unwilling victim of kidnapers. She had calculatedly placed herself squarely into the middle of all this, willingly doing anything for the story.

The more she thought, the more confusing it all became. Not only her motives and responses, but also Ryker's. There had to be more to what he was doing than just a man hunting down the killer of his family. God knows, that was motive enough for the way he acted but she was sure now that there must be something more. The connection from Louise in Forrest all the way to Lewis Kant were feasible. Extreme, but feasible. But all this about Paul Lennox and Ethan Roberts was moving onto another plane. She needed to ask questions to help her make new connections, to see where reality ended and speculation began, and if there was any truth in what appeared to be little short of fantasy. But she was unwilling to speak to Ryker who for the past half hour had been silent, hunched down in his seat, deep inside himself.

Conspiracy, Ryker was thinking. Everywhere there are conspiracies. Zack was right. He'd warned him. Like the time they'd planned to leave the farm and the old man and run away to Des Moines. He hadn't wanted to go. He didn't mind never seeing the old man again, nor even the farm although he'd miss the woods and the streams. It was never seeing his mother again. 'We can tell her, Zack,' he'd urged. 'Tell her where we're going. Come back and see her when it's safe.'

'No, that won't work,' Zack told him. 'Never will. You can't trust her. Comes down to it, she'll side with the old man and we'll be in trouble.'

He hadn't believed his brother and later, when their plans were nearly ready, he'd weakened and told his mother. She'd wept but all she'd said were prayers. She did a lot of that, praying. When the old man couldn't see or hear her. He thought, though, that everything would be all right. Then came the day and the old man and their mother set out on their monthly trip into town for supplies. An hour later, Zack announced that it was time and they started out.

They walked ten miles along dirt tracks, then five more along a paved road before Zack decided it was safe to risk hitching a lift. They recognized the first truck that came along too late to run and, anyway, on an open stretch of road there was no place to hide.

He could remember the old man's face, sharp and clear, a triumphant sneer twisting his lips as he'd looked out at them from the truck. And his mother, red-eyed from weeping and a trickle of blood escaping from the corner of her bruised mouth.

That night the old man had beaten them both, then locked them in the cellar for two days without food or water. Then he let them out and put them to work without mentioning what had happened.

Zack hadn't mentioned it either.

For two more months the old man worked them hard but there were no more beatings. Until one night he hit the bottle again. As usual, he started on his wife. She usually let it happen, resignation overcoming the urge to run. This was one of the exceptions. She ran into the barn and he caught her there and he and Zack could hear the blows and her screams.

He had slumped against a fence, arms hugging his legs, head down on his knees, trying to blot it all out.

At a different sound, he looked up and saw Zack walking across to the barn. Calm and upright. Like he was taking a stroll in the moonlight. At the door, he stopped, swung it closed and dropped the bar into place. Then he stooped and picked up something. It was a can of gasoline. It had no business being there and he remembered seeing it earlier and wondering who had left it beside the barn door, not realizing until months later that it hadn't been there by chance. Zack had walked around the barn, trickling gasoline but he had stayed, rooted to the spot, not believing what he knew was about to happen. Not even when Zack struck a match and tossed it to the ground.

The barn had burned fast and furiously. The old man's shouts fading into screams all but drowning out his mother's hopeless wailing cries.

He hadn't asked Zack a question until they were more than a hundred miles away, his brother driving the old truck skillfully and steadily. 'Why couldn't we have brought Ma with us, Zack?'

'I told you,' Zack said. 'You can't trust people. Not anyone.

159

They're all in it together. A conspiracy. You can't trust anyone.' His brother had turned and smiled at him, suddenly looking much older and wiser than eighteen. 'That's the only thing the old man said that was worth a light. Trust no one and the chances are you'll never be disappointed.'

They had driven in silence for a while before he plucked up the courage to ask, 'You trust me, don't you, Zack?'

His brother laughed. 'You? Of course I do. And you trust me. It's you and me against the world, little brother.'

And that's the way it was. For a while. But it was an unequal struggle. He didn't think about it at the time, but maybe Zack could have done better for himself without a thirteen-year-old dogging his footsteps all across Iowa and Nebraska and into Wyoming. They were lucky to get that far and, inevitably, it all came to an end. The sheriff in Rawlings had looked them over, asked a few awkward questions, and that was it. Their luck had run out. They sat in a cell in the county jail in Rawlings for three days waiting for cops to come in from Des Moines and take them back.

Zack had spent those three days telling him a lot of things, useful stuff, mainly how to survive when he got out. 'You'll be out before me,' Zack told him. 'Long time, years probably. You have to look after yourself until I can come and take care of you. Stay on your own. Don't form attachments. They can't work, can't last, can't do anything but harm. Sometimes, you'll think you can beat it but you can't. Get used to being alone.' His brother had smiled, then added, 'It goes with the territory.'

He'd asked what he meant but Zack had just smiled that secret smile. Then, after a moment, he'd continued his advice. 'Never be afraid of the dark. The opposite, in fact. Beware of the light. Stay in the dark places. There's safety in them. Danger, too, but not if you make them your own territory, your ground. Your home. That way, the dark places work for you not against you. There's safety in darkness.'

He had needed the advice because his brother was right about their sentences. He was out first. By a long way. The court had accepted Zack's statement and ignored his tearful claim to have helped. They also believed Zack when he told them that he alone was responsible. The court put him away, of course, but it wasn't prison. Not like Zack. It was a farm. Almost like being home. Most of the time it was better because there wasn't the old man to lecture and beat him. Nothing the screws and the other hardened inmates did approached the old man's drunken brutality. For a while he missed seeing his mother, but by the time he was released, eighteen years old and fit for the world, so they said, he'd all but forgotten what she looked like.

But he didn't forget Zack.

When he was released, he visited Zack but there was only a little time before he joined the army and shipped out to the Gulf. He urged Zack to tell him more things he needed to know. Especially about survival. His brother helped all he could but even Zack, who knew pretty nearly everything, couldn't prepare him for what lay in wait. In the Gulf, some of the time his brother's advice helped but he had to make his own way, keeping to Zack's rules whenever he could and the rest of the time doing things the way he figured his brother would do them if he'd been there by his side. And in a way, that was where Zack was. Right beside him, the way he'd said he'd always be.

When he came back from the Gulf the first thing he did was visit Zack who had been moved around several times and was now in a high security unit outside Chicago. Zack had changed. Now, he was more inside himself than he remembered. Part of the time it was like he wasn't really here at all but was someplace else, seeing other sights, listening to other sounds. But on some things Zack was clear and certain. 'They'll never let me go, little brother,' he told him. 'You and me, we'll have to do something about that.'

He wasn't sure what Zack meant and for a while continued visiting, asking advice, mostly taking it. Once in a while he went against his brother's wishes. Like going to work for Ralph Hardy.

'People like Hardy don't care shit for people like you,' Zack told him, his face thinner and looking much older than his twenty-seven years. He's a user and when he figures you're all used up he'll tear you in pieces and toss you out with the rest of the trash.'

'Not if I remember all the things you've taught me,' he'd said, as near as he ever came to disagreeing with his brother.

Zack had smiled. Not the secret smile, but one filled with sadness. 'Maybe,' he said and was silent for a long time. Then the secret smile returned. 'And maybe one good thing can come out of you working for Hardy,' he said. 'Maybe you can figure a way to get me out of this place.'

'I'll do it, Zack,' he promised. 'You can depend on me.'

Zack looked at him for a long silent time, then said, 'I have to, little brother, there's no one else.'

Ryker straightened his shoulders, looking ahead through the windshield, realizing that he had seen nothing of the road they were traveling for - how long? Glancing at his watch he saw that they were more than an hour out of San Antonio.

The woman glanced his way. 'We have to stop,' she said. 'We

need gas and I need the bathroom and coffee and something to eat.'

He looked at her, thinking that Zack wouldn't have approved of this. He would have dumped her before now. Dammit, his brother would never have taken up with her in the first place.

'Okay,' he said. He fished for a cigarette finding he was down to the last one in his last pack. 'Cigarettes, too,' he said.

Barbara nodded, thinking that maybe she could try something like she did the last time she'd bought cigarettes at a diner. Escape was favorite. Second best would be to call someone. Doug Carlson probably although he was far away now, and not just in miles. It was as if he inhabited another world. This time there could be no fooling, she would ask Doug to call the police, the FBI, anyone who could help. It wasn't just she who was in trouble. Like him or not, trust him or not, the president was threatened. Although, right now, she was more worried about herself. Ethan Roberts was miles away, she was right here, sitting next to a man who she was sure was planning to kill the president because of some crazy notion that he was part of a conspiracy against him.

In fact, when they stopped at the next filling station, it was easier than she'd hoped. Caught by the problem of leaving her alone in the diner while he used the bathroom, Ryker made a mistake. When she was ready to leave, he told her to wait by the cash desk, which was well away from the phones.

The woman behind the cash desk was around Barbara's age, looked tough and had seen-everything eyes. Barbara asked if she had a cell, begged to use it, and sealed the deal with twenty dollars.

She reached Doug, cutting him off as he tried to tell her that his telephone had been manned every minute since her last call. Hastily, she told him where they were, that they were less than two hours from the border and that she was sure that the man she was with was planning to kill the president.

'Okay, Barbara, keep cool. Get away if you can but take no risks. Phil Davis is only an hour away from you.'

'Davis?'

'He's in San Antonio.'

'Tell him . . .'

Suddenly, Ryker was there, snatching the instrument from her hand, smashing it to the ground and pulling her out to the Honda. He hit her hard across the face, sending her reeling against the car, then he dragged her around and forced her into the passenger seat.

When he was behind the wheel he started up the motor, backed up and then drove out of the forecourt, tires screaming. She caught a glimpse of the woman's face staring from the windows of the diner, watching their explosive departure. Surely she would call the police. Maybe not. Nowadays, when there was trouble, people looked the other way. If the woman didn't call for help then everything depended upon the call she'd made to Doug. And he had told her that Phil Davis was in San Antonio. She couldn't understand what the detective was doing so close but the knowledge made her spirits rise. Clutching at straws, maybe, but it gave her hope.

They were on the highway again, accelerating fast. 'Bitch,' Ryker snarled. 'Zack was right. It's a fucking conspiracy. Well, I'm going to end it. Then it's just me and Zack and the rest of you can go fuck yourselves. You, your friends, the heat and the fucking president. All of you.'

FIFTEEN

THE CALL from Doug Carlson reached Phil Davis within minutes. It hadn't taken Doug more than a nano-second to figure out that the morning's hot news item, the shooting in San Antonio, might well have a connection and it was the SAPD he tried first. Now, Phil listened, asked questions about Barbara's car, then spoke to Lieutenant Mike Caceres. He made requests he wasn't sure he had any right to make, responding instinctively to the angry knowledge that long before now he should have had law enforcement officers throughout the state looking out for Barbara.

Caceres had the same instincts and moved fast. 'I don't know what the hell is happening,' he said to Phil, 'But there's things about what happened here today I don't like. And I reckon that if I have to take sides, yours is the side I'm on.'

He snapped off instructions and within minutes of Phil talking with Doug Carlson a helicopter, emblazoned with the logo of the SAPD, was chopping at the air as it came down into HemisFair Plaza to collect Phil, Sam Madsen and an irritable Special Agent Larsen.

'You want me with you?' Caceres yelled against the aircraft's racket.

'None of us speaks Spanish. We might have to go into Mexico.'

'If they'll let us,' Larsen said.

Caceres grinned. 'Want me or not,' he said, 'you need me,' and followed Phil into the helicopter.

They were quickly strapped in and miked up and as soon as they were airborne, Caceres made contact with the ground. Phil handed him the notes he'd made while talking to Doug and Caceres passed on details of the car, making certain it was understood that all that was wanted was observation. No one was to try stopping the vehicle until the helicopter's arrival.

'Now,' Phil said to Larsen, 'I think it's time you talked to Washington or wherever the hell you take your orders from, and start pulling strings. We can't just go flying into Mexico without authority.' He glanced at Caceres. 'Or can we?'

'Officially,' the San Antonio cop told him, 'we have arrangements that allow us enter Mexican airspace in an emergency and this sure as hell sounds like one to me. But it won't hurt to have official clearance and maximum cooperation on the ground.'

'And unofficially?'

Caceres tapped his forefinger against the side of his nose but said nothing.

'Okay,' Phil said to Larsen. 'You heard the man. Anyway, if there's a possibility of danger to the president then I guess you want to take some kind of action.'

Larsen took the radio and made a call, talking long and urgently and gradually working up a head of steam when it became clear that the threat against the president was not being taken seriously.

A little while later, a call came in and the pilot gestured to Caceres to take it. 'They've been seen,' he told Phil a moment later. 'They're in Laredo, looks like they're heading straight for the bridge so they'll be in Mexico in a few minutes.'

'How long before we're overhead?' Phil asked.

'Not long,' Caceres told him. 'Why? What do you want to do?'

'So long as we don't lose contact, I'll feel happier on the ground. Maybe split up. You stay up here watching their vehicle, but put Sam and me in a car far enough behind them to keep out of sight, close enough to move in fast if you see something happening.'

'Okay,' Caceres said. 'I'll set it up.'

Larsen leaned across and tapped Phil on the arm. 'What about me,' he said, his face tight with anger.

'You stay with me,' Phil said. 'That's the only way I can trust you and even then not much.'

Larsen was burning but Phil ignored him after that and a short while later the helicopter touched down alongside the highway about thirty miles south of the Rio Grande. Two unmarked cars waited in a grove of trees beside the highway, with four men all looking eager for a fight.

Caceres introduced one of the four. 'My cousin Enrico Hidalgo,' he said, grinning at Phil's surprise. 'Now you know how I get unofficial cooperation.' He spoke briefly with his cousin, then told Phil, 'They're behind us now but coming fast. They'll pass here soon. You're sure you don't want to try and stop them?'

'Sure,' Phil said. 'We don't know what the man will do and so long as Barbara is in the car we can't take any chances.'

'You might have to, if he gets close to the president.'

'How long will that take him?'

'Hours. The president is in Chihuahua. From here, I guess your man will go down to Monterrey, that will take him two, nearly three hours. Then he'll drive northwest for over four hundred miles. Even without stops it will be sometime tomorrow.'

'Lot's of time,' Phil said. 'An opportunity's bound to come up.'

'Anyway,' Larsen chipped in, 'by then the president will be blanketed. No one will get within a mile of him.'

'That doesn't help Barbara,' Phil said. 'We need our man out of the car and in the open, alone.'

Caceres was becoming edgy. 'Time to get the chopper up and out of sight,' he said. 'I'll call Enrico when the Honda is close.'

By the time the helicopter was hanging among low hills to the east of the highway, Phil was in the back of one of the Mexican police cars with Larsen. Sam was in front with Enrico Hidalgo who was driving. The remaining three Mexican cops were in the other car. Phil and his companions sat in silence broken only by the gentle murmur of the motor.

About ten minutes later the radio crackled into life with a brief burst of Spanish. Enrico responded, raised a thumb to his passengers and moments later Phil saw the dusty silver Honda CR-V pass by. He watched anxiously in case Enrico was too eager but the Mexican policeman let five minutes pass before following, the second car swinging into convoy behind them.

Phil sat back and tried to relax but the knowledge that they were just a few minutes behind a man who might have the answers to a great many questions gnawed at him. He turned to Larsen. 'I think it's time you told us the missing bits,' he said.

166

'There's things about this I can't tell you, Phil. Political matters, state security. That sort of thing. Not now, not ever. Ask the Director if you like, but don't ask me. And, believe me, he won't tell you what day it is.'

Believing Larsen was one of the last things Phil would do but he didn't pursue the political angle. Maybe there would be time for that later. 'It isn't all political,' he said.

Larsen grunted, then asked Sam, 'The man you saw in the lobby at the Menger Hotel. Describe him.'

Sam turned in his seat. 'Taller than Phil, shorter than you, my build. Light-brown hair, kind of sandy. High forehead, deep-set eyes. Don't know what color.'

'Light blue,' Larsen said. He sighed, then leaned back. 'He works for Ralph Hardy. Organizer. Sets up the tricky scams, specializes in blackmail set-ups and planning hits. We're pretty sure that he takes some of the action himself, the tough ones. Maybe as many as seven, eight personal shootings we can put names to.'

Christ, Phil was thinking. He'd known that Barbara Nichols was in trouble but this sounded worse than he'd imagined.

'But it's all supposition,' Larsen was saying, 'there's nothing to prove it. He served some easy time when he was still a boy but since then, zip. A few arrests on suspicion but he always walked, never brought to trial but that once when he was thirteen years old. Jed Hollis is a very careful man.'

'Jed Hollis. That's his name?'

'Jedediah Hollis. Age forty, born in Iowa. That's where he got into trouble but his brother was the main player. Zacharia Hollis. Mean bastard. Hated everybody but to look at him you'd think he was the sweetest guy on earth. Damn near convinced everybody that he was Jesus Christ reborn except for the fact that he'd left his fingerprints all over the can of gasoline he used to burn up his mother and father. Might even have got away with that if the prosecutor hadn't gone after Jed, asking to put him away for ever. Seems that Zack figured he had a mission to protect his little brother so he confessed.'

'What happened?'

'Like I say, Jed went away for an easy five years. Served it on an honor farm. Zack went to the pen. Twenty-five years. Might have made parole after maybe fifteen but from day one he was trouble. Enough to lose any chance of parole and to have twenty more added.' Larsen rubbed his eyes. 'Meanwhile, Jed went into the army. Was in Iraq during the first Gulf War. Won himself some medals for killing the enemy, then freaked out. It happened to lots of guys.' He shrugged. 'So they tell me. I

167

don't know from personal experience.'

Phil wondered how the military had allowed in someone who had done time, even as a possibly easily-led kid, for the murder of his parents. But maybe it wasn't too hard to understand. Maybe the military had figured that talent like that was just what they needed.

'Freaked out how?'

'Started shooting at anything that moved. Not just the enemy. Birds, animals, palm trees waving in the breeze. They stood it until he took a dislike to helicopters and began blasting away at them, wounding several of his own people. He was shipped out, dishonorable discharge. Came back, drifted around Chicago for a while, which is where his brother was being held at the time, and started mixing with some real bad company. But he still managed to stay clean. Even when he helped spring his brother.'

'He broke him out?'

'Somebody broke him out. Nobody could prove it was Jed. By this time he was working for Ralph Hardy. That was when we first took a serious interest in him.'

'What about the brother?'

'Nobody heard anything about Zack Hollis for quite a while after he was sprung. Then a request came in for help on tracing a thumb print found at the scene of a crime in Toronto. It was Zack's. We knew that Jed made occasional trips across the border. We'd assumed that he was traveling on Ralph Hardy's business but discovering that his bother was there put a new light on it.'

'What did Zack do in Toronto?'

'The case was a double murder. Very unpleasant. It wasn't the last. Once he'd started, he made quite a name for himself. There were nine more cases all across Canada. No more fingerprints but there were enough similarities to convince the police up there that they were all the work of the same man.'

'Not nice people, the Hollis brothers,' Phil said. 'Seven or eight murders by Jed and ten by Zack.'

'Twenty, not ten. That was the main factor in tying the cases together. Zack Hollis killed seven women and three men and with each one he killed a small child. A parent and a child every time. Four little girls, six boys. The oldest was fifteen, the youngest eighteen months.' Larsen's fingers drummed briefly on his knee. 'I asked the Canadians one time if they ever managed to work out which way round he did it. Whether he made the parent watch their child being killed, or if the child had to watch while he murdered the mother or father. They didn't know. Not that it matters much. Either way, it isn't pretty to think about.'

Phil shook his head slowly. It looked as though he had been wrong about this not being a case of a serial killer. 'Is that the real reason why you took an interest in the murders in Forrest?' he asked Larsen.

'We took an interest because of Louise. Through Lewis Kant we knew that Ralph Hardy was somewhere in the picture and that raised the possibility, faint at the time, that Jed Hollis might be involved. And that made us think about Zack Hollis and his trademark of killing a parent and a child. No proof to any of this, you understand, but a whole string of coincidences.'

'I take it you don't believe in coincidence,' Phil said.

'Not usually.'

'So Zack Hollis didn't select Louise and her kids by chance.'

Larsen was silent.

'What about the methods,' Sam broke in. 'How did Zack kill his victims in Canada?'

'Axes and knives, sometimes a machete. Also, the adults were sexually assaulted. But not the children.'

'There's something I'm not getting,' Phil said. 'What is Jed Hollis doing, chasing all over Texas, knocking on doors of people like Senator Dillard, getting involved with Lewis Kant and Paul Lennox. Now, if what Barbara told Doug is right, he's going after President Roberts. And if that shooting in Austin is connected, maybe he's fighting battles with Ralph Hardy's men when he's supposed to be on the same team.'

'He went off like a firecracker once before,' Larsen said. 'In Iraq, shooting at his own people. Maybe it's what he does when the pressure's on.'

'But the rest of it? And where's the pressure coming from?'

'The killings in Forrest,' Sam said.

'How?'

'Remember the psych profile of a serial killer. Control is a key factor. Like you were just saying about making a parent watch while he butchers a son or daughter. Whichever way he does it, he's exercising control. And that's what Zack Hollis has been doing all his life. Taking control and keeping it. And it sounds as though, when they were kids, he controlled his brother. Even when they were adults and he was in prison, he was still in charge. That's why Jed had to get him out. He does what his brother wants.'

'So what has that to do with Forrest?' Phil asked.

'Hypothesis,' Sam said. 'Jed is running with Louise and Zack must've figured that she is coming between them, weakening his control. So he kills her and because it's the way he does these things he also kills the kids.'

'And how does that explain what Jed is doing?' Phil asked.

'This time, Zack Hollis went too far. He's attacked something Jed thinks more about even than their relationship so Jed wants revenge. He's hunting his brother.'

Phil thought over what Sam had said. Some of it made a kind of sense but there were parts that strained to fit the picture. 'Maybe,' he said. He glanced at Larsen who had stayed out of Sam's speculations. 'What do you think?' he asked him.

Larsen didn't answer for a moment, then leaned his head back against the upholstery and closed his eyes. 'Damned if I know what I think,' he said.

Phil looked at him but Larsen's eyes remained closed. He's still holding something back, Phil thought, but he decided to let it slide. For now.

For the hour and more none of the four men spoke. Twice, Mike Caceres's voice crackled through the speaker, confirming to his cousin that the Honda was still maintaining speed and direction.

It was late afternoon when they entered the sprawling suburbs of Monterrey. Enrico Hidalgo closed up on the car they were trailing, telling his passengers that the helicopter couldn't keep low enough over the city to watch a single car among thousands. Soon, they spotted the Honda, wedged into traffic maybe a hundred yards ahead, and Enrico kept it in sight. Later, as they eased out of the city centre and into faster-flowing traffic leaving Monterrey, he moved in closer and Phil sensed the Mexican's sudden tension.

'What's wrong?' he asked.

'Not sure,' Enrico told him.

After a couple more miles the traffic was thin enough for them to hang further back and it was then that Enrico called up the helicopter. He and his cousin talked in Spanish, fast and a shade excitedly.

Then Enrico pointed at a road sign they were passing. 'See,' he said. 'Either this guy is lost or he's planning something different.'

'What do you mean?' Phil asked.

'You said he was going to Chihuahua, where your president is visiting. To do that he should have made a turn to the right at one of the last two intersections. Now, if that's where he's going he must turn around. If he doesn't turn then he's not going to Chihuahua. He's going someplace else.'

'Which means,' Sam said, 'that he's not chasing after the president. He's got another target.'

SIXTEEN

FOR THE last few miles Barbara had been trying vainly to summon up a mental picture of the map of Mexico. Most of the road signs meant nothing to her and only occasionally did something strike a chord. Like Matamoros, a town on the gulf coast which she knew was on the Mexican side of the bridge crossing the Rio Grande from Texas. She had seen Matamoros on signs as they left Monterrey, signs pointing to the left which was east. Now, the distances on the road signs showed that they were heading in that direction, a fact confirmed by the setting sun that lay behind them. But Chihuahua, she was sure, lay to the northwest. So where were they going?

She dare not ask. Ryker had been silent since his furious outburst at catching her using the phone and despite her uneasiness she preferred his silence to his rage. In any case, the longer they headed this way the greater the distance between them and the president.

She lit a cigarette, aware that her throat was raw. She decided that if she came out of this unscathed she might make another effort to quit smoking. Until then, the state of her throat and lungs was the least of her worries.

Smelling the smoke set Ryker reaching for a cigarette of his own. He lit it, thinking that the woman was no longer eager to do something as personal as lighting a cigarette for him. So what? By ignoring him she was showing what she really thought. That she cared nothing about him, whether he was happy or unhappy, free or unfree, alive or dead. Which meant that she was just the same as everyone else in the world. No one gave a shit whether or not he took another breath. Except for Zack. He cared. Zack had taken care of him, confessed to the fire to save him from prison. He shouldn't have done that. Not the way things worked out, Zack going inside and doing real hard time. It was no surprise that there'd been trouble in the joint. Zack would've hated confinement, hated having to mix with dumb, ignorant people. Then there were all those fucking homos. He knew what happened in prison to people as nice looking as Zack. The cornholing bastards would have marked him out the day he arrived. No wonder that he had been so desperate to get out. But he had taken care of that. For the first time in his life he'd had a chance to help his big brother. And he hadn't failed him.

He'd planned it all himself, didn't consult anyone. Of course he'd had to hire some help but none of them knew what the deal was until it went down so there was no danger of anyone mouthing off and screwing it up. And afterwards he had taken care of the help. Permanently.

He remembered Zack's face when he finally let him out of the packing case he'd hidden in. Poor Zack. The trip across the lake had been bad. Neither of them had known there were storms like that; not on a fucking lake, for Christ's sake. Poor Zack had been sick all the way across and there wasn't a damn thing he could do about it.

But when the case was opened and Zack saw the shoreline and the snow and asked, 'Where are we?' and he'd said, 'Canada,' it had been like watching the sun come out after a storm the way Zack's face had broken into a big wide smile.

And Zack had been pleased with the way he'd dealt with the help. No smiles this time, just a nod and a knowing glance. He'd done right by his brother and he was proud of that and he knew that Zack was proud of him.

That wasn't all he'd done. He'd fixed things in Canada for Zack. A place to stay and a job. He couldn't be with him which was bad, but there was no choice. 'The cops are always keeping their eyes open for me,' he told Zack. 'So I just go on doing what I do and let them follow me all they want. They'll give up. Maybe a year, maybe more, but they'll quit. When that happens, and I'm sure it will, I'll come looking for you.'

'I might have to move on,' Zack warned. 'If I do, I'll get word. Somehow.'

172

Then they'd parted. He remembered that Zack had put his arms around him, the way nobody ever had. 'I owe you, little brother,' Zack told him.

It was more than a year before he'd risked going back to Canada. Even then he made two journeys without attempting to contact his brother. Finally, sure that it was safe, he went to the house where he'd left his brother. He was still there, had the same job, looked fit and healthy. But the eyes were different.

They talked non-stop for damn near two days, catching up. Then Zack had said, 'You came at the right time. I've about had it with Toronto. Too many fucking people, little brother. All of them breeding, bringing more people into the world where there isn't enough space now. Like them.' He jerked a dismissive thumb at the crowded streets. 'Look at them, having kids, doting on them, educating them, training them. For what? To make more fucking kids. Somebody's got to stop it.'

This time, they made an arrangement for messages. Zack said it was necessary, that he was sure, this time, that he would soon be moving on.

About six months later Ryker read about the killings in Toronto. At first he didn't make a connection but then he spotted that someone was watching him. So he played it safe, let them follow him, even though it made some of the work he was doing for Ralph Hardy trickier than usual. Then he saw the message in the Dallas newspaper, the way Zack had planned it. He let a few more months pass, then slipped the tail and went back to Canada.

By then, there'd been more killings like those in Toronto. And when he saw Zack he knew that it was right for him to do what he was doing, even if the Canadian cops were going crazy trying to find who was doing it. He couldn't remember Zack ever looking this happy.

And he couldn't ever remember Zack wanting to talk so much, tell him things, extend his education was how he put it. But, sometimes, Zack held back, saying how his little brother knew as much as he did and that he had no right lecturing him. He had smiled the secret smile and said, 'We don't want no lectures and speeches muddying up the water between us, do we.'

It was like old times, listening to Zack talk, telling him things. 'Sometimes it isn't easy, trying to change the world. You'll learn, if you try it. There'll be days when you can't rest, nights when you can't sleep, then more days, more nights, seems like they're going on forever. And there's not a damn thing you can do about it because that's the life you're leading. You just have to learn to live with it.'

And Zack had warned him of the dangers. 'You have to keep

covering your tracks. Don't take chances. Don't let anyone make a connection. And make plans in case there's trouble. You need an escape hatch. A way out when things go wrong. And they will. One day.'

He'd asked his brother to tell him about the way he did what he did but Zack had misunderstood and kept telling him about the killings, how he started out threatening to kill the kid and making the mother or the father scream and beg and grovel for mercy for the kid. They would offer to do anything, beg him to do anything he liked to them, if he would only let the kid go free. He always took them up on it. He would've done that anyway, even if they hadn't begged him. But it was better that way. He made the women do things they wouldn't do with their own husbands, made the men suffer the way the big cons in prison had made him suffer. And then, when he was bored with it, he killed the kids anyway. Then, when the mother or the father knew that they'd done what they'd done for no reason and there was no escape and he could see in their eyes that all that was left was total despair and acceptance that there was no escape, he finished the job.

But that wasn't what he'd wanted to know. It was the planning that interested him. The set-up, the hunting, the capture. Okay, so the things Zack did afterwards were interesting enough but once you'd heard one you knew what was coming. The planning, that was different every time.

One time, he'd thought to ask about the way Zack always did some things the same. Like always taking a child with its mother or father. That didn't sit comfortably with what Zack said about never letting anyone make a connection. The cops must've made the connection. They had to know it was the same man. And that made him wonder about the tail that had been put on him in Dallas soon after the Toronto job. Maybe the cops already knew it was Zack. But if they did, they wouldn't know where he was. Just so long as they both were careful. Zack in his task, and himself in making contact.

And all the time he was rising up the ladder in Ralph Hardy's empire and he'd been able to make only one more visit to Canada. By then Zack was famous. Ten cases, twenty less people to pollute his world. After that, he hadn't wanted to take the risk. He was becoming too well known to the cops. Not as famous as Zack. He'd never be that famous. But well-known enough to make poor odds at keeping clean on a trip to Canada. That was sad. He missed seeing his brother, hearing him talk, but it was safer this way.

The trouble was, every day that passed there were more and more things he needed to talk about to Zack. Like Louise and Billy.

He closed his eyes for a moment, felt the car swerve and snapped them open again. He concentrated, watching road signs, then turned off the highway onto a dark, potholed road.

That last thought had thrown him. Louise and Billy and Jo-Anne didn't fit with Zack. Why was that?

What was he doing here? In Mexico, for Christ's sake. Something to do with the president? His head was hurting again. Maybe he should stop for a while. Up ahead, he could see the dim shapes of houses. No people were about, a couple of beat-up old cars and a farm truck were the only signs that anyone lived here.

He stopped the Honda, turned off the motor, and sat staring at the green neon sign outside a building along the road. The sign, advertising Carta Blanca beer, gleamed steadily through the growing darkness.

'They fixed the sign,' he said.

Beside him, the woman stirred and he could smell her fear. 'You've been here before?' she asked, sounding ready to disbelieve him.

Yes, he'd been here before. What was it? A week, ten days? It seemed like a fucking lifetime but he could remember it sharp and clear. He'd been driving a rented Ford Focus and had parked it right here, just down the street from the Carta Blanca sign that had been spluttering on and off.

SEVENTEEN

TURNING OFF *the motor of the rented Focus, he killed the lights. Ahead of him and across the street stood the bar, its green sign flickering uncertainly.*

Winding down the window of the Focus he smelled the still, warm air of the overcast night. It stank the way he'd expected the air in Mexico to stink.

Lighting a cigarette he flicked the match out the window, and breathed smoke to take away the smell of this godforsaken little town.

He sat for a few minutes, barely moving, thinking of nothing. When he had finished the cigarette he tossed the butt end out, trailing sparks

Easing the heavy caliber automatic from the deep inside pocket of his sweat-stained jacket he screwed on the silencer, then checked the .22 pistol he wore strapped to his left ankle. He didn't need to check the knife, which as always bulked his hip pocket.

Climbing out of the Focus he walked across the rutted surface of what passed for the town's main street. He was halfway to the bar when the flickering green light finally gave up the ghost and went out and with it went the dull glow of light from the bar's windows.

At the building he could make out the telephone line looping down to the bar. Taking out the knife, he snapped open the blade, cut the wire, then drove the knife firmly into the peeling woodwork beside a window. Around the corner, he laid the silenced automatic on the sill of another window, butt outwards.

As he reached the door the neon light spluttered back into life, casting its still flickering deathly green glow over him.

From inside the bar where the inside lights had also come back on he heard voices and a burst of laughter .

Opening the door he walked into the heavy, fetid atmosphere and one of those sudden silences that come when strangers enter a local watering hole anywhere in the world.

The room was narrow and long with a low ceiling from which dangled half a dozen fly-spotted bare light bulbs. A dozen or so posters advertising long-forgotten bullfights and football matches tried to brighten walls from which most of the paint had long since flaked away. Stained linoleum covered the floor and there were maybe a dozen tables with chairs, all empty.

The men were all standing at the bar; one with his back to him, the other three around the bar corner, their faces bent towards beer glasses. No one was looking his way, but he knew that they all were watching him.

Walking up to the bar, he stared at his reflection in the ageing mirror. Pale blue eyes stared back at him out of a narrow expressionless face, thinning sandy hair lay flat to his sweating scalp. Like always, he didn't look like what he was; the men around the bar would take him for a potential patsy.

A door in the wall behind the bar banged open and a tall, thin mournful-looking Mexican came through it muttering to himself.

He didn't speak Mex, why the hell should he, but in the dozen years he'd lived in Texas he'd had to pick up a few words because the lazy sonsofbitches who pumped gas and ran the bars and the supermarkets couldn't speak American. From some of the thin man's words and his manner and the oily rag he was using to wipe his hands he knew he was cursing the generator that supplied light to the bar.

No words passed between the barman and the other Mexicans but somehow a message was communicated and the man with the rag looked his way, grinning to show tobacco-stained teeth.

'Yes, señor, you want drink?'

He nodded. 'Beer,' he said.

The man reached behind him for a bottle of Carta Blanca, opening it in the same movement that pushed the bottle across the bar. As an afterthought he slid a grimy glass alongside.

Ignoring the glass, he raised the bottle and took a sip. It was warm and flat but he didn't care because he didn't plan on drinking any more than that first sip, something he's had to do to relax the spics. Taking out a handkerchief he mopped sweat from his face, then flapped his jacket as if to cool himself knowing that the gesture showed that no gun was hidden beneath the coat.

'I need directions,' he told the barman.

The barman looked at him and this time so did the others.

'There's a house someplace near here, an Americano lives there. Old guy. Lives alone.'

The barman's eyes wavered, his shoulders contracting in a shrug of feigned incomprehension.

The man nearest to him turned and looked his way. He was short, stocky, about forty, balding with a thick, drooping moustache. 'This man, he is amigo . . . a friend?' he asked.

'Friend of a friend,' he told him.

'South of here,' the Mexican said, 'Maybe twenty minutes in car. You got car?'

He looked at him, hearing the lies and knowing that this was the man he would have to kill first.

He glanced across at the others; two were mid-twenties, thick black slicked hair with the eyes of men who liked handing out punishment but were mere takers of orders. The last man was maybe sixteen or seventeen, nervous, not knowing how to look tough. He was the one he would use, he decided.

'I have a car,' he said. He nodded thanks and turned to leave. He was halfway to the door before the stocky man spoke as he knew he would.

'Bad to find in the dark,' the Mexican told him. `Maybe we show you the way.'

He paused, glanced back, his face expressionless, his eyes not giving away the fact that the stocky man had just signed four death warrants. 'Thanks,' was all he said.

He waited as the four men moved towards him, letting them set the pattern. The stocky man led the way outside, the two toughs hung back letting him precede them. The boy hovered, uncertain and sweating with nervous excitement.

Outside, he paused to accustom his eyes to the darkness, then moved forward following the stocky man. As he came abreast of the window where he had laid the automatic, he stumbled, swore as he banged against the wall, and smoothly scooped up the weapon in his left hand.

As the stocky man turned the corner of the building he moved faster, taking those behind him by surprise. Turning the corner, he already had the automatic up and pointing and he squeezed the trigger, the soft plop of the gun vanishing into the explosion of air that left the lungs of the stocky man as the bullet smashed into his spine.

Before the next two had cleared the corner he had turned, pulling his knife free of the window frame as he did so. The first man to round the corner was on his right so he used the knife, driving it up hard under the rib-cage and then, as the body drooped lifelessly forward, he shot the second man in the face.

He stepped back around the corner to meet the boy who had heard but hadn't recognized the sounds of death and was standing bewildered and afraid in the green flickering glow of the neon sign.

He drove the silencer into the boy's mouth, hearing his teeth shatter and said quietly, 'You understand English?'

The boy nodded, his eyes shining with pain and fear.

'You're gonna drive me to the old man's house,' he told the boy. 'And just so you don't try any funny business, I know the house isn't south of here like your buddy said, so you better not make any false turns. Understand?'

The boy nodded again, his teeth chattering against the metal of the silencer.

He pulled the gun free of the boy's mouth and yanked him into movement. As they passed the corner the boy looked sideways at the bodies of his companions, and a thin whine escaped his lips.

Ten minutes later they were outside the house. He told the boy to drive on a few yards, then stop and turn the car. The boy did as he was ordered but nerves were fast overcoming him and wheels slid into a gulley by the roadside where they stuck fast and spun futilely until he stalled the motor.

'Get out,' he said, his voice bleak with irritation. Now he would have to steal a car.

The moon was gleaming fitfully now through thin clouds and the white-painted walls that surrounded the house loomed blankly in front of him. Iron gates, high and locked securely, barred the way. Let into the right-hand pillar was a security intercom.

'Who's in charge?' he asked the boy.

The boy's face was wet with sweat. 'Huh?' was all he managed to say.

'The head honcho, el jefé, que nombre?'

The boy swallowed hard. 'Lopez,' he said.

'Okay, this is what you do. Call him down here. Say one word that even sounds wrong, you're dead. Got it?'

The boy nodded fast. Moments later, he was jabbering softly away on the intercom.

He knew that there were eight guards, four on duty, four off. Hardy had been certain about that, telling him that Lensky will be alone in the house with just the four guards to take care of. Mexicans. Nothing to worry about.

He had already accounted for three of the off-duty men and the boy would soon join them; when Lopez came down to let them in he would be taken care of and that would leave just three more. Everything was going well. The assignment was proving easier than he'd expected even if the hardest part of it was yet to come.

When he heard footsteps coming down the path from the house, he slammed the butt of his pistol hard against the boy's head, and lowered him to the ground, then thrust the gun into the inside pocket of his jacket.

When Lopez reached the gates he moved swiftly and surely, seizing the man's hair with one hand and slicing the knife into his throat with the other.

Holding the body against the gates, he frisked the pockets until he found a bunch of keys and moments later he was inside.

He stood for a moment, looking down at the boy, mentally checking off what was likely to happen in the next hour. He couldn't think of any need he would have for him but there was always the possibility of something unexpected so he hoisted the unconscious boy onto his shoulder and carried him back to the stalled Focus and dumped him in the trunk.

He circled the house, a large, U-shaped single-storey building that smelled of money, checking windows and doors. Security was lousy; most were unlocked and many windows were wide open to let in air.

One of the guards was making coffee in the kitchen in the right-hand wing of the U, the remaining two were sitting on a verandah overlooking the swimming-pool, playing cards. He could hear music in the other wing and briefly a woman's voice singing. The radio, maybe.

In the kitchen, he killed the guard with his knife, then headed for the verandah. Now, only one of the card players was there. The verandah was well-lit and he couldn't get close without being seen, so he shot the man with the silenced automatic. The man flew backwards, his chair clattering across the tiled surface of the verandah. The other man came outside both hands occupied, carrying drinks. He shot him, too.

He was ready to go into the house but just in case the old man should look out the window and see the bodies, he flicked off the verandah lights.

From the shelter of the bougainvillea hanging from the verandah's stucco arches, he peered through a window into what appeared to be the living room of the rambling old house, then used the blade of his knife to slip a catch and moments later he was inside the house.

He stood for a moment, listening for any sound that might be Lensky.

The sudden sound he did hear, that of a woman's voice, was unexpected.

EIGHTEEN

RYKER'S HEAD snapped around and he stared at the woman sitting beside him. Almost at once, he realized that she had not spoken. The words had been inside his head. He sat for a moment, confused, then, suddenly, lights hit his eyes, reflected from the rear-view mirror. Now, he saw that he was in the woman's Honda, not a Ford Focus. That was last time.

In the rear-view mirror the lights died. Staring back along the street, he saw another car come around the corner. It stopped, too, and out went the lights. He waited, watching, but as far as he could make out in the darkness, no one climbed out of either car.

He thought about the house a few miles down the road, trying to figure out why he needed to go there. Was it to do with the president? Or Zack? Or what?

He started up the Honda but didn't turn on the lights. He moved off slowly, passed the bar and turned to the right and was soon clear of the little town.

It took him almost half an hour, longer than last time, even though, then, the Mexican kid had driven badly. At least the kid had used headlights. Negotiating the narrow bumpy road in darkness was a bitch but he managed it and eventually glimpsed the wall of the house off to the left.

He drove past until he saw the burnt-out hulk of the Ford Focus, doors, trunk lid and hood all sprung open like straining blackened wings. 'Remember,' Hardy had said, 'All the time keep covering your tracks.' Well, he'd certainly covered the tracks he'd made with the Mexican kid.

It had been complicated. Now he remembered how Hardy had warned him it would be. But he'd worked on it for weeks, covering all the angles; like Lensky who, retired or not, knew too much about too many things. And then, somewhere along the line, he'd begun worrying about Hardy. He was mixing with trouble. Talking up a deal where he was going to run the entire goddamn country, so he said. But he needed to take care of some people. Some were trouble for his friends, some were trouble for him, Hardy told him.

So the job became more and more complicated and Hardy was forever bitching because he wanted things done fast. But Ryker had to move slow, because complications were what caused problems. Like fixing Lennox so he wouldn't be a problem for Ethan Roberts. He'd wanted to organize a stunt like the one that helped reelect Dillard but Hardy insisted on something different. Hardy told him there would be help because Roberts would see to it that they had cooperation. 'Official cooperation,' Hardy had told him, grinning like a cat, 'Top of the mark cooperation, better even than the kind you can buy.'

Ryker was remembering things more clearly now. Maybe it was the surroundings, all those things that had happened the last time he was here.

He hadn't liked the sound and smell of any of Hardy's ideas for the job, especially the part about help they didn't have to buy. Everything had to be paid for. Somehow. But Hardy wouldn't let go. And he kept adding complications. Ryker figured out why eventually. It was because Hardy wanted to clean up some long-standing problems of his own. Like Max Lensky and Lensky's brother-in-law and the brother-in-law's woman and child and then it had all become very messy and he wished he could have talked about it all to someone. To Zack.

He turned the Honda, careful not to drop the wheels in the roadside gully the way the kid had done with the Ford rental.

He thought about the woman sitting beside him. Maybe he could deal with her the way he'd handled the kid. Except he couldn't burn the Honda to finish her; he needed it to get out of Mexico. Maybe the old Chevy was still in the garage. He could dump her in that. Or the Jaguar, but that had probably been taken away. It didn't matter which. Not to him, and it certainly wouldn't matter to her.

He drove back until he reached the gates. 'Get out,' he told her.

This night there was no moon and the white-painted walls that surrounded the house looked gray and forbidding. Like a prison, he thought. Like the place where they'd thrown Zack and from where he'd sprung him.

He hoped it wouldn't be long before he saw Zack again. There were things he wanted to talk to him about and questions to ask. Important questions and important things to say. But he couldn't quite remember what they were, letting his mind get all silted up with thinking about the last time he'd been here in Mexico, but he'd remember soon.

The iron gates were wide open.

He pushed the woman ahead of him, along the path that led towards the house, hoping he'd see Zack soon.

A HASTY conference between Enrico Hidalgo and the men in the other car had produced information that added complications to something that was already as tangled as anything Phil had ever confronted.

As they started up again in pursuit of the Honda, Enrico reported.

'A week ago there were several killings here,' he told them. 'Three men died over by the bar. Then many more were killed at a house east of here, among them an American named Max Lensky.'

At Phil's inquiring glance, Larsen told them, 'Lewis Kant's brother-in law.'

'Who did it?' Phil asked.

'So far, nobody knows anything. A car stolen from the house was found at Matamoros but otherwise the investigation is stalled.'

Phil peered anxiously ahead but could see nothing. Since darkness had fallen they had lost the use of the helicopter and he was uneasily aware that in country like this, and driving without lights, they could pass the other car within a few feet and never see a damn thing.

'We're heading east,' Sam said. 'Maybe the house where those killings took place is where we're going.'

'Why, for god's sake?'

'The chances are that Ralph Hardy will know about the house and if he does, then Hollis will know about it, too. Maybe he figures it's a good place to hide out.'

'Maybe he was here before,' Larsen admitted. 'If Hardy wanted Kant taken out of the picture then he might have wanted Lensky eliminated for the same reason.'

'Which is?' Phil asked.

'Damned if I know,' Larsen said, not making his claim to ignorance sound very convincing.

For a few minutes no one spoke as they bumped slowly along the road.

Then Sam broke the silence. 'I've been thinking about Zack Hollis's murder spree in Canada,' he said. 'You said that all the adult victims were sexually assaulted. Well, the patterns killers like him evolve usually stay the same. No fundamental changes occur. At least that's the way the profilers claim. Well, we all saw the medical report on Louise and the kids. The kids were untouched. Same with Louise. She wasn't raped.'

'Not then . . .' Larsen stopped.

Phil turned to him, trying to make out his expression in the darkness. 'Go ahead, Jake' he said. 'Tell us what else you've been keeping secret.'

Larsen was silent for a moment, then Phil sensed rather than saw him shrug. 'I told you about the night Aaron Stone killed his wife and son, after Harry Stone beat Louise. Well, Harry didn't just beat her. He raped her. She didn't tell Stone for fear he'd hurt his son but he killed him anyway.'

'So why did she tell you?' Phil asked.

'Jesus,' Sam said softly, interrupting. 'That was almost five years ago. And the little girl, Jo-Anne is four. Was she the result of the rape?'

Phil heard Larsen sigh. It was something he did a lot. Irritation? Exasperation? Just plain habit? 'Yes,' Larsen said in answer to Sam's question.

'So, if Jo-Anne wasn't Jed Hollis's kid then we're way off course thinking he wants to take revenge. Especially against his brother.'

'There's still Louise's death.'

'No,' Larsen said. Having gone further than he'd intended there was no point in stopping now. 'As far as we know, Louise had no connection with Jed Hollis. Never met him. Very probably, she never even heard of him.'

'For god's sake,' Phil said, tight with anger. 'You knew this all along and never told us. What else is there? And why is Jed Hollis running all over the goddamn country chasing the man who killed Louise and those kids? Don't tell me all that he wants is a brotherly reunion, maybe to have a family head count, decide which of the murderous bastards has top score.'

'Whoever he's hoping to find,' Larsen said, his voice flat, 'it won't be his brother Zack.'

Phil recognized certainty in the FBI man's voice. 'Go on,' he told

Larsen.

Larsen's hesitation dragged on, then he said, 'Okay, there's no reason for keeping it quiet now. We set up a joint operation with the Canadians on Zack Hollis. We kept Jed under surveillance right from the start, since the time we knew his brother left his thumb-print in Toronto. Sometimes Jed gave us the slip. Not sometimes, often. He was like a goddamn ghost. Flitting in and out of places right past some of the best men we had. I suppose he had to be good at things like that, doing what he did for Ralph Hardy. I can tell you, heads have rolled at the Bureau over Jed Hollis. Organizing and sometimes making hits all over the goddamn country for Hardy while he's supposed to be under FBI surveillance. Anyway, some of the time things went better for us than other times, but he was a problem. That's why it took so long. Almost ten years. And all the time we knew, but couldn't prove, that he was making contract hits in this country, and Zack was racking up more victims in Canada. But we got him in the end. Zack, I mean. And his little brother led us to him.'

'Got him? He's back in prison.'

After another pause, Larsen said, 'We trailed Jed up through North Dakota into Saskatchewan. He met up with his brother. We trapped them in a little a town called Estevan not far from the border. It didn't go how we planned. There was a lot of shooting. Two officers went down and Jed Hollis got out. Zack didn't. He was dead when we broke in. Jed disappeared and, anyway, we had nothing on him.'

'So if Zack Hollis didn't kill Louise and her children, who did?' Phil asked.

'I don't know,' Larsen said. 'I really don't.'

His tone failed to convince Phil.

'But whoever did kill them knew about Zack's methods,' Sam said. 'Okay there were differences. No sexual assault on Louise and the method used on Jo-Anne didn't match. Zack sounded like he was a butcher and that matched with Louise and the boy. Jo-Anne was different. Whoever killed her was neat, precise. Like a surgeon.'

'Are you suggesting there were two killers?'

'Dammed if I know what I'm saying,' Sam admitted. 'For all I know, Jed Hollis could be chasing his own goddamn tail.'

'Maybe you'll soon have some answers,' Enrico said, letting the car ease to a standstill and using the handbrake so his stoplights didn't glow in the dark. He pointed and, faintly, the others could make out the shape of Barbara's silver-gray Honda parked alongside high gate posts set into a wall.

'About time,' Phil said, opening the door and stepping out into the soft, warm night air.

RYKER KEPT one hand on his automatic, the other gripped the woman's arm. The house was dark and silent. Not like last time, when there had been lights and music playing inside. Even the cicadas were silent. Tonight was more humid than he remembered. Sweat was slick on his face and body, and he could feel it on his legs.

A thin layer of dust covered the floor and the heavy Spanish-style furniture in the room and leaves had blown in through open windows. In one corner someone had piled a heap of bright-colored Indian rugs.

'Why are we here?' the woman asked.

He pushed her away from him, further into the room. He took the knife from his pocket and when she saw it she opened her mouth and he knew she was going to scream but he was too fast. He hit her, his fist connecting with the side of her head, sending her spinning onto the couch. Slashing strips off one of the rugs, he used the pieces to bind her hands.

By now her eyes were open and clearing.

'Just keep still and stay quiet,' he told her. 'I have things to do.'

And he needed time to think.

He moved swiftly from room to room, checking back periodically that the girl wasn't trying anything. The house was empty. In the kitchen he fumbled around until he found the mains switch and turned on some lights. Through the windows he saw that others had sprung on, illuminating the verandah and gardens.

On the kitchen floor he saw stains that could have been blood and remembered the guards.

Someone had cleared up the mess but hadn't been too careful or taken too much time over it.

He went back to where he had left the girl. 'No one's here,' he said.

For a moment Barbara was silent, then asked quietly, 'Who did you expect?'

He shook his head. 'Zack, maybe. Or Louise. The kids. Billy and Jo-Anne.'

Hesitantly, not having the least idea how he would react, Barbara said, 'Louise is dead. And Billy and Jo-Anne. They died in Forrest. Don't you remember?'

Of course he remembered. And he remembered that she knew how they had died. 'How do you know how they died?' he asked.

Again she hesitated but he seemed calm. 'I saw the photographs the police took at the scene.'

'No one should die that way,' he said. 'Louise all slashed up that way. Billy axed. And Jo-Anne. How could anyone do that to her? Her eye, for Christ's sake.'

Barbara stopped breathing, trying to swallow but her throat was dry and constricted. She could feel her heart hammering. She could remember almost word for word what she had told Lewis Kant about the killings. Like now, she'd been afraid to say too much for fear of tipping this man into an act of violence against Kant. So she had picked her words when she described Louise's wounds and the injuries to the boy.

She hadn't said how Jo-Anne had died. Not a word.

But he knew.

Ryker barely breathed, his mind racing. He knew. Sweet Jesus, he knew. How could he have forgotten? He must have blanked it out but now he could see it clearly. The timber houses along Lee Street were small and tidy. He'd waited until dark and the house lights were out. He knew that the old lady who lived closest didn't hear too well. He knew because he'd had the place checked out carefully, the way he checked out all the jobs carefully. This one was no exception but it was an easy mark and so he hadn't wasted valuable manpower in setting it up. Luis Delgado was dumb but he was good enough and had turned in a thorough report on the neighborhood.

On the porch, he had slipped on a pair of thin surgical gloves, then eased open the flyscreen, unlocked the door with a skeleton key that Luis had already checked out for him, and went inside.

He went into the kitchen, picking up things, looking at them, putting them down again. Some he took with him, not planning now, just reacting to words inside his head.

The crippled kid's wheelchair was folded up by the foot of the stairs and he went up fast, two steps at a time, softly and calmly.

In the woman's bedroom he'd stood looking down at her, trying to imagine how it must be to have a woman that you didn't have to pay for. Someone who didn't just lie back and open her legs for you when you handed over a few dollars but welcomed you with loving arms and washed and cooked and made a home.

But it was no use thinking about such things. Zack had told him it wasn't possible. 'You're like me, little brother, so I know what I'm telling you is true. A man like you can't have a life like the lives of other men. It isn't possible. Don't even think about trying it. You'll fail. You'll lose everything you've worked for.'

He was so wrapped up in his thoughts that had forgotten what he was doing here and when the voice came from close behind it was like a jolt of electricity.

'Who are you? What do you want?'

It was a child's voice and he turned fast to see that it was a small boy, wearing pajamas, holding on to the door, his legs crooked. Billy.

He moved without thinking, snatched at the boy with one hand yanking him into the room, the other hand raised and then swinging downwards.

He hadn't remembered picking up the small kindling axe in the kitchen and he was surprised when it smashed into the boy's shoulder sending up a spray of blood. He heaved at the axe, pulling it free as the boy screamed shrilly, and smashed it down again into his skull.

Then he was spinning around to see the woman sitting up in bed, her eyes open and unfocussed and he reached out for her, his hand slipping a knife from his pocket and slashing left to right across her throat, then right to left slicing her breasts, then left to right again ripping into her stomach, and finally digging deep across the mound of curling black hair at the vee at the top of her thighs.

He was out of breath, leaning against the end of the bed.

He hadn't planned on doing it this way. Christ, he was a shooter. That was why he carried guns, that was what he did. Why had he picked up an axe? He looked at the knife in his hand, not recognizing it, then stabbed it down into her leg.

He didn't move for a moment, controlling his breathing and waiting until his pulse rate settled.

Calmer now, he knew why he had done it this way. Maybe it was Ralph Hardy who had ordered the woman's death, but it was someone else who had decided upon the method. Another voice telling him that now it was up to him to continue the work that had begun in Canada. Zack's voice.

He stepped away from the bed, checking that although there was blood on his gloves and coat, there was none on his shoes.

He went out of the room, down the stairs and into the kitchen, planning to go out through the back door. Then he heard a voice. High-pitched, calling softly.

'Mommy. Mommy.'

The girl. He'd forgotten about Jo-Anne.

Hardy hadn't asked for the boy, he was only interested in the woman. It was for Zack that he had killed the boy. No one had spoken of the girl.

He slid open a drawer and fumbled for a moment, gripped something, then went into the hallway, looked up and saw a tiny figure dressed in yellow pushing at the door to the woman's bedroom, and he went up the stairs, wraithlike.

189

The girl was in the room now, standing clutching a doll in one hand, the other rubbing sleep from her eyes. He picked her up from behind, one hand closing over her mouth. He saw the door to the bathroom and stepped inside, turning on the light.

Kneeling on the bathroom floor he looked at the little girl, stared into her eyes, hearing himself telling her not to be afraid, that he wouldn't harm her, and seeing the look in her eyes that told him she would remember his face for as long as she lived. As long as he let her live.

And he knew that he would never forget the look in her eyes. Her eyes. Eyes.

He rested the point of the scissors on her cheek, angled slightly upwards and inwards. Then he smiled reassuringly at her. She wouldn't be a victim of Ralph Hardy, who didn't care whether she lived or died. She wouldn't even be Zack's victim, although he might prefer it if her life should end.

No, she belonged to him.

So, he smiled again and for a moment he thought that beneath his encircling hand the girl was smiling back at him.

Then, almost gently, he pushed in the scissors.

'I had to do it,' he said, looking at Barbara intently, trying to see if she understood. 'He was my brother and he had a task to perform and he was stopped and there is no one else to do the work so I had to pick up where he left off. I had to.'

He couldn't understand why he had forgotten so much. How he could have forgotten the house in Forrest and what he had done there. They could have been the family that he'd wanted but which Zack had told him he could never have.

He had never really believed that but he couldn't argue with Zack. He owed him too much. But maybe this time his brother had been wrong. Maybe he could have had a family like that. Louise and Billy and Jo-Anne.

But he had sacrificed them. For Zack, because he owed him. Owed him more than he could ever repay. Especially after what had happened the last time he went to Canada.

190

NINETEEN

AT FIRST, when the cops surrounded the shack on the outskirts of Estevan he'd thought they must have trailed Zack but they were not just Canadian cops; Americans were there, too. FBI agents. So they must have followed him.

He'd been so careful. Switching cars in Minneapolis, again in Duluth, then thumbing a ride to Fargo, then buying an old heap from a farmer for the all-night drive across the border.

When the lights hit the building Zack started shooting right away. Then bullets were slamming into the shack, burying themselves into the timber, smashing out the windows. They fought back sending one of the police cars up in a torrent of orange flame and roiling black smoke. Then the gas tank of the car he'd used exploded and in the bright glare he killed one of the cops and Zack picked off another.

Then he heard a gasp and turned to see Zack was lying slumped against a leg of the rough wooden table, his face running with sweat in which gleamed the reflection of the flames outside. The front of Zack's shirt was soaked with blood.

Zack smiled at him, his teeth white. 'End of the road, little brother,' he said.

'Not yet, Zack. We'll make it.'

'No.' The voice was strong and firm. 'You can, there's still time. There's a way out. Like I always told you, you need an escape hatch for when things go wrong. Some old hunter built the shack but I guess it was a bootlegger had other ideas. In the cellar there's a tunnel, behind a pile of beer crates, brings you out down the road a piece. You'll make it.'

'We'll make it. I can carry you.'

'No. That way they'll get us, both of us. On you're own you've a chance, a good chance.'

'Zack . . .'

'No!' His brother moved his hand weakly towards the wound in his chest. 'This is no flesh wound. It's the real thing. Okay?'

For a moment he hesitated, then another burst of gunfire sent bullets into the walls.

He looked into his brother's eyes.

'Over there,' Zack told him, inclining his head. 'Under the rug.'

Yanking the dirty, moth-eaten rug aside he saw a hatch

'In the corner,' Zack used his head again to indicate.

He looked, seeing two gasoline cans. 'No, Zack, not that way.'

'You need time, time for you to get through the tunnel and away. They'll still be here waiting for it to cool down when you're safe across the border. Now do it!'

Crouching low as another fusillade of bullets echoed around the building he reached the cans and began sloshing gasoline all across the floor.

'Okay,' Zack said.

He stared at him, seeing the liquid running in streams beneath his brother's legs.

'Zack,' he said again, pleading.

'One more task for you, little brother.' Zack smiled the secret smile he remembered so well. He raised his gun and clicked the trigger onto an empty chamber. 'Seems I'm out of bullets and you wouldn't want me to feel pain now, would you.'

'I can't.'

'Of course you can. How many men have you killed? What with the war and all, I reckon you must have higher score than me. One more won't hurt you.'

'No, Zack,' he said, knowing that he had no choice.

There was another explosion of bullets and he heard his brother yelling, 'Now!'

And he screamed at Zack, 'Forgive me,' as he fired into his chest.

And again, and again, screaming, 'Forgive me, forgive me.'

Then he lit the gasoline as he scrambled through the hatch into the cellar, pulling the door shut behind him and dampening the roar of the flames. He threw aside the crates, found the entrance to the tunnel and crawled away into the darkness and the silence, hearing only his own sobs until, eventually, they stopped too and he came out into the clear air and looked back, just once, to the shack burning in the distance and the cars and men clustered around, the smell of smoke and their shouts borne faintly on the wind.

'I'll never forget you, Zack,' he whispered into that wind. But already he was forcing himself to do exactly that. He had to forget what he had just done. He had to. Otherwise, he'd end up going crazy.

But he could never really forget.

Never.

TWENTY

WHEN THE lights had suddenly come on Phil and Sam were at the far side of the swimming pool, Enrico and Larsen were moving around the outside of the house to their left, the other Mexican police officers to the right.

For several moments all them froze in position, waiting, but when there was neither sound nor movement from the house, they all began moving again, slowly and carefully.

When Phil reached the verandah he glanced at Sam, indicated that he was going over the wall. Sam nodded, watching the house, his eyes unblinking.

Phil wasn't sure what he was stepping into but it was good to know that at least he had Sam on his side.

Cautiously, he clambered over the low wall onto the verandah, the thorns of a bougainvillea snatching at his clothing. Then he edged towards the window. Nothing.

Moving to his left he checked another window. Still nothing. As he reached the third window he heard a voice from inside. A man's voice, saying, 'I had to do it, for what I did to him.'

Raising his head, Phil risked a glance into the room. A man sat with his back to him. Facing him, her mouth suddenly wide in utter disbelief, was Barbara Nichols.

The man also saw the look and moved, faster than Phil could imagine, snatching at Barbara and dragging her across to the doorway and through it without wasting so much as a glance towards the window.

Phil turned and yelled at Sam, 'No shooting, tell them he's got the girl.'

Then he moved on around the verandah, checking each window.

Behind him, Sam Madsen relayed instructions to the others then went in through the window where Phil had been when he'd called out. Inside, Sam eased towards the doorway. Cautiously, he peered around the opening, seeing a tiled hallway and three more doors, only one of them closed.

He edged along the hallway, his shoes hissing softly on the tiled floor. Sam reached the closed door and rested his ear against it, listening. From inside he heard a slight sound, muffled, that could have been a voice.

Leaning back so that his head and body were clear of the door, Sam called out, his voice clear and firm. 'There's no way out of here, Hollis. So let's do it nice and easy. Let the woman go, she has no part in this.'

Sam listened but all that he could hear was his own breathing.

INSIDE THE room, Ryker was listening, hearing nothing but the woman's throaty rustle of breath. He couldn't hear his own breathing, not a sound.

He looked at her, his gun warning her to stay silent. But she didn't. 'Hollis,' she said. 'Is that your real name?'

He nodded, annoyed that she was speaking but his ears were attuned more to the door and his eyes intent on the window.

Listening to the man, his words mostly whispered as if to himself, Barbara had been able to piece together enough to know that the truth was just about as bad as it could be. This man, the man she knew as Ryker, was not Ed Garrett; was, it seemed, named Hollis. And he was not a grief-stricken, vengeance-seeking husband and father, but a vicious killer. This man with whom she had been intimate was a cold-blooded monstrous murderer.

Hatred filled Barbara. Of him. Of herself.

Behind her back she strained at the bonds on her wrists. She had to get away. She had to. She strained at the bonds again and for a moment thought she felt them give.

'Time to go, Hollis,' she said. 'Time to pay for killing a woman and her children. Time's up, you murderous bastard.'

Ryker swung his hand, slapping her hard across the face, sending her crashing to the floor. 'Shut the fuck up,' he snarled. Then, he hit her again, standing over her as she tried to scramble up onto her knees. 'Calling me names. You let me fuck you, didn't you. What'd you do that for? For a fucking story, for Christ's sake. You fucking tramp. You're all the fucking same. Zack was right.'

Suddenly he felt her hands on him, grasping at his leg and for an instant he wondered how she had managed to slip off the bonds but then realized she had found the Glock strapped to his ankle.

He flung himself to one side, sprawling on the floor, rolling over and coming to his feet with his Smith & Wesson in his hand.

But the Glock was aimed straight at him and he saw the knuckles of her hand whiten.

On the wall facing him was a large mirror and he stared into it. Looking back at him were light-blue eyes, deep-set in a brooding face that was narrow and expressionless.

He had a fleeting, unsettling sensation that he was looking into the face of a stranger. And that he had been this way before

Then the woman squeezed the trigger and he felt a sudden pain, like a slap on his arm. He looked down, seeing blood.

Slowly, he raised the gun. 'Why?' he asked.

Then he heard a sound behind him and turned his head to see a shadowed figure of a man standing at the window, featureless, black against the outside lights. In the man's hands, rock-steady, he gripped a revolver.

He swung his body around towards the man in the window, the Smith & Wesson moving in a slow and steady arc.

'Zack?' he asked.

The man in the window did not speak.

'Forgive me, Zack. Sweet Jesus, forgive me. God forgive me.'

Still there was silence and Ryker steadied his gun hand, his eyes narrowing; then he pulled the trigger, the movement sudden and hard. Too hard. The bullet hit the window frame beside the man's head.

From across the room, Phil Davis looked into the eyes of the man he had been trailing, knowing that there were many questions yet to ask and simultaneously knowing now that he would never have the chance.

Before the man could adjust his aim, Phil shot him three times, the second and third bullets smashing into the spreading red target on his chest driving him back until he crashed against the wall and slid slowly and limply to the floor.

Phil looked at Barbara who was staring down at the body. She let her hands open and the gun fall to the floor. She looked up, her eyes empty. She was trying and failing hopelessly to find words to speak but none seemed right and even if they had she didn't think she had the strength to speak them.

In the sudden, pounding silence, Sam Madsen came in through the door fast, his gun steady. Then he lowered the weapon, his eyes on Phil who, somehow finding a thin smile, said, 'I guess it's over.'

TWENTY-ONE

IT WAS two weeks since Phil and Sam had returned to Forrest and the first time they had seen Barbara, other than on television.

Her reports broadcast over WNTA had all had a hollow ring. Lots of surface glitter, a small amount of innuendo, and almost no substance whatsoever. He imagined that Barbara was embarrassed at her failure to break through the official white-out but who could blame her. His own reports had gone to the Chief and from him direct to Special Agent Larsen in Quantico with copies to Washington and from there they had vanished into some unfathomable black hole.

Phil brought three coffees over, edging one onto Sam's desk where his soon-to-be-ex partner was emptying his desk drawers and deciding what to pack into two large cartons, what to hand on to his successor, and what to junk. From the state of the overflowing wastebaskets, junk was winning.

'I saw your reports,' Phil said to Barbara.

'They were bullshit,' she said.

This time her use of the word didn't jar. It was exactly right.

'The curtain came down on you, too, I guess,' he said.

'Curtain? Barbed-wire fence with machine-gun towers at fifty-yard intervals. Total black-out by the FBI, the White House. You name it, they slammed the door in my face.'

'You did well with what you had.'

She looked at him for a moment, clearly unconvinced. 'How about you?' she asked. 'What's life like here in Forrest?'

He shrugged. 'Pretty much the same.'

After a moment, she asked, 'What do you make of it all?'

He shrugged again. 'A mess.'

'You can say that again.'

'How would you sum it up? If they'd let you.'

Barbara shook her head slowly, then said, 'We know there are ties between the White House and organized crime, we know the president tried to have Lennox framed for murder, with the help, unwitting, maybe, of the FBI; we know all this and there's not a damn thing we can do about it. However you look at it, we're a pretty sorry trio, aren't we.'

She looked from Phil to Sam, for the first time noticing what Sam was doing. 'Leaving?' she asked.

'Yes.'

'The San Antonio Police Department's newest recruit,' Phil told her.

'San Antonio?'

'Start next Monday,' Sam confirmed.

'Promoted, too. Sergeant,' Phil said. 'He'll be working with Mike Caceres,' he added. 'A good cop. He made that frame-up look like what it was. Paul Lennox owes him a lot.'

'I don't think that Mike is the kind of man to take advantage of that kind of debt,' Sam said.

'Let's hope not,' Barbara said. 'Lennox has enough problems as it is. After he was taken in for questioning the polls showed a twenty percent shift against him. That was enough to put Ethan Roberts in front for the first time since Lennox was nominated. Lennox has to recover. He must. With everybody ganging up to keep Roberts smelling of roses the only way to get him out of the White House is to defeat him at the election.'

'Lennox will get my vote,' Sam said.

Barbara looked at Phil who nodded, saying, 'Mine, too, I guess,' although he doubted he would exercise his right this time around.

'He'll appreciate that,' Barbara said. 'He thinks highly of you.'

'He does what?'

'He knows what you did, and how much he owes you. And Sam, and Mike Caceres. He's very grateful and he's not the kind of man to forget the people who help him.'

'How do you know all this?' Phil asked.

'I went down to see him in Houston last week for an interview.'

'I'll look out for it,' Phil said.

She shook her head. 'Not that kind of interview. He interviewed me. For a job.'

'I'm surprised,' Phil said. 'I had you down for a long and successful career in television.'

A slight reflective smile touched Barbara's lips. 'I'm a bit surprised myself,' she admitted.

'How did you do?' Phil asked.

The smile widened a little. 'I leave tomorrow. After the election, well, we'll see. I can always come back into television. But, maybe, if I do a good job and Lennox becomes president, then who knows.' She looked across to Sam. 'So, in the meantime, maybe I'll see you around San Antonio.'

'I'll keep my eyes open,' Sam said, which Phil knew was a weighted remark.

Sam picked up one of the two cartons and went out the door.

'New worlds to conquer for Sam and I,' Barbara said. 'What about you, Phil?'

'Same old same old.'

He was, Phil knew, looking forward to getting back into the rut of routine. Monday would be his forty-fourth birthday and he didn't need the excitement any more.

'Will you come down to San Antonio for a visit?' Barbara asked. 'I expect Sam would like that.'

'He'll think I was checking up on him.'

I'd like it, she thought, but decided against speaking. They both had too much baggage. Especially that they'd gathered in the past few weeks.

'Well,' she said, heading for the door. 'Take care of yourself.'

The phone on his desk rang and Phil reached out to pick it up. Glancing up, he said, 'You too.' But Barbara had gone.

It was Tony Rodriguez calling from the front desk. 'There's been a fight over at O'Leary's Bar,' the desk sergeant said.

'Yes?'

'The uniforms have dealt with it, but they say you might like to take a look at something in the back room.'

'Okay,' Phil said.

He was on his way out to his car before he remembered that Sam was leaving and his own birthday was looming. It didn't need a detective to figure out what awaited him in O'Leary's back room.

Oh, well, Phil thought. There are worse ways to spend a Friday night.

About the Author

Bruce Crowther's previously published work includes some 15 crime novels and a similar number of non-fiction books, mainly on cinema and popular music.

Resulting from the popular music books, in particular those on jazz, he has become a sought-after authority and reviews records for magazines and on-line. Some of his work in this field can be seen on his website: www.jazzmostly.com.

From the mid-1980s, he was deeply involved for twenty years as researcher and advisor with what became one of the world's largest databases of popular music, both in print and on-line.

He has written for television and the stage, and for several years hosted a weekly radio show.

Dead Man Running, marks his return to his first love, crime fiction.

1619230R00107

Printed in Germany
by Amazon Distribution
GmbH, Leipzig